TECHNICOLOR TERRORISTS

ANDRE DUZA

deadite
press

deadite press

DEADITE PRESS
205 NE BRYANT
PORTLAND, OR 97211
www.DEADITEPRESS.com

AN ERASERHEAD PRESS COMPANY
www.ERASERHEADPRESS.com

ISBN: 978-1-62105-141-1

Printed in the USA.

Send in the clowns.

— Stephen Sondheim

THE HOLY GHOST CLAW

"So, what's in the crate?" the thumb-headed wharfie asked Harley Cooper.

Standing in the shadow of the Brenda Raye, an enormous cargo ship docked at Berth 12, the two men watched an old 12' x 12' wooden crate lower toward the pier on a crane arm. The deck of the vessel was a windowless dystopian cityscape of stacked shipping containers. Deck-hands leaned over railings marveling at the bustling Port Newark nightlife. On the pier, wharfies unloaded crates, operated cranes, and moved cargo around on forklifts. A large flatbed truck sat idle 10-feet away from the descending crate.

"A new beginning," Harley proudly replied as he crossed his arms over his chest and rubbed away the damp chill of night on Newark Bay. His eyes never left the wooden crate. Gleaming with reverence, he watched it descend as if it was a naked woman.

The wharfie looked Harley over with mild contempt. Harley had reached a level of success that enabled him to delegate the shit jobs to underlings. However, the traveling carnival business was in the toilet, thanks to fully immersive amusement park experiences, and to the internet where oddities on par with Daddy Long Legs and the Inside Out Man could be viewed with the touch of a finger. With no money to pay the talent scouts, Harley Cooper was back to trolling for sideshow freaks.

"Yeah. Well, whatever it is, z'got the seamen all spooked."

"Being out at sea for such long periods of time…It must take a toll on one's mind," Harley replied without looking away from the crate.

He had been riffing for days on what he'd do with all the money he stood to make from this new find, and on the idea of restoring some form of prestige to the Toxic Brothers' Traveling Carnival.

Harley Cooper was the face of the Toxic Brothers'. Their carnie lineage traced back to the days of PT Barnum, for whom Reinhold Tocsek worked for a short period in the 1880s. He had even rubbed elbows with Joseph Merrick. Together with his brother Zelko, they claimed to have given birth to the old Ten-n-One Sideshows.

After Reinhold's death in 1922, then Zelko's in 1925, Toxic Brothers Incorporated found a home as part of Atlantic City's Steel Pier working alongside acts like the Diving Horse, the Human Cannonball, and the Highwire Motorcycle Act.

Celebrities of the day clamored for a guest spot as Carnival Ballyhoo. The carnival became a staple of the famous pier and of the Atlantic City experience until the pier closed down in 1976.

Harley's father was instrumental in reviving the TBC as a traveling carnival, moving from city to city in a convoy of dirty, white tractor trailers and Gulfstream RVs. Harley secretly pined for the romanticized portrait of the sideshow business that his father's stories painted.

"I don't think so," said the thumb-headed wharfie. "I know these guys."

"Is that why they asked you to come over here?" Harley said pointing with a glance at the small cluster of seamen watching suspiciously from afar.

"Nah. You know. I could see that they was upset about something. So I asked them.

"Upset?" Harley nervously inquired. "About what?"

"They was scared to talk about it."

"Really?"

"So, C'mon…" the wharfie nudged. "What's in the crate?"

"So, they didn't they tell you anything?"

"No. Their exact words was, 'Don't ask.'"

Harley thought for a moment, and then said, "Funny. That's exactly what I was going to say."

Harley had spoken to the port manager by phone a short while ago on the drive over. The man relayed a worrisome radio-communication he'd had with the Captain of the Brenda Raye as the ship approached port.

Captain (anxious): Is the buyer there to pick it up?
Port Manager: The "package" from Spain? Yes. He's on his way. Why?

Captain: I want this thing off my ship and as far away from me and my crew as possible.
Port Manager: What's the problem? You didn't open it?
Silence...
Port Manager: You were specifically instructed not to open the crate.
Captain: A coupla my guys...They heard voices comin' outta the thing. We thought there was somebody inside, so we opened it.
Port Manager: Son of a Bitch!
Silence...
Port Manager: So what'd you find?
The Captain hesitates...
Captain: "It...asked us not to say."

"I'll tell you like I told him," the port manager warned when Harley arrived in his office a short time later. "You're aware that human trafficking is a serious crime."

"I'm well aware of that. And you needn't be concerned." Harley replied, and then he pulled a card from his shirt pocket and handed it to the man, a C-note folded against the back of it. "A free pass for you and your family to come see the sideshow... We'll be appearing in Merrywood, PA next month. Until then, I trust that you will keep this between us."

The port manager slipped the bill into his pocket and stared at the card with a straight face.

"Merrywood, you say," the man smiled.

The 12' x 12' crate came to rest atop a wooden palette. The thumb-headed wharfie refused to detach the cable unless Harley told him what was inside.

Instead, Harley fished a business card from his shirt pocket and handed it to the man on the sly so as not to alert the seamen.

"What's this?" Thumb-head started to say, and then he flipped the card over and bugged his eyes out at the C-note folded against the back.

Harley dropped his schpiel, "A free pass for you and your family to come see the sideshow... We'll be appearing in

Merrywood, PA next month. Until then, I trust that you will keep this between us."

"Since you put it that way," the wharfie smiled as he slid the card/bill combo into his pocket and proceeded to detach the cable from the crate.

Afterward, Harley walked up to old wooden crate and examined it with eyes full of hope and wonderment. He dragged his fingertips along the Spanish lettering stenciled diagonally across the face ("No Abrir") and put his ear up to it. He tapped his finger against the side and waited for a response.

Thumb-head stood behind him, his face in a curious twist. He looked over at the seamen, who, despite their distance from the crate seemed equally anxious to see what happened next.

A forklift pulled up alongside the crate and startled Harley. A wiry man, cut from the same cloth as Thumb-head, leaned out and yelled over the engine at him. "You want it on the truck; right?"

It seemed rather obvious to Harley, who returned an expression that said as much.

"Gotcha." The forklift driver said.

Harley and Thumb-head backed away from the old wooden crate as the forklift positioned itself to transfer it to the back of the waiting flatbed truck. The seamen watched from a distance.

Six weeks later…

1:15am

It was like a sauna inside the large, 10' x 30' enclosed military frame tent. Candles balanced on fancified iron supports. Their low light danced on canvas walls bowed outward by hot air, and on the faces of the eleven sheeple who stood facing an animated man in a shirt and tie. A tan blazer lay crumpled on the floor a few feet behind the man.

"What say you, elitists and intellectuals in your ivory towers? What *scientific* explanation will you try to force on us regarding this miracle that has befallen us?"

The animated working-stiff preached with an enthusiasm suggesting absolute faith. His sleeves were rolled up like he meant business. When he spoke he flared his lips showing too many teeth and he placed too much emphasis on his D's and S's. His eyes gleamed as he read aloud from a leather-bound bible held open in one hand. He pointed at the ground to punctuate the divine sermon that poured down from the heavens and out through his mouth.

Standing shoulder-to-shoulder, in two rows, the sheeple stared in brain dead reverence, broadcasting glazed expressions that said, "I'll believe anything you say."

One of the sheeple—a young man wearing cargo pants and a Polo shirt—cleared his throat for the umpteenth time.

The working-stiff preacher paused at the interruption.

With his head pointed down, the young man coughed into his fist several more times. He looked up and was ambushed by ugly scowls, and squinty-eyed disgust.

The preacher resumed speaking where he had left off. As they settled back into their trance-like focus, the other 10 sheeple sucked their teeth, and shook their heads, and whispered under their breaths.

Again, the young man coughed and hacked.

"For the love of all that's Holy!" cried the preacher. "Have some respect!"

"You could at least go outside," a disgusted woman added. She appeared visibly sickened.

The young man looked up, meeting the angry, hovering faces, and said, "Sorry… Won't happen again."

But the angry faces weren't convinced.

"I promise!"

The preacher let his glare linger after everyone else had looked away from the young man. At some point he snapped out of it and realized that the congregation was waiting for him to speak.

Reluctantly, his eyes returned to the bible in his hand. He scrolled down to a section of black text highlighted in pink (Mark 13:6,7,8) and began to read aloud.

"'For many shall come in My name, saying I am Christ;

13

and shall deceive many. And when ye shall hear of wars and rumours of wars, be ye not troubled: for such things must needs be; but the end shall not be yet. For nation shall rise against nation, and kingdom against kingdom: and there shall be earthquakes in divers places, and there shall be famines and troubles: these are the beginnings of sorrows.'"

The preacher looked up at his flock and cast an ominous gaze on each one individually, underscoring the severity of his words. He skipped the young, phlegmy man fearing that the sight of his stupid face, which he wanted to punch repeatedly, might throw him off his game.

"Are we not in the midst of these prophecies?" asked the preacher. And then he went down the list.

"'Nation shall rise against nation, and kingdom against kingdom.'"

"—911."

"—Iraq."

"—Afghanistan."

"—And soon Iran and North Korea."

"'Earthquakes…'"

"—The Tsunami in Sumatra."

"—Haiti."

"—Japan."

"'Famines and troubles…'"

"—The economy."

"—Hurricane Katrina."

"I ask you, my children, are we not—"

A cell phone rang. The ringtone was set to George Carlin performing "The Seven Words You Can Never Say On Television." It was coming from the phlegmy young man's pocket.

Gasps leapt out of the crowd. Faces twisted horrified. A woman, who looked like she was about to cry, slapped her hands over her ears. Another man plugged his ears with his fingertips, squeezed his eyes closed, and recited the Lord's Prayer on a continuous loop under his breath.

Visibly unfazed, the young man dug the ringing cell phone from the pocket of his cargo pants and checked the flashing screen on the front. His eyes lit up. Within that brief span, the ringtone repeated several times.

The preacher lunged at the young man, growling, "You blasphemous sonofaBITCH!"

Two men ran forward to stop him. The preacher slammed into their arms and continued pushing forward with his chest.

"How dare you make a mockery of God's word! How DARE you!"

With the phone to his ear, the young man calmly raised his hand and signaled 'hold on a sec,' to the incredulous preacher, and then said, "I gotta take this."

"Hello," he said into the phone. He put on a listening face and occasionally nodded his head and said "Umm hmm," as if some big secret was being relayed to him.

The other sheeple in the tent looked to the preacher, and then back to the young man on the phone.

At some point the young man looked over at the preacher and then said into the phone, "Yeah…He's here."

The preacher's face reddened, sweat breaking across his forehead. He relented to the two men who held him back and stared curiously at the young man.

The sheeple did the same.

"Okay. I'll tell 'em," the young man said into the phone and then he hung it up and slid it back into his pocket.

He put an innocuous, thin-lipped smile on his face and walked to the front of the tent. He nearly touched shoulders with the preacher as he passed him.

The sheeple were tense with anticipation.

Who was that on the phone? What did he or she say? Was it some kind of sign?

Even the preacher was on pins and needles.

The young man cleared his throat. This time, the backwash was especially phlegmy. His smile became like a straight line surgically sliced into the meat of his face. His eyes became slits pinched at the corners and stretched impossibly thin. The corners of his mouth oozed further apart.

"I have something to show you all; a sort of test from the master," he calmly stated. "For this to work, I'm going to need a moment of complete darkness. So, could I please have someone put out the candles?"

"What for?" asked the preacher. "What kind of test?"

The young man pointed his slit eyes and his long, skinny smile directly at the preacher and said, "You'll see," and then, with a nod, he volunteered a woman to blow out the candles.

The woman nervously complied and the room went dark. Uneasy voices whispered to one another for comfort.

"Some of you will not like what you're about to see," the young man warned. "Some of you may find it too much to handle. Those of you whose faith is true, however, need not worry."

The uneasy chatter grew louder.

"Lights please?" The young man requested. His voice was different, several octaves deeper, and rumbling with an unpleasant tone.

Someone struck a match. A hand, seemingly disembodied, floated in the darkness and touched the flame dancing at the tip of the matchstick to the candle wick.

***

The Toxic Brothers' Traveling Carnival was currently located on the outskirts of a nowhere town called Merrywood. It sat alone on a flat, to lumpy, to flat horizon, surrounded by earth tones like a pocket of alternate reality cut into a rural folk-painter's wet dream. Made popular by a vulgar, punk tune from a few years back, Merrywood was swirling with a thick, lazy atmosphere that guided the townsfolk through long uneventful days.

During business hours the sky within the carnival's fenced-in borders blinked and flashed. Pitch-men waxing old-school spoke in loud, colorful proclamations scored by spooky-cool Hammond-organ licks. The Toxic Brothers' theme tune would pour from the main-speakers. Bells rang to signify a winner at one of the many Dollar-a-Toss booths, or the start of a generally underwhelming ride.

The rides were only fodder to placate the family-types,

who had been known to take offence to the sideshow in the past. The jumble of red and white-striped tents, long-tall, bottom-lit banners, and flashing light bulbs lining each structure radiated a peculiar glow that could be seen from as far away as the Pennsylvania Turnpike at night.

Screaming poured from inside the military frame tent.

"They're gonna wake up the kids," whispered a woman wearing an oversized Paramore Concert Tee and denim shorts. She was sitting in a circle of picnic chairs further down the grassy area from the military frame tent.

"Wonder what it is this time?" said the man sitting next to her.

Groups of people were camped out on the lawn, their beach chairs and blankets and tents filling a grassy area that stretched half-a-mile down rural Ellsworth Road to a large open field packed with cars and church vans and a fleet of dirty, white tractor trailers.

Prayer groups and churchified jam-sessions took place on the grassy stretch. Other people sat around smoking cigarettes and swapping stories.

Recessed further back into the grassy area, a wall of trees marked the entrance to a densely wooded area. Occasionally people went back there to relieve themselves, and to smoke marijuana, and to have sex.

There were children here with their families. The youngest was around seven or eight-years old. It was late and most of them were asleep.

They were all waiting for the Toxic Brothers' Traveling Carnival to open at 11am-sharp tomorrow morning. More specifically they were waiting for their turn to witness the Rust Resurrection. It was the latest addition to the carnival's infamous sideshow.

A rush of panicked sheeple pushed through the front flaps of the military frame tent and escaped to the night. In an instant their voices went from slightly muffled to piercing and obtrusive in an otherwise drowsy milieu.

A few of the lawn crew rushed to console them. A few others stood around in shock. One man was doubled over with his hand on his knees, vomiting all over the grass. A large piss-stain decorated the front of another man's pants.

"He was…It was…I don't know what it was, but it was horrible!" A woman cried.

"Dear God, I can't get it out of my head!" a man screamed, rubbing his hair feverishly in a circular motion.

A loose crowd gathered outside of the military frame tent. People in the crowd were craning their necks to see past the sliver of light between the tent's front flaps.

Across the wide blacktop, a 15-foot fence wrapped around a dormant ghost, shantytown painted surreal. Caricatured faces loomed from banners, and signposts, and tent-faces. They were frozen in screams of delight or of fear or smiling big—too big. A strange, humpback metal dragon-thing stood, heavily shadowed, in a static, serpentine pose in the middle of the place. A mini Ferris Wheel stood near it.

A police siren wailed and made the crowd jump. It wasn't like any normal siren, but people understood it as such. The sound was actually made up of Robert Plant's opening wail from "The Immigrant Song," run on a continuous loop, with background music and all.

Across the road, the front gate opened and a vintage Volkswagen Bug painted with living, florescent swirls sped out, swerved, and tore down Ellsworth Road toward the commotion outside the military frame-tent. A single orb attached to the roof of the car flashed red and blue.

The Volkswagen, with its writhing, pulsating fluorescent swirls, screeched, and slid, and finally stopped near the crowd that had formed. Robert Plant's voice was snatched away in mid-wail. The car sat there silently. The orb flashed and dowsed the crowd in red and blue. And then…

The driver-side door swung open and bounced against its hinges. Absolute darkness inside. An oblong shoe broke the surface of black. A leg stepped into the light. It belonged to a clown dressed in a security officer's uniform and big, floppy clown shoes.

The clown got out and looked around as if to evaluate the situation at hand. He was muscular to the point of parody.

The bulk was all in his upper body, which sat on top of a tiny waist and stick-thin legs. Beady little eyes squinted and shifted from behind a white, grease-painted face decorated with sardonic licks of color. The muscular clown was twirling a nightstick and smacking the blunt tip against his palm as he calmly walked to the back of the car, pivoted on his heels, and stood there facing the crowd.

Another clown got out. He was twirling a nightstick, too, and he was equally muscular. Though painted differently, he looked to be from the same clown tribe. The second clown walked over, pivoted on his heels, and stood next to the first one.

Another clown got out of the Volkswagen and stood next to the second clown.

They kept coming. Five. Six. Ten. Twelve. Twenty.

A wall of 20, overly-muscled clowns dressed in security officer's uniforms and those big, floppy shoes stood shoulder-to-shoulder on Ellsworth Road twirling nightsticks and castigating the crowd with their eyes, and their body language.

The crowd was all kinds of dumbfounded. People scoffed and wondered aloud.

There was a loud POP!

The quizzical chattering ceased.

A flatulent whine, like a balloon deflating, followed the loud noise. The deflating sound was coming from one clown who had suddenly stopped what he was doing. He had a worried look on his face. His muscular torso was rapidly shrinking in sections (left bicep, right pectoral, right arm, shoulders, latissimus) until the security officer's uniform hung on an emaciated frame.

The other clowns stopped dead and glared at the deflated clown, who shrugged his shoulders and made an "Oopsie!" face.

"Hey! What gives!?" someone in the crowd yelled.

A wave of low grumbling spread throughout.

An angry man squeezed through the first tier of quizzical bodies and addressed the wall of clowns. "Is this you people's idea of a flippin' joke, because it's definitely not funny!?"

"Heeyyy! Giveit-ah rest why don't cha!" the deflated clown stepped forward and said. He spoke with a cartoonish accent.

The angry man walked right up to the deflated clown's face and said, "No! *You* give it a rest!"

"I'm warnin' ya, shorty."

The angry man was tall.

"I'm warning *you*, buddy! You people better get your keisters in gear or you're liable to have a dozen lawsuits on your hands." Then the angry man turned to the crowd and yelled, "Am I right?"

Some people agreed.

"I'd suggest you take a few steps backwids, Johnny Handsome."

"Or what!? Huh!?" growled the angry man, who by most accounts was rather unattractive.

The deflated clown snatched a revolver from the holster on his hip and pointed it right between the angry man's eyes.

"Oh! Lemme guess. It shoots water...or...or...one-a-those little flags with 'Bang' written on it, right?"

The clown pulled the trigger. The angry man's head exploded. Pulverized flaps of skin flayed outward and flailed in the blast exposing chewed meat and gnarled bone. Blood and brain-matter painted those standing nearby in red.

People screamed and ran away.

The police siren belted out its peculiar wail. The background music thumped underneath. The orb atop the VW flashed. Its blinking rhythm grew frenetic and produced a strobing effect that gave the angry, headless man's wild, boneless thrashing an aggressive beauty.

The wailing and the music stopped. The red and blue flashing returned to normal. The angry man's noodle legs crumbled beneath him. His headless body fell straight down.

The night became eerily silent. Residual screams jumped out from random points within the crowd as discombobulated minds played catch-up and people began reacting to the angry man's violent death.

A minute later some slacker teen yelled, "Look! Over there!"

The slacker was pointing at the angry man's headless body, which had just sat up. It was sitting there, in the grass, with its shoulders slumped and its arms hanging down. Screams were put on pause.

The headless body jerked suddenly.

The crowd jumped.

And then the headless body reached up with its arms and felt around the mangled stump sitting on its shoulders. The angry man's head popped through the stump. He didn't look angry anymore, but rather relieved to be out of the fake shoulder prosthetic his real head had been stuffed inside.

The man looked around at the horrified faces, and smiled. His face was marked with smears of red laced with sticky chunks. His hair was badly disheveled and matted down with reddened moisture.

Some people clapped and cheered. Someone complained that the children didn't need to witness that.

"A good parent would've had their kids in bed by now," said an anonymous voice in reply.

"A good parent wouldn't have had their kids out here in the first place," someone else shot back.

Several others agreed.

Using the sleeve of his shirt, the formerly angry man wiped an area of his face in a circular motion. A circle of skin, white as clown grease paint, gleamed from underneath a pink, Caucasian hue that had apparently been painted on. The man continued to wipe with his sleeve. The wiping motion became less controlled. A sardonic clown-face began to reveal itself.

When he was finished wiping, the clown reached up and grabbed a clutch of his matted hair, and peeled the "average-white-guy" wig off his head. A frazzled, bottle-red Mohawk popped up from underneath.

Holding the wig in his hand, he made a "TA DAAA!" motion with his arms.

More people clapped and cheered. Others in the crowd were still in shock.

"All parta da show, pee-ple," said the deflated clown.

"Dude!? You're a clown!?" Some thunderstruck guy said to the man with the frazzled Mohawk. Looking like his world had been rocked, he turned to the crowd. "I've been hangin' out with this guy all friggin' night!"

"That's called dedication, kid," replied the Mohawked clown whose name was Spiro Ton. He had a voice like a mischievous fox. If foxes could talk, that was, and spoke with the same cartoon accent that clowns used.

Some portly woman hollered, "What about what we just seen in there!?" She was pointing at the military frame-tent.

The phlegmy young man in cargo pants and a Polo shirt stepped forward peeling away what looked like skin from his neck. It was a mask. Underneath it was yet another clown face. This one had a horse-shoe of blue hair wrapping around the sides and back of his head. His name was Whacko Ton.

"Like the man said, Slim, it's all part of the show," Whacko said to the portly woman, laughing as he spoke.

***

"I gotta say, Harley. I think it's a bad idea," said the chubby-faced geezer.

"I agree. There'll be other towns," said the man seated across from him, who was just as old. A third, slightly younger man sat next to him.

Harley Cooper sat with his thoughts at the head of the rectangular, Formica table feeling somewhat ambushed by the three worried, old faces further down the table.

The inside of the Gulfstream RV marked "Administration" was cramped and disorganized. There were two small desks holding up layers of scattered paper, manila folders, and wrinkled, scribbled-on legal pads. Second-hand flat-screen computer monitors waded in the mess. A rectangular booth next to the modest kitchenette was where the meeting was taking place.

The worried faces belonged to Harley's business partners. They were meeting to discuss the best way to handle the crowd outside the gates.

Harley wasn't ready to leave Merrywood just yet. Not when there was so much money to be made. Rust Resurrection was the carnival's most successful attraction to date. In a day and age when traveling carnivals, and especially sideshow attractions, were a dying breed, Harley wasn't about to fuck with the formula.

A little over a month ago, he was actually considering closing down the sideshow for good. With only two freaks left (Louie 2D and MISTer Cloud), it was costing more money to run than it was taking in. People were complaining about false advertising because of the banner lines that suggested a whole stable of them. Harley told them that he kept the old banners flying for nostalgic reasons.

Harley rested his chin on his interlaced fingers and said to the worried old faces, "So, lemme get this straight. You chuckleheads wanna just close up shop in the middle of the most successful run we've had in…in forever because a bunch-a-religious nutjobs are treating this thing like it's the second coming?"

"I'm not so sure that it isn't."

Harley rolled his eyes, arched his ass and fished a cheap lighter and a silver cigarette holder with his initials engraved across the front from his back pocket. He thumbed it open, plucked out a cigarette, lit it, and took a long drag.

"Please tell me you're not serious?"

"Yeah, we're rakin' in the cash, Harley, but at what expense? No offense, but, it just seems like you're so blinded by dollar signs lately that you can't see what's going on right under your nose."

"Which is?"

"Which is that that…*thing* in there ain't like the other freaks."

"A-men to that," said another worried face.

Harley closed his eyes, exhaled in frustration, and then scanned the worried old faces to validate their sincerity, which he simply couldn't fathom.

"Really guys? I mean…*Really*?!" he said. "Cause if

what you're sayin' is true, then I hafta say that I'm extremely disappointed in the lot of you. Okay, so maybe the crowds are gettin' a little outta hand. I'll give you that. But—"

"Out of hand is an understatement. And the Tons ain't exactly helping the situation if you ask me."

The Ton Brothers worked as offbeat clowns. On a typical day, they would run through the standard clown repertoire for the crowds waiting in line and pick people's pockets as they dazzled them. Occasionally they worked as security.

There were six main brothers; Vigo, Spiro, Whacko, Presto, Bully, and big brother Drago, who had left the carnival just over a year ago to find his own way. No one was sure how many Tons there were altogether—sometimes seven or nine or twenty. It didn't make any sense, but not making sense wasn't uncommon at the TBC.

"So, we'll hire outside security," Harley said.

"I thought you were against that?"

"That was back when we were lucky to break even."

"You mean last month?" quipped chubby-face.

Harley glared at the man. "So what would you pessimistic old farts have me do; send 'em all home? We turn 'em away now and we'll have a goddamn riot on our hands. The best thing to do is let the people see what they came here to see. They'll go home and tell their friends, and *they'll* tell *their* friends. The more, the better as far as I'm concerned."

If Harley Cooper knew one thing, it was people.

"Just imagine the kind of figures we'll be looking at by the time this thing hits the National News."

If Harley Cooper knew two things, it was people and making money.

"That's when we pack up and leave. We do it at night, real quiet-like. Leave 'em wondering what happened. We lay low for a while. Let their curiosity perc-o-late. We stir the pot with a few anonymous phone calls to the tabloids. 'I saw that freak from the carnival,' kinda thing. You know? Just be really vague. They love that shit. Gets their minds working. Then we pop up out of the blue somewhere, like nothing ever happened."

24

If Harley Cooper knew three things, they were, people, making money, and showmanship.

"Do you even hear yourself Harley?" whined the youngest of the old, worried men. "You're talking like this thing's been smooth sailing the whole time. Didju forget about the old woman?"

He was talking about the old woman who collapsed of a heart attack after leaving tent six last week. An ambulance came and whisked the woman away. They said that she could barely speak, that she had tears in her eyes, and a look on her face like she had seen God in the flesh. She died in the hospital a few hours later.

"Little old ladies die of heart attacks e-v-e-r-y-day, my friend."

"What about the other two people who had to be carried outta there? We're damn lucky they only just fainted."

The young-old man looked for support from the older men sitting near him, but neither would look him in the eye.

Harley was shooting beams of controlled anger at the young-old man. In his mind he was throttling the guy while money rained down all around them.

"I don't mean no disrespect, Harley. You know me…I get carried away sometimes. Specially when it's something as dear ta me as this place. All I'm sayin' is that the way things've been goin', it seems like only a matter-a-time before someone else—"

"That's enough!" Harley barked..

The young-old man paused, disappointed, and then said, "All right, then. Let me ask you a question."

Harley furrowed his brow and tilted his head to the side thinking, *Here we go again.*

"Just one question is all and then I'll shut up."

"Wouldn't that be somethin'," Harley quipped.

A few seconds passed.

"Well. What's your question?"

"Oh. Sorry, I was just gonna say, doesn't it make you uncomfortable at all?"

"Uncomfortable? In what way?"

Harley knew exactly what the young-old man meant. He had experienced it himself while in the Rust's presence. If the feeling had a voice, it would have said, "Do you realize what is sitting in that cage only a few feet from you?"

Rust wasn't the first freak that spooked him. Daddy Long-legs, Mr. Insignificant, and Lickity-Split were a few former freaks who came to mind.

Harley could see in their faces that the other men shared the young-old man's sentiment.

"Look. None of you are new to this business. Between the three of you, you've put in what; 30 plus years? I would think that in that time you've seen enough shit that falls under the category of 'strange,' that you'd come to accept that just about anything's possible. So I just don't get all the fuss about this one freak."

The worried old men looked at each other.

"I don't know how to explain it, Harley," said Chubby-face. "That thing…it's just…different."

"Different?" Harley scoffed. "That's why they're called freaks, ya dipshit."

***

"What'd you do this time?" Words came down from the ceiling like pressurized steam hissing from a cracked pipe.

"That you, Indo?" replied the 37-1/2 inch aluminum storage tube that leaned against the wall in the corner of Harley Cooper's personal RV. The tube was capped on both ends. A shoulder strap stretched from end-to-end. An 18-year-old boy was wrapped up like a poster inside. His real name was Louis, but around here everybody called him Louie 2D.

"Who else?" Indo hissed.

Usually the freaks were acquired by Harley Cooper or one of his scouts after scouring the tabloids or following up on peculiar "sightings" in some bumfuck town out in the middle of nowhere. But Indo was a walk on.

Harley had given him the nickname "Indo" after several, unsuccessful attempts at pronouncing his real name. He

26

named Indo's Sideshow Attraction, MISTer Cloud.

"What's goin' on out there?" Louie asked. "I heard the Tons bustin' a gut about something a while ago. Something about a priest in a military tent?"

Louie could tell by the way Indo's voice dragged that he was in mist form. He must have entered the RV through that crack in the window that Harley always meant to tape up.

"Clowns being clowns."

"And you didn't do nothing? I thought you was against all that stuff? I thought you said the Tons was a bunch-a-criminals."

'That stuff' meant pranking people in line and causing general mischief on the carnival grounds. And Indo, with his noble intensity and his, 'I am one who is summoned to right wrongs,' rap delivered in that mocha-smooth African accent of his, was the antithesis of that kind of behavior.

He was a bit of an enigma to the other carnies, having only been with the Toxic Brothers for a little over six months. From the start, Indo shunned the behind the scenes social gatherings meant to solidify the familial bond amongst the carnies. He rarely spoke unless spoken to, and even then his responses were never more than a few words. This led to speculation that he was hiding something.

"Sometimes the end justifies the means."

"I don't get it."

"We often hold our spiritual leaders to unattainable standards. In doing so, we sometimes fail to see them for who they really are."

"What's it like out there?" Louie asked, shifting directions.

"Nice try. But I will not consider releasing you until you tell me what you did."

"I don't wanna say…You're gonna be mad at me."

"Goodbye, Louis."

"No! No! Wait! I'll tell you. But you have to promise me that you'll—"

"Good*BYE*, Louis."

"Okay! Okay!" Louie pleaded. And then, following a moment's hesitation, he confessed, "Cooper caught me…

jerkin' off to a picture of his wife."

"Sylvia?!" Indo gasped. "Are you mad?!"

In spite of his flagrant philandering, Harley Cooper talked about his "Sylvia," like she was the best thing that ever happened to him.

"I couldn't help it," Louie whined. "You seen the picture on his desk."

"The mermaid?"

"Yeah."

Sylvia Cooper had been a performance artist in her youth. The Jersey Mermaid was her most popular act.

"You *must* learn to control your urges, boy, or they will be the death of you."

"You gotta help me, man," Louie begged. "I can't stand it in here."

Because of his perverted inclinations, Louie was branded the black sheep of the Toxic Brothers' family. Because of his size and his unique body type, he was bullied by some of the other carnies. They knew not to push him too far as Louie had a violent streak. He would use his flat body as a weapon, wrapping himself around the head of his adversary and attempting to smother them. And the tips of those paper-thin fingers cut like knives when he got to swinging them.

Louie had a problem with women. He liked to stalk them and leer and sex them up with his eyes. On more than one occasion, he stowed away in some unsuspecting woman's car as she left the carnival. He'd hide out in their homes and watch them eat, sleep, and bathe from tiny cracks in the walls/ceiling/floor. He preferred the naïve, submissive type, and usually blonds.

As a result, Louie was a mainstay on Harley's shit-list. He knew that he was lucky to be alive, lucky that 'Louie 2D: The Two Dimensional Boy' still turned a profit. Otherwise he'd have probably gone the way of Mr. Insignificant and Daddy Long Legs. No one knew for sure what had happened to them, but the rumor was that Harley had them 'taken care of.'

"Look…" Indo began. "I know I said I would look after you, but…"

"But what?"

When he wasn't working, Indo liked to drift in the wind and survey things from on high. What he saw in Louie was a troubled teenager who had most likely suffered abuse as a child. So he took pity on the boy.

"By releasing you I would be doing you a disservice," Indo said, his voice sounding further away than the last time. "Let this be a lesson to you, boy—"

"Wait! You don't know what it's like in here! I can't move! I can't breathe! I can't see anything!"

A few seconds passed. Louie swallowed the warm lump of paranoia that had been inching its way up his throat and called out one more time, "Hey! You still there?!"

He cried like a baby when there was no response. At some point his sobbing was interrupted by muffled voices coming from outside the RV. He listened to see if Indo was among them and heard signs of a commotion.

***

"There's No-buddie else! I swear it!" the handsome man with the overly gelled hair cried as he struggled against the grasp of two other men.

The handsome man was dressed in jeans and a vintage T-shirt with a wrinkled black blazer on top. He looked fairly young—maybe in his mid-to-late 30s—but too old for the clothes and the hairstyle.

The two men had the handsome man pinned against the wall of an RV. The man on the left was bald and built like a powerlifter. His arms were a tangle of swollen muscles and veins. His shoulders were broad, yet rounded on top, and they appeared to eat his neck. He had throw pillows for a chest. They rested on top of a hard, round gut. He was shirtless and wearing suspenders over a sweater of hair. He went by the name Brahm Howser.

The man on the right had a short ponytail of oily black hair and was covered in colorful tattoos. He wore a sleeveless vest decorated with throwing knives.

A bulky dwarf stood on the shoulders of a second dwarf who was a bit taller and skinnier than the first. Standing eye-to-eye with the handsome man, the bulky dwarf stuck his chubby index finger in the man's face and said, "You can say it 'til yer blue in the face, kid. It ain't gonna make it any more true."

"Any truer," the taller, skinnier dwarf corrected.

The bulky dwarf cast a glare downward.

"What?"

"I think the words you were looking for were 'isn't going to make it any truer.'"

The bulky dwarf's glare persisted.

"You know…cause you said 'it ain't gonna make it any more tr—"

"I know what I said, ya fuck!"

The bulky dwarf sucked his teeth and then he looked directly into the handsome young man's eyes. They were like a deer's with long curly lashes that belonged on a woman.

"I'll make a deal with you, kid," said the bulky dwarf. "You tell us where *your* friend is and maybe…just maybe, I'll ask *my* friends here to go easy on you."

"So whaddowe have here…an *inter*loper?" came a voice from behind.

A lanky clown with straight, black hair pouring down both sides of his face emerged from the shadows. He had a long face with harsh bone structure underneath and eyes spaced too close together. His face paint skewed more rock-and-roll than clownish. He wore a dark colored suit that looked slept in. His name was Vigo Ton and he was the oldest of the remaining Ton boys.

Vigo's accent was more subdued compared to his brothers', but the trademark zaniness was still discernable underneath his restrained cadence.

His younger brother Spiro walked beside him. Spiro's red Mohawk was shaped into hardened spikes that stood nearly a foot tall. Together the clowns seemed to glide forward on wheels.

Spiro was reaching into his pocket as they approached. He pulled out a ten-dollar-bill and handed it to his big brother on the sly. He had bet Vigo that the intruder was Sebastian

Storm, a two-bit, Atlantic City Illusionist with a thing for clowns. Storm was akin to a stalker, always showing up uninvited, wanting to hang with them and learn the tricks of the trade so that he could rip them off in his act.

It was obviously not Storm.

Vigo took the money, flipped his hand, and the bill was gone. He tapped his pocket afterward and teased under his breath, "Nice doin' business with you, brother."

"Another one," the bulky dwarf said to the clowns. "Can you believe it?"

Brahm Howser held up a rectangular object—a walkie talkie. He tossed the walkie-talkie to Vigo, and said, "He had this with him."

"He's stickin' to his bullshit story that he came alone," added the bulky dwarf. "Artie heard him talkin' to somebody on the call box, though."

Artie was short for "Artie-ficial." It implied that Brahm's size was the result of steroids.

"Fuck off, midget," Brahm shot back.

The bulky dwarf paused and then shook his head from side-to-side. "Midget" was like "Nigger" to him. He hopped down from the taller dwarf's shoulders and stalked toward Brahm Howser with his body on swell.

"Down boys," Spiro said like an evil fox scolding a pair of feisty dogs.

The bulky dwarf stopped and balled his lips.

"You'd do best ta watch your back...*Artie*," he pointed at Brahm and warned.

Brahm turned away from the bulky dwarf before he finished speaking. He dug into his pocket and tossed a small, square object (a wallet) to Vigo Ton.

"He had this, too," Brahm said.

Vigo snatched the wallet from the air, and then he handed the walkie-talkie to Spiro, and opened the wallet. He slipped the contents from their compartments and tossed them aside one-by-one.

Drivers' License.

Credit cards.

Andre Duza

A condom.

And $27.50 in cash.

He double-checked the empty compartments and found a business card tucked deep into one of the slits.

Don Hanson
Reporter
Between the Lines Times

The name on the card matched the one on the Driver's License.

"Un huh," Vigo knowingly commented. He walked up to Handsome Don Hanson and looked him over. "Sooo, you're a reporter. Come ta pull back the curtain on old Rust, I gather."

"I was just doin' my job, man. I don't mean any harm."

"That's what you backstabbin' assholes say when you're standing face-to-face with somebody. Then you go sit at your computer and make up all kinds-a-lies."

"Um Hmm," the bulky dwarf instigated.

Don shook his head, "No."

Vigo leaned closer to Don's face.

"So where is he...the one you came with?"

"I'm tellin' you, bro. I came alone."

"He ain't cher bro...*bro*," said the bulky dwarf.

Vigo put his hand up as if to say, "I got this."

"Then what's the walkie for, if you came alone?" he asked Don.

"Uhh...to communicate with my boss."

"You're a terrible liar."

Spiro stepped forward holding the walkie-talkie up to his mouth. He was smiling, as usual. He thumbed the "Talk," button.

Psssht

"Ki. Ki. Ki. Ma. Ma. Ma," Spiro taunted into the speaker with a big, dumb grin on his face. "You hear that, chum? That means we're out there, and we're comin' for ya."

Vigo smacked his younger brother upside the head...

32

"Hey!"

…and snatched the walkie-talkie from his hand.

Psssht

"Listen here, slick," Vigo said into the speaker. "If you give two shits about your friend, here, you'll come out from wherever you're hiding."

He waited, but there was no response.

Psssht.

"Last chance, slick."

No response.

"Shoulda just leveled with us, *bro*," said the bulky dwarf who seemed much less intimidating now that he was looking up at Don.

Vigo handed the walkie-talkie back to Spiro.

"Not much of a friend if you ask me," he said to Don.

"Cause there *is* no one else. I'm telling you the truth," Don pleaded. "I swear."

Vigo leaned away and patted Don on the shoulder.

"I know you are."

"So whadda you wanna do?" asked Brahm Howser.

"I could put him on the wheel…use him for practice," the knife thrower offered. "That'll scare the truth out his ass."

"I'll handle it," Vigo replied and then he put his arm around Don's shoulders and nodded to the two men holding him against the RV.

Don panicked when the men released him. He was looking up at the sky where just a few seconds ago he thought he had seen a partially formed man's face made of cloud wisps that had somehow floated down to a hover ten feet above him. The cloud wisp man had appeared disgusted or angry and he was casting his ghostly indignation down at Don's molesters with tiny white irises surrounded by open air corneas. When Don looked up again, the face was gone. And a little voice in his head reminded him that there were no clouds in the sky tonight.

Vigo tightened his arm and squeezed the struggle right out of Don. He furrowed his brow at the handsome man's sudden interest in the night sky. Following Don's gaze upward, Vigo saw nothing out of the ordinary.

33

"The social butterfly," Spiro suggested as the reason for Don's sudden start. That was what the Tons called Indo behind his back.

Vigo made a "Hmmph," sound in response to his brother's suggestion and then put on a consoling face and said to Handsome Don Hanson, "It's okay. It's okay. Caaalm down."

Don refused to look Vigo in the eye. He looked like a child stuck in the single-arm embrace of an older male relative with pedophiliac tendencies.

"You and I are just gonna have a little talk is all."

Vigo walked Don around to the side of the RV where the others couldn't see them. Spiro crossed his arms and smiled. The others pointed their ears toward the side of the RV and listened. They heard hints of a whispering voice and then...

An explosion of sound and electric light erupted around the side of the RV. The light sizzled and hissed. A phantom wind kicked up dirt. Within the explosion there were moist, ripping sounds, and anguished screams, and chipmunk laughter, and thunderclaps. A loud musical sting meant for movie jump-scares scored the event.

The group around front flinched at the unexpected burst of light and noise, except for Spiro, who stood with his arms crossed gleaming pride.

A second later there was darkness and relative silence.

Vigo came walking around the corner with his arm around Don, who looked like he had stared down the Devil and lost. Some awful sight had numbed his expression and aged him about ten years. He was shivering and barely able to walk. His hair had gone white.

Vigo walked up to the group, grabbed Don by the shoulders, and shook him until the handsome man's eyes began to blink and his mind emerged from beneath a heavy fog. The dwarfs, the knife thrower, and Brahm Howser stared quizzically, wondering what had just happened. The bulky dwarf walked up to the side of the RV and leaned to see around the corner. He saw nothing out of the ordinary.

"Now... What was that you were saying about your friend?" Vigo asked Don.

It took a moment for Don to summon his voice.

"I...I don't know his name," Don replied. He was breathing faster than he could speak. "I met him in a diner a couple miles from here. He overheard me asking the waitress about this place and came over to my booth."

Mouths hung open in reverence of Vigo's twisted influence.

"Ain't that a son-of-a-bitch," muttered the knife thrower.

"The Tons don't fuck around," Spiro proudly stated.

"What did this guy look like?" the bulky dwarf asked Don.

Don thought for a second, and then shook his head.

"He was...He was..." He said, thinking. "I can't remember..."

"Whaddayou mean you can't remember? Was he...tall, short, fat, skinny, black, white," then the dwarf let his eyes roll over to the clowns, and said, "...other?"

Don thought hard.

"I really can't remember."

The bulky dwarf turned to Vigo and remarked, "Looks like your little trick didn't work."

Ignoring the bulky dwarf, Vigo tilted his head and peered deep into Don's eyes.

"What did he say to you?"

"I told him that I was looking for somebody to help me sneak in. I said I'd pay him, but he said he'd do it for free. He said that we could help each other."

"Help each other? How?"

"I don't know. He kept talking about payback, though."

"Payback, huh," Vigo remarked. "So, it's someone affiliated with the carnival."

"He said he used to work here," Don said.

"Doin what?" asked the bulky dwarf.

"He didn't say."

"Isn't that convenient."

"He kept talking about Vegas, too. That's where he's gonna go after he's done here."

Vigo's eyes widened. He looked over at Spiro who said

what he was thinking.

"Sig?"

Vigo nodded, "He always had a hard-on for Vegas."

Sig was short for Mr. Insignificant.

"He's goin' after Coop!" The words leapt out of Spiro's mouth as soon as the thought came to him.

"For what?" asked the knife thrower.

"For kickin' 'em to the curb the way he does when the freaks stop earning," said the bulky dwarf. "It was only a matter-a-time before somebody let Coop know how they felt about that shit. Can't say I blame 'em, neither."

The statement resonated throughout the small group and for a split second they understood Sig's pain.

"But this ain't exactly a good time, if ya know what I mean," the bulky dwarf added motioning toward the front of the carnival where the crowd waited beyond the gates.

"He's right," Spiro said to Vigo. "He'll ruin everything."

"So, what's the plan?" the bulky dwarf inquired.

Vigo pondered a strategy. One of Sig's many talents was the ability to blend into any environment he found himself in, so locating him wouldn't be easy.

"Where's Coop now?" Vigo asked.

"He's in the administration trailer meeting with the other bigwigs," replied the knife thrower.

Vigo faced east and peered down the row of Gulfstream RVs as far as he could see.

"Me and Spiro'll check the admin trailer. The rest of you spread out and search." Then he singled out Brahm Howser and said, "Brahm. You go and let my brothers know what's happening. Tell 'em we can use their help. Remember... This is Sig we're talkin' about. He won't change unless he absolutely has to. So he's most likely still in human form. If that's the case, you won't find him if you're actually looking. The trick is to distract your mind with something else."

"Like all the money we stand to lose if that sum-bitch gets his hands on Coop?" the bulky dwarf suggested.

***

Harley Cooper stormed out of the RV marked "Administration" and slammed the door so hard that the lock didn't catch and it bounced back open. He turned, halfway down the short stairs, reached out and closed it with half the vitriol. Then he snatched a cigarette out of thin air, lit it, and took a drag that lasted for an hour.

The other partners had overruled his decision to extend their stay in Merrywood. How could they not see things his way? How could they turn their backs on such an opportunity?

The "Administration Trailer" sat at the head of three rows of Gulfstream RVs at the rear of the carnival grounds, three to a row. Fluorescent graffiti murals rendered hard and loose decorated many of the RVs. Each mural was designed to correspond with the carnie who lived inside—the Knife Thrower, Brahm Howser (aka the current Strongman), the Little People, and the Ton Brothers.

The graffiti murals on the RVs had been painted by Harpo Ton, an ancillary brother who was known as the sensitive clown.

Bunch-a-weak-kneed faggots! Harley fumed. *Let's see how they like it when I take everyone with me and start my own carnival!*

Harley was so angry that he could spit fire. For now he was spitting expletives. Walking around and chain-smoking.

Behind the rows of RVs, a line of old-school carnival tents harkened to a different era. This was where the current freaks lived. The tents had been with the Toxic Brothers since the glory days when the freaks were the main attraction.

These days the tents' formerly taut skin had gone flaccid. Cracks and tears held together by haste-handed stitch patterns and duct tape decorated their saggy faces. There were grease-stains and grime, sun-baked to a permanent bond.

Inside, the floors were a dirt/natural-shag blend—but mostly dirt: hence the freaks were known as Dirt Dogs. The natural shag was laced with creepy crawly things that crunched and squished under foot and staked claim to clothing and bedding and inside shoes. The tents' trademark vertical stripes had faded from brilliant red, to pink, to white with hints of cloudy pinkish hues.

Memories jumped out at Harley as he strolled along the carnival grounds. The corridors between tents were like desolate neighborhoods populated by red-faced and white-striped architecture.

Each sign he passed, each banner, each ride, each Dollar-a-Toss booth, filled him with a sense of sadness. He pacified the sadness with cigarette smoke and thoughts of all the things he would do with the money that he stood…that he stands to make from the suckers outside.

Fuck the partners and their decision. They weren't only betraying him. They were betraying everyone who stood to benefit from the Rust Resurrection.

Harley took a long drag from the cigarette and held it while an idea gestated. He had previously hinted at bonuses for everyone should the crowds for Rust Resurrection keep coming. He could use the partners' decision to stomp all over the employees' giddy anticipation. Their anger would overwhelm the partners and force them to rethink their decision. It was perfect.

Harley turned and headed back toward the tents grinning from ear to ear. He exhaled a plume of cigarette smoke into the sky, and then said, "Harley Cooper. You're a Goddamn genius."

"When life closes one door, another one always opens," said a male voice that Harley instantly recognized. It had come from over his left shoulder. "It might not happen right away…It might not happen in a way that you expect…but it will eventually happen."

Harley stopped walking and choked on his exiting breath.

"You remember when you said that to me?"

"Sig?" Harley queried, sounding utterly confused. He was about to turn toward the voice.

"You keep staring straight ahead! You snively sonofa-whore! This right here is *MY* moment! See! You move when I *TELL YOU* to move!"

Harley understood the clicking sound that followed as a revolver being cocked.

"Now C'mon, Sig," he said. "Is this about my letting you go?"

"You know exactly what this is about...*old friend!*"

"The decision was nothing personal, Sig. You know that. I have to think about what's best for the—"

"What's best?! You signed us over to that...*place* and you're talking about what's best?!"

That '*place*' was the Koechner Institute, a Government facility that dealt in clandestine research. Harley sent the freaks there when they were no longer of use to him. It was a nasty little arrangement that he had only agreed to after years of veiled threats by lanky G-men in dark suits and mirror shades who would turn up unannounced wherever the carnival set down. They appeared like curious ghosts armed with hidden cameras, strange, handheld gauges, and meters meant to ascertain the freaks' authenticity.

Harley tried not to dwell on the freaks' fate once the lanky G-men came for them. For him it was as simple as a phone call. The G-men liked to come at night, while everyone slept. Harley would lie awake beneath the covers, listening for them. But the G-men never made a sound. Bastards were like Ninjas.

"So, this isn't about your being let go?" Harley said to Sig, playing dumb.

Harley faced the darkness between the rides up ahead, unsure. His powers of persuasion were dampened by the fact that he didn't have a visual reference from which to determine whether or not Sig was buying his line of bullshit.

Sig shoved the gun against the back of his head.

"Hey! Whatareyoudoing?"

"All the people you sentenced to die in that...that... slaughterhouse...I should just put you down right now. But I wanna hear you admit it."

"Slaughterhouse? Come on Sig. Let's talk about this. I'm sure it's just a big misunderstanding."

"...I watched them pull DL's legs off one-by-one, just to

see how he worked? Did you know that!?"

DL was short for Daddy Long Legs.

"Do you have any idea what that was like? He sacrificed himself so that I could escape. Before I left he made me promise to avenge his death, and the deaths of all our brothers and sisters. Do you know what today is, Cooper?"

Today is the day when I set the wheels in motion, Harley mused. Or at least it would have been, until Sig turned up...

"Today is collection day. See!"

Sig pushed his arm forward and forced Harley's head to slump.

"Okay! Wait! Just wait! Lemme explain first," Harley said loud enough for his voice to be heard from a distance.

Sig eased back on the gun.

Harley lifted his head and twisted it from side-to-side. And then he said, "It's not as simple as you think."

"It never is. Is it?"

"I had no choice. I swear. I didn't even want to do it at first but they—"

"Not so fast. First I want you to turn around so that my friend here can see your face. You see, she had a hard time accepting that you were capable of such...heinous behavior. So I want there to be no mistake."

Harley was busy formulating an excuse in his head, something to buy him some time at the very least.

"Well...She's waiting," said Sig.

Harley took a deep breath and turned around expecting to see some floozy that Sig had picked up, maybe a fan of the show.

What he saw instead made him shudder and instantly go limp. He exhaled until his lungs were completely empty and for a moment, he forgot how to breathe. He collapsed to his knees. His skin was white as a ghost. His eyes were wide and channeling regret.

"S...Sylvia!" he cried, in shock.

***

The bulky dwarf walked along smiling at the series of vengeful vignettes that flashed across his mind. Though he often denied ever fantasizing about being normal size, he was quick to jump to that very fantasy when it came to assholes like the Brahm Howser who didn't take him seriously due to his diminutive stature.

Bulky had a habit of picking unwinnable fights. His would-be opponents usually blew him off in the end, which he chose to view as cowardice. That he had balls to call them out showed that *he* was no coward.

He heard a voice coming up ahead. It was Harley Cooper's voice, and it sounded like he was crying.

Bulky adopted a hunched posture and crept up to the edge of the nearest structure, a ticket booth. He peeked around the corner and saw two male silhouettes about 30 feet away; one kneeling, and the other standing over him with a gun in one hand and what looked to be a woman's severed head dangling by the hair from the other hand.

Bulky gulped down a rush of dismay and watched. He could hear Harley blubbering about his beloved Sylvia.

"I'm so sorry," Harley wept. "You didn't deserve this."

Bulky put the pieces together as he watched. He told himself that if not for the gun, he probably would've said or done something. Instead he continued to watch. Part of him derived pleasure from seeing Harley Cooper on his knees, but it was a small part. He was mostly horrified by the scene.

Harley was reaching out to the dangling female head and caressing the sides of her face as he cried like a baby. As he did this, Sig shoved the gun-barrel up into the mangled stump and pushed until it protruded from the woman's wide open mouth. And then without warning, he pulled the trigger.

A flash of blue light leapt from the barrel. Harley's head snapped backward. Debris spit from his brow where the bullet pierced.

"Holy Shit!" Bulky gasped and stumbled backward. He regained his footing and crept back up to the corner of the ticket booth and peeked around, scared that Sig might have heard him.

He saw Harley lying on his back twitching like an epileptic. The woman's severed head lay on the ground by his feet. Sig was gone.

Bulky could hear the others from the search party approaching. They had heard the gunshot.

"Over here!" he called out to them.

***

9:00am

The grassy area was mostly quiet save for the animals and insects that foraged at dawn. People were still asleep in their tents and sleeping bags and on picnic chairs. The early birds marveled at the ominous black clouds that chased away the gestating blue sky. People were perusing the internet on cell phones and iPads and laptop computers. Word began to circulate about a tornado possibly touching down in or near Merrywood later in the morning. Doubters were referred to articles and video clips stating the same. Local reporters expounded on the rarity of such an event with elaborate Doppler Radar presentations and charts and stock footage of funnel clouds doing their twisty hula dance across wide open plains, and of the aftermath.

People started talking about leaving. The optimists in the line hung onto the word "possibly," in the News' warning, and to the fact that tornados were extremely rare in this part of the country.

As the clouds grew darker and more turbulent, some people headed for the parking lot, disappointed, but satisfied to have chosen safety. Parents in attendance with their children were encouraged to leave for the children's sake. Some of them left, and some stayed. The line trickled down to half its original size.

"Shouldn't they be preparing to open?" A man at the front of the line wondered aloud. He was craning his neck to see further into the carnival grounds, expecting to find workers going through pre-opening chores "Be my luck I'll have waited all this time just for them not to open."

"Please don't say that," whined the next woman in line. She had a gaunt, sickly appearance and wore a knit cap over her bald head, her voice weighted down by emotion. "I can't do this again." She crumbled into the arms of a young girl standing with her and cried loudly into her bosom.

More voices jumped out of the crowd.

"This is ridiculous!"

"Yeah!"

"Better believe I'll have something to say if they try to deny us entry!"

The grumbling trumped the morning animal calls. People tried to calm the crowd to no avail. A soft, feminine voice eventually broke through the ruckus. It was more what she had said, "I thought I heard a noise last night…like a gunshot. It came from inside the gates. Didn't anybody else hear it?"

Apparently someone else had. People speculated, but nothing came of it.

"It could've been anything," they determined.

Further back, the girl in the oversized Paramore Concert Tee was forever talking about nothing at all. She was pretty enough that most of the men feigned interest.

Concerned folks in passing cars pointed up at the blanket of clouds with blackened bellies that turned the day to night and shouted warnings about the tornado.

The people in line smiled and waved and gave stock replies about God keeping them safe. Someone mentioned that the weather was one of God's tests. Children riding in back seats made funny faces. Some people made faces back at them.

Suddenly, a man in tattered clothing appeared from behind one of the refreshments booths on the carnival grounds. He limped forward underneath the tempestuous sky with one arm held against his ribs. A dark red blotch stained his shirt in the same area.

Sig staggered up to the front gates, clutched the fence,

and hung from his arms while he gulped air. Afterward, he lifted his shirt and slid a revolver from his waistband.

"He's got a gun!" someone yelled.

At the very front of the line, enthusiasm turned to puzzlement, and then to fear. People gasped and backed away from the gates as Sig pointed the revolver at the deadbolt holding the chain that snaked between gates holding them in place.

He fired three times. People screamed. Sparks leapt from points of impact.

The third shot bore through the deadbolt and it released its hold and fell to the ground. Sig worked the chain loose and let its weight take it on a downward slide, and then he made roving eye contact with several members of the crowd.

Well, don't just stand there! his face projected.

Voices leapt out from layers deep within the carnival grounds. Sig whipped his head toward the voices and stared, and then he ran away in a panic.

The crowd stood there, unsure. There were rumblings of dissatisfaction.

The clouds were stirring overhead. There was lightning, but no thunder. The air was damp and cold. An occasional wind kicked up dirt and tiny refuse. People squinted and turned away from the gust.

A minute later, a pair of clowns appeared from behind the same refreshments booth. One had bone straight black hair and the other had a spiked, bottle-red Mohawk.

Vigo Ton whipped his hair away from his face. He had a hunting knife in his hand. He quickly hid it by his side when he noticed the crowd watching from across Ellsworth Road.

Spiro had a retractable baton, fully extended.

"Which way?" Vigo yelled at the crowd.

Nobody moved. Finally, the girl in the oversized Paramore Concert Tee pointed toward the rollercoaster. The sideshow was located back there, too.

Vigo took off running. Spiro started to follow him, but then stopped when he noticed the chain and the mangled deadbolt lying on the ground. He looked up and saw that a number of people had taken tentative steps toward the entrance.

"I don't think so," Spiro sneered at Sig's plan to use the crowd as a distraction, and then he smiled at the crowd and said, "Nothing ta see here folks."

"All part of the show. Right?" said an angry man who recognized Spiro from the exploding head gag.

"Hey! What's going on here?! Who was that guy?!" Another man demanded to know.

"Was that for real? Was he...bleeding?" a woman asked.

A gang of clowns appeared from deep inside the carnival. Brahm Howser, the knife thrower, and a few others were with them. They ran up to Spiro.

The first clown to reach him said, "He got Harpo!"

This clown was on the portly side. Blue dreadlocks dangled from beneath a slightly oversized top-hat perched at a tilt on his head. His name was Presto Ton.

"I know!" Spiro replied. "We almost had him back by the bumper cars."

He looked over Presto's shoulder at the small group standing behind him. At that very moment the bulky dwarf came running up to the small group, huffing and puffing. There were more dwarfs behind him.

The dwarfs stayed close to the tents and booths to hide from the powerful gusts of wind that came and went unpredictably and pushed their little bodies off step with ease. Bulky stood with his back pressed against the wall of a nearby booth and fixed a glare on Brahm Howser.

Spiro nodded his head toward the front gates, which the wind had pushed slightly open, and said to Brahm, "Make sure they don't get in!"

"But I wanna help," Brahm replied.

"This-siz a family matter now." The big sardonic smile painted on Spiro's face contradicted the tone of his voice, and the anger that fattened his eyes.

Spiro was known as the funny one; the one who was always pulling pranks. It was quite a shock to see him looking so serious.

Brahm hesitated.

"Don't you think we should find out what happened before we rush to—"

"We'll do it your way when he kills *your* brother!"

"We all cared about him, Spiro."

"I don't know about you, but I'm gonna see this thing one way or another," came a voice from the other side of the fence. The voice belonged to a large man.

Brahm looked up at a swarm of angry faces focused on their small group. At the front of the swarm, a big, bearded face with crazy eyes glared at them through the diamond-shaped fence-links.

"Enough pussy-footin' around in nere!" the bearded man said. "You let us in now or else we're comin' in!"

"Handle it," Spiro said to Brahm. "The rest-a-you can help him."

Spiro turned and took off running toward the rollercoasters. His brothers followed him.

Brahm glared helplessly at Spiro's back as he disappeared behind a Dollar-a-Toss Booth.

A gust of wind came along and rattled the fence and pushed the front gates open even more. Brahm hurried over and pulled the gates closed.

"Oh, no you don't!" said the bearded man as he marched forward and pushed against the gates.

The fence flexed, but Brahm was unmovable. There was a moment when the large, bearded man realized that he was outmatched, yet he persisted to no avail. He turned to the crowd behind him for help. Some of them were already venturing forward.

"C'mon! They're tryin' ta keep us out! We have a right!" he yelled to the crowd.

People came forward and startled rattling the fence in defiant protest while the bearded man and a few additional men pushed on the gates.

Brahm dug his feet in and pushed back.

The fence shook, and rattled, and leaned drastically. Some people started climbing over.

More people joined the men pushing against the front

gates. It was becoming difficult for Brahm to hold them closed. He glanced over his shoulder and saw the knife thrower standing there in a stupor. The dwarves were further back hiding from the wind.

Brahm's blood began to boil. He was pissed at Sig for killing Cooper, which he had mixed feelings about, pissed at Spiro and his brothers for their rash behavior, which was only going to make matters worse, pissed at the impatient folks on the other side of the fence, who were making it difficult for him to think straight, and pissed at his colleagues for doing nothing to help him.

He cast a demonic grimace at the crowd on the other side of the fence and then lifted his foot and stomped down hard.

"GET THA FUCK BACK!" he roared.

The ground shook.

A wall of bodies stumbled away from the fence. Some of them fell to the ground. People climbing the fence were thrown off.

The knife thrower stumbled and fell on his side. The dwarves held onto whatever they could.

There was a moment of confusion as people were unsure what had happened or how to respond. A metallic pop broke the silence. Seconds later a 10-foot section of fence fell over and slapped the ground 100 feet away. It started a chain reaction that pulled the rest of the fence down with it, section-by-section. The falling sections approached Brahm like a vertical tidal wave of flexible metal. He jumped back and watched the wave pass him and continue on until the entire front of the carnival was exposed.

Brahm looked down at the section that smacked down at his feet and then he looked up at the crowd. People were climbing to their feet and massaging sore areas, and protesting being thrown from the fence. Someone mentioned a lawsuit.

The knife thrower picked himself up off of the ground, turned to Brahm Howser and said, "You were supposed to keep them out."

***

Sig hurled an empty Snapple bottle down a side corridor between tents, hoping that the sound of it shattering would send his pursuers off in the wrong direction. He then ducked into the nearest tent to escape the cluster of footsteps that was gaining on him by the second.

It was dark inside the tent. Sig stood there perfectly still and listened. He barely heard the bottle shatter in the distance. Outside the wind howled and whistled. When it reached its peak it was such that it bowed the sides of the tents and made banners and decorative flags snap like whips. The powerful sound of the wind, as it ripped and tore its way through the carnival, made it next to impossible for Sig to hear anything. But then, during a latent period, he heard the slapping of rubber soles getting closer.

The footsteps stopped right outside the tent and were replaced by voices that he recognized.

"We got 'em now!" Presto Ton celebrated.

"Shhhh! Let 'em know we're coming, why don't-cha," Vigo scolded.

Their voices were so close that Sig was unsure if they had fallen for the bait or if they were preparing to rush the tent he was hiding inside. But then something else stole their attention, an approaching stampede of thunderous footfalls and voices laced with crazy determination, and aggression, and malice. It sounding like an ancient army set on pillage.

"Awe SHIT! They musta got in!" said Presto, or maybe it was Bully.

The voices outside the tent died away. Either his pursuers had crept off toward the shattered glass, or away from the rampaging crowd, or they were skulking up to the tent.

Sig took a deep breath, and then fingered the tent-flap aside and peeked out.

All clear.

Sig exhaled and marinated in the massive swell of relief. A peculiar sensation crept up from behind, and suddenly he felt as if he wasn't alone in the tent.

He spun around thinking that the Tons were sneaking up behind him. Instead, he found himself surrounded by darkness. But the darkness wasn't natural. It had a texture to it and a fuzzy stillness. Shapes hiding layers deep teased his eyesight.

Sig squinted. Random objects began to take shape. He saw fake stained glass windows hanging on the walls like paintings and rows of folding chairs facing a stage. No. It was an altar.

Tall, bulky spotlights with tripod legs stood like napping sentinels on either side of the altar. Fat cords snaked from the backs of their slumped heads. There was a cage on the altar. It looked about 15' x 15' with rusted, tubular steel bars for walls and a door in the middle. The top edge of the cage brushed against a lower section of the tent's cone ceiling. A velvet rope cordoned off the cage to ensure that visitors maintained a distance of at least five feet. A kneeling-pad wrapped around the cage. The pad was dented from knees upon knees.

Beyond the tubular steel bars, a darker mass huddled in the corner. The mass was huge and had a familiar shape. Sig squinted at the mass, and watched, and waited. And then he remembered the mini flashlight in his pocket, and fished it out.

He crept closer to the cage. His focus was farsighted, so he didn't see the four-foot signpost until he nudged it with his shoulder, jumped back, and pointed the flashlight at it.

The signpost teetered as if it might fall. Sig reached out and steadied it, and then he leaned forward and perused the framed sign sitting on top. A photograph of a weeping statue of Christ floated above small text.

Sig's eyes scrolled down to the text below the photograph.

Rust Resurrection

Originally stolen, in 1953, from a church in Toledo, Spain, after reports that it wept real tears, this 15-foot statue of Jesus Christ was recently donated to the carnival by an anonymous source.

Sig had heard about the Rust Resurrection from reporter Don Hanson, who told him that the thing was "creepy-as-all-get-out." Hanson hadn't seen it himself, but he had heard from a friend, whose friend's friend had supposedly seen the thing a couple days ago. One of the cooks at the diner said that he had seen it, too, and backed up the friend's, friend's description.

"So, it's just a statue that leaks rusty water from its eyes?" Sig had asked the cook.

"You just have to see the thing for yourself," the man had replied, and then he disappeared into the kitchen shaking his head and mumbling under his breath, "Eeeh-vrrybody's a skeptic."

"Why the Hell's it in a cage is what I wanna know?" asked a woman who had been eavesdropping on their conversation from a few booths away.

"Cause it adds to the mystery," Sig had knowingly replied.

He was aware that Harley had been hurting financially and the private joke amongst some of the old freaks was that he would eventually resort to fakery to keep the sideshow running. Sig assumed that to be the case with the statue.

"Maybe it got tired of listening to everybody's prayers?" Don Hanson had quipped.

Sig remembered how everyone had looked at Don then, like he was crazy, but the reporter continued to riff on the subject.

"Can you imagine how much it would suck to have to hang around in one fixed position while people lay all their problems on you and beg you for shit? Day in and day out… for years and years…Man, I'd be crying, too."

At the time, Sig had guessed that Don Hanson was high on marijuana, and he was right.

Sig flipped the flashlight to an underhanded grip and pointed the beam at the hulking mass inside the cage. Dust wandered lazily through the light and added a murky, underwater ambience. The dusty yellow hue fell upon a giant statue of Jesus Christ huddled in the corner of the cage.

Sig shuddered at the monstrosity. He knew it was only a

statue, but it was much larger than he imagined, its appendages were strangely elongated, and the look painted on its face spoke to real live awe or reverence. Its emaciated body was a canvas of faded Caucasian fleshtones flecked with patches of rust, and scratches, and dings. Its skin was textured like dried latex paint and it possessed an ugly thickness from having been painted over during repeated restoration attempts.

Angry cracks decorated the statue's joints. Its head was long and skinny and tilted upright as if it was counseling with God or begging. Its eyes were a washed out shade of blue and had no depth, like they had simply been painted over the suggestion of ocular pits sculpted into the vague template of a face. A hint of rouge brought out its cheekbones. Its narrow lips were slightly parted and enclosed within a beard of light brown hair that was much too neatly man-scaped for 31AD. Its hair was a hood of brown that crested over broad, boney shoulders. A crown of thorns rested on top of the hood. Blood trails had been painted over a painfully furrowed brow.

So this is what all the fuss'z about? Sig thought as he approached the cage feeling largely underwhelmed by the Rust Resurrection. Although it was facing upward, Rust's eyes were locked on Sig and following him without moving. In them Sig sensed apprehension and fear. The emotions seemed strangely present and not something that a sculptor could reproduce. But it was still just a statue.

Sig got close enough to see tears of rust flowing from the statue's eyes, or what appeared to be tears, and he commented under his breath, "Neat trick Cooper."

The statue suddenly moved...or he thought it did. Maybe just a twitch of its left eye, maybe nothing at all, but Sig was sure that he saw *something*.

He leaned away, momentarily startled, and then focused the beam directly on the Rust Resurrection's face. Even seated, the thing was tall. Its living blue eyes were looking down at him like he was a roach skittering toward it and there was nowhere to run. It lips were trembling and its chin quivered like it was trying not to cry.

Sig was incredulous.

51

"No más?" came a unisex whimper from behind lips that barely parted.

As he stared at the thing, a cynical sneer took shape of Sig's mouth. He stepped up onto the kneeling pad and stood right up against the tubular bars of the cage and said, "What are you, some kinda animatronic thing or something? Some kinda puppet?"

Rust snatched its face away from Sig and threw up its wiry arms and hid its face behind massive hands with long, bony fingers that were spread apart and curled into claws. A single blue eye peeked out from between its clawed fingers.

Though rigid, Rust's movements were strangely articulate and possessed an awkward fluidity and grace that seemed way beyond what Harley Cooper could afford.

But it was still just a statue; a big, weird, expensive, animatronic statue.

"Ningún mas! Por favor? Pido de usted" [No more! Please? I ask of you!]

"Shhh!" Sig hissed at the giant statue, or whoever was controlling it. "They'll hear you."

"Yeah, Rusty," came a slapstick voice from the entrance. "Quit yer bitchin', or else we'll hear you..."

Sig tensed up.

"...and Ole Sig here wouldn't want that."

Sig turned, reluctantly and saw Presto Ton standing at the entrance with a look on his mostly white face that said, "Gotcha!" He was holding the tent-flap open with his hand. In the other he brandished a foot-long pipe of some kind.

"It was an accident. I swear it was!" Sig asserted.

"I got 'em!" Presto yelled over his shoulder and then he turned back to Sig. "You killed baby brother. That's a capital offense, buddy boy."

"Hágalo marcharse!" [Make him go away!] Rust said to Presto. "Haga todos ellos marcharse! Dígales que no puedo contestar sus rezos! Dígales que no soy a quién ellos piensan que soy! Dígales—" [Make them all go away. Tell them that I cannot answer their prayers. Tell them that I am not who they think I am. Tell them—]

"Would you S-H-U-T...T-H-E-H-E-L-L UP!" Presto yelled.

The giant statue stopped whining, but continued to sob and shiver.

"You mean you ain't controlling that thing?" a bewildered Sig inquired.

Presto shook his head "No," and then responded, "Haven'cha heard? Ole Rusty here is the real deal."

More clowns appeared at the entrance and focused their extreme ire on Sig.

Sig snatched the revolver from his waist and aimed it at Presto, who was standing at the front of the group. The last thing he wanted was to pull the trigger, but he was willing to do what was necessary to get out of the tent in one piece.

Presto stood defiant and glared down the barrel at the forced reticent gaze floating behind the gun.

"They're coming!" yelled an ancillary clown.

Vigo pushed his way to the front of the group.

"There's no time!" the same clown yelled at Vigo.

"Back off!" Vigo growled at his concerned, ancillary brother. And then he pointed his knife at Sig and bore down on him with eyes gleaming hatred and said, "This ain't over."

"Harpo jumped me from behind, man! I didn't know who it was!" Sig pleaded. "I blacked out and when I came to, he was dead."

In fact, Harpo Ton lay convulsing at Sig's feet with a chunk missing from his throat, when he came to.

"You know how it is with 'the change.' You know how much I hate it. Why would I turn on Spiro? Why would I do that? We've always been cool, he and I. I've always been cool with all you guys."

"I don't care. Our little brother's dead and you did it. That's all that matters."

"I didn't know! I swear!"

"Not my problem."

Vigo kept pointing the knife at Sig as he backed up to the entrance, turned, and ordered his brothers to leave.

Sig kept his aim locked on the front of the tent as the

Rust Resurrection panicked and started to thrash against the tubular bars as if hope had left along with the Ton brothers. The noise from the cage was such that it overrode the howling, whistling wind, and the approaching stampede. It rattled at a timbre that Sig could feel in his bones. Rust's painted bulk scrapped and thumped against the cement floor. Its rigid skin stretched, and crackled.

The ground began to vibrate from the impact of a thousand feet. The air filled with overlapping voices waxing fanatical.

Sig took off running toward the entrance of the tent and slammed into a wall of ugly zeal. He lurched backward and into a balance dance. The stampeding crowd continued forward and gobbled him up before he could regain his footing.

Sig hadn't even hit the ground yet when he found himself ricocheting between legs kicking forward. He bounced around like a pinball with noodle limbs. There was no time to react before he was kicked or stomped or shoved into a sloppy tumble again and again. He could hear his bones shatter. He cried out, but his voice was lost in the overall din. Eventually his hearing went muddled from too many blows to the head. His vision was next to go. He felt an intense swell of adrenaline manifested as kinetic heat. That meant the change was coming.

But these people were innocent. Harley Cooper was to blame for their frenzied zeal. Sig's alter ego had gotten him into enough trouble tonight. He fought against the change, willing it into submission.

People fell over each other and were kicked around and trampled on. They screamed and cried out for help, but no one listened.

Sig was barely conscious when the stampede settled. He was lying face-down with his nose mashed into the dirt floor of tent six. Razor sharp fragments swished around inside his mouth and cut his gums. He tongued the jagged peaks of chipped and broken teeth that they left behind and tasted blood. He was breathing rapidly and inhaled a bunch of dirt. It made him sneeze and cough. The fit left him teary-eyed.

Every inch of Sig's body was alive with pain. He tried, but couldn't move anything below his neck. His hearing came and went.

Still he fought back the change.

Sig lifted his head and looked through his blurred vision, through the murky, underwater sheen, and saw people kneeling in front of the cage with their hands clasped together in prayer. The faces he could see were damp from a continuous flow of tears. Their mouths were moving, presumably in prayer. Their eyes were glassy and bursting with reverence.

Upon the altar, the Rust Resurrection continued to thrash inside the cage. It stomped the tubular bars with its feet, and banged against them with closed fists, and grabbed them, and shook with all its strength. Then the statue planted its feet on the ground, thrust its body upward, and pushed against the roof of the cage with its back. Its painted face was painfully arranged, like a wailing infant.

And then the giant statue threw its hands over its ears, pointed its skinny face at the ceiling, and stretched its mouth open wide.

The crowd recoiled from the sound that came out. The walls of the tent flexed outward. At the front of the kneeling crowd a woman's head began to inflate as if it was filling with air and then it popped like a balloon and sprayed cerebral slop. The same thing happened to the man kneeling next to her, and again to the man next to him.

The crowd reacted as if Rust's voice hurt their ears. People were screaming and wearing other people's blood as they ran away from the headless bodies that crumpled to the dirt floor of tent six. Some people continued to pray. Eventually their heads exploded too.

***

Leaning against the wall of Harley Cooper's personal RV, a 37-1/2 inch aluminum storage tube jostled and then lifted off the ground. An 18-year-old boy named Louie 2D was still rolled up inside, unable to move. A circle of light appeared at one end. Louie sensed that it was the bottom. A draft rushed in carrying with it a shrill trumpeting sound that stabbed his sensitive eardrums and gave him headache.

What the hell is that? Louie thought.

Louie slid his eyes toward the circle of light and glimpsed a pair of black shoes. The tube began to shake. He felt himself sliding out.

Louie hit the floor and bounced. He had been rolled up in the tube so long that his body adhered to the shape. As he struggled to unravel himself, he spied a chubby-faced old geezer, standing over him with the empty tube in his hand and eyes radiating concern.

Louie rolled back and forth trying to unfurl his body and making little progress. He reached out to Chubby-face and said, "Gimmie a hand!"

The chubby-faced geezer pinched Louie by the shoulders and yanked him unfurled as if he was opening a beach towel. Then he placed Louie on his feet and helped him to stand against his body's repeated attempts to return to its rolled state.

"How long you been in there?" asked Chubby-face.

"I don't know," Louie replied trying to think. "What day is it?"

"Friday."

"Since Thursday. Cooper didn't tell you?"

"No," Chubby-face said, ashamed.

"What's happening out there? What's all that noise?"

"The shit hit the fan. Cooper's dead. The crowd got through the gates and charged Rust's tent."

"Dead?"

Chubby-face nodded. "We tried to warn him that something like this would happen."

A rise in the ruckus outside the RV. Rust's piercing holler vibrated the RV walls and made both men cover their ears.

"You have to get outta here!" Chubby-face yelled over the ruckus.

"Where am I supposed to go?!"

Heading toward the door of the RV, Chubby-face replied, "Beats me, kid!"

"Where are you going?!"

"As far away from here as possible!" He opened the door and let in a rush of noise.

"Wait! Where's Indo?!" Louie yelled. "Have you seen 'em?!"

"I don't know! He wasn't in his tent!" Chubby-face paused on his way out the door, looked back, and said to Louie, "Take care of yourself, kid!"

Moving during lulls in the wind, and the stampeding feet, Louie slithered from tent-to-tent covering his ears to block out the sound of Rust's trumpeting wail, which was now broken into extended verses of rampaging mastodonic fury. Its footsteps shook the ground.

Louie squeezed underneath each tent he came to, peeked out, and waited for another lull. The wind was picking up, starting to whistle. Up in the sky, clouds raged with contemptuous swirling. Lightning flashes set random spots aglow.

The massive statue stumbled into view as Louie watched. A sloppy pile of zealots clung to its legs. Rust lurched and staggered forward, dragging its long, lithe appendages weighted down by bodies.

More people dangled from the statue's arms. One man swung from its right armpit. Childlike fear warped Rust's features as it focused its trumpeting wail at the swarm of zealots. Without the confines of the tent to trap and thus amplify its voice, the impact of the shrill pitch was less devastating. Heads remained intact as a result. But the sound still hurt people's ears. Louie's ears were more delicate than most, now starting to bleed.

Rust did everything to get the people off. It twisted, and writhed, and kicked, and stomped, and swung its arms. People were flung into booths, and tents, and amusement rides where they hung like macabre Christmas Tree Ornaments.

Bodies littered the ground twice and three-times squashed. More people dropped to their knees in prayer at the statue's feet only to be kicked or stomped. Squishy carrion chunks stuck to the bottom of Rust's feet causing it to slide off balance.

The statue's legs became entangled in a tent's guylines and the frightened thing tripped and fell on top of the tent. Sun baked canvas enveloped the statue like plush bedding.

Luckily it wasn't Indo's tent. That was Louie's destination.

He slithered underneath and into Indo's tent during another lull. The tent-wall bowed and flexed as the wind flared up. The dirt floor trembled to Rust's thumping stumble-dance.

Louie stood up and held onto the nearest heavy object—an antique armoire passed down through generations of tenants—and squinted to see through the cloud of dust kicked up by the wind. The dust cloud tricked his mind into thinking Indo had not left.

"Indo," Louie called out hoping that his friend would solidify before his eyes. But that never happened.

Louie moved between solid objects, holding on for dear life as he scanned the large room for some indication of where Indo might be, wishing that he would return and protect him from the madness outside.

The dirt cloud thickened. Coaxed by the intensifying wind, tiny grains of dirt attacked his orifices. Louie turned away and squinted. The virulent dirt-cloud was laced with papers, and books, and various light-weight objects. One of those objects—a newspaper—slapped him in the face and stuck there, inhibiting his vision.

Louie pinched the paper—USA Today—away from his face and grimaced at the headline that stared back at him.

RARE AFRICAN EXHIBIT KICKS OFF CROSS COUNTRY TOUR IN PORTLAND, OREGON.

Under the headline a promotional photo for the ART AND MYSTERY OF AFRICA EXHIBIT circled in red marker. A beautiful woman made of wood, partially formed from the torso up and boasting a life-like expression, was prominent in the photo. Her face was filled with exotic majesty. Her eyes were alive, seeming to beckon Louie. He had to look away lest he fall victim to her intoxicating gaze.

"He found her," Louie said, momentarily excited for Indo, who was forever lamenting about his beloved Atieno, and of how she was taken from him by his summoner.

But it meant that Louie was on his own now, without Indo to look out for him. As that fact sunk in, he began to feel sick.

The wind intensified and kicked up more dirt. Louie was lifted off his feet. He wrapped his arms around the leg of a table and held on for dear life.

The tent walls bowed, and then flexed. The ground shook. Outside Rust Resurrection screamed bloody murder.

Louie closed his eyes and prayed. He didn't even believe in God.

PAPERCUTS

Kurt Sadler floated partially submerged in a happy trance as he followed his normal route along the outer border of the Utopia Springs Estates. It was the tail end of his morning run and he was coming up on completely whupped. Generally a morning run left him feeling rejuvenated and ready to kick some figurative ass. But not today. Not even with one of his favorite tunes— "Talking in your Sleep," by the Romantics— streaming from his headphones.

A trembling, huffing ball of golden brown fur was attached to Kurt's right wrist via a retractable nylon leash. The furball's name was Rucksack. She was a needy little thing the likes of which Kurt never, in a million years, thought he'd own.

Rucksack was a Pomeranian. Pomeranians were lapdogs. Lapdogs were for snobby chicks and gay dudes. Any straight man who owned one was pussy-whipped.

Now Kurt had love for the little shit. It was a conditional love, however, that didn't extend to dragging the hindering little furball with him during his run. This was *his* time. Time to reflect. Time to micromanage and schedule his day down to the minute. These were the tools Kurt used to allay the squall of anxiety that slapped him awake every morning. As such the morning run had become an integral requirement of a good day.

Nancy Sadler was aware of her husband's contempt for the chore, but she had no clue how deeply it ran. Her idea of the family unit consisted of herself, Kurt, their seven-year-old biological daughter Lili, and their other daughter, Rucksack. Kurt should see it that way and get over it. But he bristled at the comparison. Lili was his life.

Kurt would often try to sneak out. Nancy played right along. Sometimes she would pretend to be asleep until he was halfway out the bedroom doorway.

"Don't forget Ruck Ruck," she'd purr from beneath the covers, lethargically. Ruck Ruck was Nancy and Lili's pet name for the little shit.

Sometimes Nancy would appear out of nowhere with the dog cradled in her arms. Rucksack had a tiny face with a mouth full of daggers that seemed to never close. Her entire body shook when she panted, which she did endlessly. Kurt imagined that Rucksack's was a helpless, painful existence, the sad result of human vanity.

"Baby needs go potty," Nancy would coo with pouty eyes and her bottom lip sticking out.

That pouty-faced expression and that baby voice used to be part of her sexual repertoire before she forgot she was a reasonably attractive woman. It made Kurt long for those days, days when the mere thought of Nancy didn't invoke negative feelings. These feelings weren't conducive to marital longevity. Even if the marriage counselor said that they were normal and sometimes healthy as long as you confront them.

Rucksack couldn't keep up with Kurt's pace. The little dog was starting to choke from the constant tugging on her collar. Kurt scooped her up in his arm and carried the dog like a football.

The cookie cutter suburban community was laid out in a starburst pattern. Five rows of cul de sacs converged on a large circle of paved land with a small sitting park in the center. There were 21 homes per row; 10 on the left side, 10 on the right, and one sitting at the head of each cul de sac curve.

Kurt lived on Huntsacker Lane, which had been experiencing a slow exodus and thus had become a stain on an otherwise blustering suburban landscape.

Currently there were 10 vacancies on the block starting from the seventh house in on both sides and extending to the big house on the peak of the curve on the left, and then back to Colin Sachs' house on the right. Colin lived next door to the big house at the cul de sac's peak—612 Huntsacker.

Pete and Sasha Willingham were the last residents to occupy the revolving door that was 612 Huntsacker. Like the others before them, they had left the place in a hurry one night and never came back. There had been 4 families in all since the Utopia Springs Estates was built in 2007. The house and the events surrounding it had become the scourge of the Estates Community.

The entrance to the Utopia Springs Estates was marked

by a sliding iron gate that stretched between corner sections of decorative stone embossed with a rectangular plaque that was lit from the bottom. Engraved letters read UTOPIA SPRINGS ESTATES: A SECURE COMMUNITY.

Just beyond the gates a small guard shack sat in the middle of the narrow road that reached back 100 feet to the paved circle and out to the rows of cloned edifices.

Kurt jogged into the front gate and waved to Felix, the morning-shift guard. Felix waved back with a half-devoured pastry in his hand. He was always eating something.

A secure community... Kurt sarcastically thought.

A black Mazda packed full of boxes sped past Kurt. His reclusive neighbor Colin Sachs was slouched behind the wheel, his baby face hidden behind cheap shades that were too large for his head, and a patchy, unkempt beard. Colin waved like it was a chore to do so.

Kurt stopped and waved back. He mused about the unfortunate series of circumstances that had recently befallen Colin as he watched the car drive down the road and out the front gate like a bat outta hell.

I guess he finally had enough.

Kurt jogged through the circle park huffing and puffing, and continued toward Huntsacker Lane. His house was the fourth one in on the left side.

He heard someone whistle and knew instantly that it was meant for him. Based on the direction it had come from, he knew who it was as well. Begrudgingly Kurt looked up from the pavement.

Ted Woodruff, a short, stocky man who looked like an asshole cop, walked out of his house and down the pathway between his and the neighbor's lawns as if he had been anticipating Kurt's arrival. .

Fearing a lengthy interaction, Kurt snatched his eyes away and pretended not to hear or see Ted approaching. He put on his "Leave me alone, I'm running" face and continued at a hurried pace. When it became evident that Ted wasn't going to give up without some form of communication, Kurt waved without looking and said, "Morning, Ted."

"Morning Kurt. You got a minute?"

"I saw." Kurt said on the run.

"Saw what?"

Reluctantly Kurt stopped and put Rucksack down. He could have kept jogging. He probably should have.

"Colin Sachs. He zoomed past me down by the gate. Looked like he was leaving for good."

"Really? Huh... Guess he finally had enough."

"Yeah. That's what I said. Poor bastard."

"Shoulda left a long time ago, if you ask me," Ted remarked.

Kurt frowned at Ted's candor, even more eager now to end the conversation.

"Well...have a good one," he said as he gestured toward his house. "Oh...Lili said she left the ball with Caleb, by the way."

Eight-year-old Caleb was Burt and Kathy Murphy's kid. The Murphys lived at the corner, across the street from Ted. Ted had been asking about the ball. His daughter Sue Ellen claimed that she had found the thing at the circle park. Ted's wife Alicia took Sue Ellen there every Saturday where she would play for hours while Alicia gabbed it up with the other milfs who came and went with their children.

There was some debate among the kids of Huntsacker Lane about who had seen the ball first. Sue Ellen's bid for ownership was the loudest and most persuasive. She was basically an eight-year-old version of her father, a bully.

The ball itself was a strange thing. Big as a beach ball with a handle on top in the shape of a hand. The kids loved the damn thing, but their parents were mystified by the warped face that decorated its surface. None of them could recall a movie or a television show or a book from which the character was derived, which made a few of the parents wonder if whatever it had come from was appropriate for children.

"Whoa. Hold your horses," Ted said. "I wanted to run something by you."

Kurt rolled his eyes mentally.

"Yeah?"

"So, I've been thinking…If we're gonna do this right, we're going to need a treasurer. The fellas all agreed that you'd be the perfect man for the job with your background in accounting."

Kurt mostly avoided confrontation, however Ted was the type who would view anything short of emphatic refusal as acceptance, and Kurt had no intention of being treasurer of anything, let alone a goofy organization like the "Guardians of Utopia."

Rucksack was darting in and out of Kurt's legs. He had to keep lifting his feet to stop the leash from tangling around them.

"Thanks for thinking of me, but I'm gonna have to decline. I barely have time for my family, as it is."

"Then you *make* time. Especially for something like this."

Kurt felt his blood pressure rise.

"What does my acting as treasurer have to do with catching Cecily's attacker?" The words came out hard and cool, even more so than Kurt had intended.

Three weeks ago Cecily Sigworth awoke to a feeling in her gut that told her someone was in her bedroom, hiding in the dark, a man who was not her husband, Jim.

Jim worked the late shift and wasn't expected home until morning. Cecily had called out to no response and then made a run for the door and was grabbed from behind. She never saw her attacker, but remembered that he smelled like B.O., and that he weighed next to nothing, so he must've been small. A police officer told her that it was more likely her heightened adrenaline that made him feel that way. She said that the man held her down and groped her and that he had used some kind of edged weapon to slice her about the arms, back, and legs, which left deep lacerations like paper cuts on steroids. He shoved her face into the carpet so that she couldn't breathe and she ultimately passed out.

It was determined that no rape had occurred, and that the attacker had probably recognized Cecily from one of her photos, and followed her home. Cecily had a part-time gig as a plus-sized clothing model for a local department store.

"Jim says she still has trouble sleeping, you know," Ted commented.

"I'm sure she does, Ted. But once again, that has nothing to do with my…"

"Don't you wanna see this guy brought to justice?"

"Well, of course I do, Ted. But who knows if this…groper is even out there still?"

"So we should just go about our lives like nothing ever happened?"

Kurt paused, annoyed that he had been goaded into a semi-flustered state by an intellectual caveman like Ted Woodruff.

"You heard that cop, Ted. It's likely that this pervert moved on, especially since we've been making ourselves visible with the neighborhood watch patrols."

Ted responded with a series of pensive nods that told Kurt he was about to turn on the guilt.

"Well…if you're busy, you're busy, I guess. I suppose I could see if Ron Stanky would be able to do it."

Ron Stanky was a failed stock broker with a gambling habit as big as his wife's fake tits, which looked hard as titanium bowling balls and completely contradicted the rest of her sluggish, rotund body.

Although he knew Ted was playing him, Kurt felt obliged to end the discussion on a good note. Otherwise Ted was liable to warp his refusal into outright dismissal and use it to paint him in a negative light with the other fellas.

"Tell you what, Ted. I should be done with this project I'm overseeing at the office by the end of the month. Maybe then I'll have some more time."

Ted pondered Kurt's statement and then nodded.

"See. Now that wasn't so hard was it?" he said with a semi-satisfied grin.

Kurt looked down at Rucksack who had been tugging at the leash. She was looking up at him with eyes pleading for sustenance.

"I hear ya, girl," he said to the dog. "She's hungry," he informed Ted.

"Un huh," Ted replied. "So, when you gonna get a real dog?"

When you get a fucking clue, Kurt thought.

"Good question," he chuckled, and then turned to walk away…"I gotta get her home before she starts pitching a fit."

"We wouldn't want *that*," Ted quipped. "Oh, by the way, we're meeting tomorrow night at my place. I know you're busy and all, but I promise it won't take up too much of your precious time."

You don't quit, do you? Kurt thought as he scooped Rucksack up in his arm and patted her on the head.

"What time?" Kurt's reply sounded like a concession.

"Seven O'clock. Sharp."

Kurt pretended to peruse his mental calendar. He knew that barring some work-related emergency he was definitely free this Thursday at 7pm.

"I'll be there."

A loud noise invaded the morning calm. It sounded like a garage door being yanked into a slow, upward crawl. A motorcycle engine gargled and then roared. It was coming from the house directly across the street from Kurt's.

The garage door yawned open and Austin Wallace rode out on the back of a midnight-black Yamaha Shadow. He was covered in black leather that was shrink-wrapped to his toned physique. Yellow tubing ran up the sides of the padded suit. His face was hidden behind the tinted visor of his helmet.

"Here comes pretty boy," Ted groaned without moving his lips.

Kurt guffawed and shot an annoyed glance at Ted.

The engine's bestial rumble hurt the men's ears as Austin rode by without looking their way.

Kurt waved but was left hanging.

"Good morning to you, too," remarked Ted.

The rest of the morning unfolded like a typical day. Nancy had breakfast (bacon and two eggs over-hard) ready for Kurt when he returned from his jog as unspoken gratitude for taking Rucksack out with him. Kurt lapped the food up with affection, brushed his teeth, and gave Nancy a peck on the cheek on his way out the door.

He perked at the sound of a motorcycle in the distance as he tossed his briefcase into the passenger seat of his car and stood there waiting for Austin Wallace to appear at the mouth of Huntsacker Lane.

He flagged Austin down and apologized for the men in the neighborhood who had been giving him shit since he moved in two weeks ago.

"I feel compelled to convince you that I'm not 'one of *them*,'" he said over the rumbling engine.

"Aren't you a...*Guardian*?"

"Well...yeah. I guess I am," Kurt replied, embarrassed. "It's just the Neighborhood Watch. The name change was Ted's bright idea."

"I figured as much."

"He's kind of an A-hole."

"Figured that, too."

"Well...I just wanted to officially welcome you to the neighborhood...and to let you know that we're not all assholes around here."

"That remains to be seen," Austin said and then he rode off.

Kurt kept revisiting Austin's parting remark as he went about his day wondering if his neighbor included him in that assertion. But then some work-related issue would come along and distract him.

Work was as mundane as usual. There was no drama from the entry-level knuckleheads and no last minute assignments that required his staying late.

The neighborhood rugrats were playing with the bouncy ball with the ugly, warped face again when Kurt turned onto Huntsacker on his way home. Lili was with them. She waved to him and smiled when he drove up.

Kurt stopped and lowered the window.

"Hi Punkin," he said to her, smiling warmly.

"Hi Daddy."

"You kids know to stay on this side of the block, right?"

This side of the block meant south of the border of vacant houses.

"We know Daddy," Lili replied.

"Mr. Woodruff already told us like 40 times," remarked the smart-assed chubby boy in the Pittsburgh Steelers Jersey. His name was Roger Stanky, Ron's kid.

Kurt shot Roger a dirty look.

"You kids be careful," he said.

"We will, Daddy."

He was about to say something else when the bouncy ball came out of nowhere and Lili screamed and jumped out of the way to avoid being hit. She picked up the ball and ran giggling and screaming after the child who had hurled it at her. The other children screamed and ran from her. Kurt smiled at their youthful exuberance as he drove off.

Dinner was boring, but not terrible. Afterward Kurt helped Lili with her homework. Then he knocked around with Rucksack for a bit. At some point he got too rough and Rucksack yelped. Nancy came running and Kurt quietly longed for a bigger dog that he could wrestle with like he did with his German Shepherd, Spanky, when he was a kid. The night ended with Kurt and Nancy spooning in bed to *Pawn Stars* on the History Channel.

That was Monday. Tuesday through Thursday afternoon played out similarly.

The rush hour traffic out of Philly was especially rough on Thursday evening. Kurt deferred to the radio while he inched along I-76 West. He bobbed his head to a few good songs and disagreed with talk radio pundits. He traded fleeting glances with a woman in the next car over, whom he considered way out of his league, and felt flattered.

The dashboard clock read 7:30pm when he drove through the entrance to the Utopia Springs Estates. The meeting of the Guardians was scheduled for 7pm.

Kurt was on cloud nine from the interaction with the pretty woman and hadn't realized that it was so late. The neighborhood children had all been summoned in for dinner, which left Huntsacker Lane eerily quiet.

Kurt grunted at the thought of Ted Woodruff's response to his tardiness and compared it to what the entry-level knuckleheads at the office must have felt when he confronted them and pointed at his watch upon their arriving late for work.

Nancy would give him shit for skipping dinner. Depending on how he left it, that could boil over into later in the evening when he planned on hitting her up for his bi-monthly dose of pussy. He assured himself that he wouldn't let that happen.

Nancy was on the phone with her best friend Donna and hadn't even started dinner when Kurt ran in the front door and straight to the bathroom. Usually that would have been cause for a spat, but tonight it worked out in his favor.

He changed his clothes and interrupted Nancy with a passionate embrace. She told Donna to "Hold on," and then she lowered the phone and focused her attention on Kurt, who was waiting for her to do just that.

"Where's Lili-bo-billie?" he asked her.

"She's having dinner with her classmate Stephanie's family. Remember? I mentioned it yesterday. You said it was okay."

Kurt didn't remember any of it.

"Oh yeah. That's right," he replied.

Remembering the time, Kurt kissed Nancy deeply and slid his hand down her back and over the jutting contour of her ass, ending with a squeeze that forced her groin into his. She responded with a reciprocal thrust and remarked, "Oh my!" Then he backed off and left her wanting more.

Kurt jogged half-a-block to Ted Woodruff's house, where the meeting of the Guardians was already in progress.

Alicia Woodruff greeted him at the door, her face filled with concern. He heard raised voices coming from deep inside the house. The voices belonged to Ted Woodruff and Austin Wallace. Kurt was surprised that Austin had decided to attend the meeting.

"What's goin' on?" he asked Alicia. "Is everything alright?"

Alicia responded with quizzical unease and directed him to the basement stairs. He walked through the living room where a group of wives lined the plump sectional couch nursing champagne glasses and acting like they weren't eavesdropping on their husbands. Kurt said his greetings on the move.

"Where's Nancy?" asked one of the women.

Kurt acted like he didn't hear her and descended the basement staircase gingerly. The tension in the basement was palpable. It hit him like a hot wind wafting up from a subway vent on an especially humid summer day.

"I knew it was a mistake coming here!" Austin Wallace yelled at Ted.

"Why's that? You got something to hide?" Ted replied.

"Guys! Guys!" Kurt interrupted as he rushed over and stood between the two men. "What the hell is this?"

"Pretty boy here doesn't wanna answer our questions," Ted accused.

"Questions?! Yeah..." Austin protested. "Try accusations!"

"Accusations about what?"

"Genius here seems to be implying that I might be this... *groper.*"

Ted chafed at the "Genius" comment. There were 3 men seated around a 50" Plasma TV mounted on the wall in the lounge area of Ted Woodruff's man cave. Ron Stanky was there, and so was Steve Mifflin from across the street. The TV was turned on with the sound muted. An ornate pool table loomed in the background. A rectangular lamp faced down at the plush green surface of the table and illuminated four more men standing around it holding pool sticks.

He saw Burt Murphy and Jim Sigworth back there and two other men with whom he had traded small talk in passing. Generally, Kurt kept his neighbors at an arm's length, and his feelings for these men as individuals ranged from non-existent to generally warm. As a group, however, their xenophobia was intimidating. And Ted Woodruff was King Dumbass.

Austin Wallace was Ted's (and, by default, the Guardians') latest target.

Ted had overheard Alicia comment to one of the other wives over the phone that Austin was "a hot piece-a-man with a body to die for."

"The attack *did* happen around the same time you moved in," Ted asserted. Then he directed his intensity at Kurt. "Don't act like you haven't thought about it, too."

"Actually I haven't."

"I shoulda known you'd take his side," Ted replied after an incredulous pause.

"Well, you're kinda forcing the situation, Ted."

"What?"

"You've had it in for him since he moved in, for starters. I mean, it's no wonder why he blows you off in public." Kurt scanned the other men and stopped on Cecily Sigworth's husband, Jim. "You're not buyin' this are you, Jim?"

Jim shrugged his shoulders and looked away.

"Un-believable," Kurt responded. "And I can't believe the rest of you guys allowed it to get to this point."

"That's because they agree with me. Maybe if you'd gotten here on time you woulda heard the facts."

Kurt rolled his eyes and then replied in a dismissive tone, "The facts."

"You're wasting your time, Kurt," Austin warned.

"No. I wanna hear these facts."

Austin let out a disgusted breath and left the room.

"Figures," Ted commented under his breath.

The basement fell silent as the men listened to Austin's heavy footsteps move swiftly across the floor above. They heard a door slam. A few seconds later a voice yelled down the steps. It was Alicia Woodruff.

"Honey?"

"Yeah, babe," Ted replied.

"Everything okay down there?"

"Right as rain, babe."

"You need anything?"

"We're good. Thanks."

"You guys are ridiculous," Kurt scolded. "What sense does it make that Austin would be the groper?"

"You don't think it's strange that somebody would move into this neighborhood of all places. *This* neighborhood? The guy's got a successful business from what I hear, so it's not like he couldn't afford to live somewhere else."

"Yeah, I admit it's a little…strange, but—"

"If you were lookin' for a house, wouldn't you have done your research and found out enough about this place to stay away?"

"Maybe he didn't do his homework. I dunno."

"Well, that's just foolish."

"I agree with you, Ted. I'm sure he had his reasons, though."

Kurt couldn't imagine what those reasons might be other than that Austin was a dunderhead, which didn't seem to be the case.

"Like coppin' a feel on our wives?"

Kurt heard someone snigger. A few of the men were nodding in agreement.

"Why does he keep dodging our questions, too…if he's so innocent?" Ted added.

"You come off like a bully, Ted."

"A bully?"

"That's right. I'd probably feel the same way if I were in Austin's shoes. Yeah, you would think anyone with a brain would steer clear-a-this place, but to assume then, that he's going around groping suburban housewives…"

In this case, suburban housewives was code for slightly overweight and boring.

"…that's a pretty big leap, don't you think?" Kurt continued. "I mean, look at him. You really think he's hard up for women? The guy owns a chain of gyms. He's probably got tail coming out his friggin' ears."

"Sounds like you got the hots for him."

Kurt tensed up.

"No. But your wife does."

Someone gasped over by the pool table.

Ted's demeanor quickly shifted from playful to angry. His face questioned, *What'd you say?!*

"Come on, Ted. I don't think it's any secret how the women in the neighborhood feel about the guy."

Shocked female tonnages sounded off at the top of the

basement steps. Downstairs, the men puffed up and traded doubtful glances as if to say, "Not my wife."

"You all know it's true. My Nancy's guilty of it, too."

Kurt had caught Nancy stealing a glance or two whenever Austin rode by on that motorcycle of his. If he asked her, she'd probably say that he wasn't her type, or that he was "oh-kay if you're into that sort of thing," which was more than he could say for some of the other wives who weren't so subtle about what they'd do to Austin if given the opportunity.

Kurt could see Ted's mind working. It was written all over his big, dumb face.

"My point is that maybe you're all letting your insecurities get in the way of clear thinking." Kurt added when it seemed like Ted was going to blow a fuse or maybe stick his bottom lip out and start to pout. "What about what the police officer said?"

"Why are you so into this guy?" Ted instigated. "You know something we don't?"

"You get a sense about people, Ted."

"A sense…" Ted quipped to his audience. "So now he's a psychic."

Kurt rolled his eyes and exhaled loudly.

"This is pointless," he said and stormed out of the basement.

***

Cavanaugh's Pub was filled with people in their 20s and 30s, most of whom appeared much younger than Kurt remembered looking when he was their age. It didn't help that Austin still looked like he could pass for one of them, even though he was closer in age to Kurt.

Young men were huddled in packs ogling girls with pretty faces and asses that would have been considered fat in Kurt's day.

Something that passed for music played on the jukebox. On one of the TVs, a bobble-headed news anchor reported on the aftermath of a freak tornado that tore through the outskirts of Merrywood, Pennsylvania two months ago and claimed a death toll in the triple digits. Haunted survivors recounted seeing Jesus at a carnival, and people took pity on them.

Some loudmouth at the end of the bar was going on about how strange that was, how tornados never happen in Pennsylvania, not even way out in Pennsyl-tucky, where Merrywood was located.

Kurt had run into Austin in Center City on his way to the garage where his car was parked. He had left work early—at 2pm—because he could. Austin had just come out of one of those electronics shops run by shady Middle Eastern types, with a bag in his hand.

"Better make sure you got a warranty," Kurt walked up and said. He felt bad when Austin responded that the owner was a client of his.

He was sure that Austin would decline his offer to buy him a drink. He figured he was too much of a health nut for that, especially at 2:27pm on a Friday afternoon.

But here they were in the bar.

"You said that?" Austin nearly choked on his drink—a screwdriver that was heavy on the screw.

"I did," Kurt confessed as he fidgeted in his barstool attempting to find a position that made him appear younger than his chronological age, if that was at all possible.

"Shit, man!"

Kurt's body language conveyed remorse.

"I know. It was like one of those times when you regret saying something as soon as it comes outta your mouth"

"What did Ted have to say to that?"

"He just sort of puffed up like I was questioning his manhood. They all did."

"Greeaaaaat."

"If it's any consolation, I included my Nancy in it, too."

"Oh. Well that makes it all better."

"Trust me, if I could take it back I would," Kurt said on his way to leering at a buxom woman who walked past them. He lingered on her as she sauntered her fine ass into a booth at the back and flirted with the young man sitting across from her.

I was better-looking than that guy in my 20s, he mused. *You mean I could've scored chicks like that?*

"Tell me their wives didn't hear you?" Austin asked.

Kurt hesitated and then nodded, "Yes."

"Oh-ho-ho-MAN!"

"You shoulda seen the looks I got on the way out."

"I bet. So, how'd you leave it?"

"I told them I was gonna have that cop come back and reiterate his stalker theory."

Austin finished his drink and held up his empty glass for the bartender to see.

"Well, I appreciate the effort, man…but in the future, please…don't do me any favors," he half-joked.

"Hey. At least I got 'em off your back."

"At *least*," he chuckled.

"Another round?" the bartender interrupted.

Austin nodded and said, "Thanks."

The bartender eyed Kurt's glass, which had been half-empty for some time now.

"I'm good. Thanks," Kurt said. "Can't put 'em away like I used to."

He watched the bartender make Austin's drink and raised his eyebrows at the amount of vodka he poured in the small glass. "Used to be that was considered a double," he commented as he directed Austin's eyes to the man's fast hands.

Austin seemed disinterested.

"Y'shoulda just walked out, you know," he said a few minutes later.

Kurt got the impression that Austin was more troubled by his revelation than he let on.

"I did. Probably shoulda left a little sooner, though. It's just that Ted is such an asshole."

"And you felt like you had to knock him down a peg. You can't let guys like that bring you down to their level, man. That's how they get cha."

Kurt didn't reply. Instead he took a long sip from his drink.

"Well, what's done is done," Austin added. "No use crying over it."

Some time passed.

Austin persuaded Kurt to have another drink.

"You should come down to one of my facilities when you have some time," Austin said out of the blue. "We'll put some muscle on you. Maybe then your wife'll fantasize about you instead-a-me."

The two men shared a laugh. Kurt's was hiding a slight unease with Austin's statement.

"Wouldn't that be something."

"I'm serious. Come on down. The main one is on 9ᵗʰ and South, right down the street from the Whole Foods. S'called Human Power. I'll set you up with one of our trainers at a discount."

"What's it like a...private gym or something; right?"

"Private training facility."

"What's the difference; if you don't mind my asking?"

"Our clients work out by appointment. We cater to people who, for whatever reason, don't like the idea of working out in a traditional gym."

Kurt nodded in reverence of Austin's entrepreneurial vigor. For a while the men drank and people watched.

"So, ah...why *did* you decide to move to the Estates?" Kurt asked rather directly.

Austin stopped in mid-swig and rolled his eyes over to Kurt as if he suddenly expected Ted Woodruff and his suburban thug-squad to jump out from behind walls and under tables and surround him.

"Excuse me?"

Kurt looked at him for a moment, reading his face. "You mean you don't know?"

"Know what?"

"About 612 Huntsacker."

"The big house at the end of the block?" Austin asked visualizing the place in his head. "What about it?

"What did the realtor tell you?"

"Not much. I mean, I didn't ask."

"You mean you didn't even inquire about the area, the neighborhood, nothing?" Kurt asked in a high-pitched voice.

"I had my buddy, Hoff come look at the place to make sure it was structurally sound. He's done a ton-a-contracting work for me at my facilities. I walked around the neighborhood just to get a vibe for the area, which seemed fine at the time. You gotta understand...I'm from the city, man. Sure, I lived in a condo downtown, but people still get mugged on occasion. That's why I carry a gun."

"Really?" Kurt replied, somewhat startled by the info, and instantly curious to know if Austin had the gun on him now.

"Center City's a small world, man. People know who I am. They know that I own that 'cool new training facility on South Street.' I know a couple of business owners in the area who've been targeted by muggers in the past. I figure you can never be too careful."

If he had the gun on him, Austin wasn't giving any indication of it.

"What the hell do I have to worry about way out in the burbs...aside from boredom?" he gave Kurt a look and added, "...and crazy neighbors?"

Kurt pretended to laugh and lifted the glass to his mouth. It was empty.

"I was just looking for a place away from the city. Somewhere I could come take a break from all the drama down here, if you know what I mean. Like I said, Center City's a small world."

Kurt wasn't quite sure what Austin meant by 'drama,' but he guessed it had something to do with women. The guy probably had a harem of hot, in-shape babes.

"You know, the realtors...they dress up the vacant properties to look lived-in whenever they're about to show one of them? We used to warn people, but the real estate agency called the police on us...on Ted, actually. They told us not to interfere. But people always find out anyway. That's what the Internet's for; right? It's as easy as Googling 'Utopia Springs Estates.' That's why everyone was so surprised when you moved in."

Austin was looking at him with a 'what the fuck' look in his face.

But Kurt had said too much already. As a rule he never talked about what had happened. None of the remaining neighbors did. Someone had mentioned that talking about ghosts could actually conjure them up. After the horror stories they had heard from the various owners who had fled from 612 Huntsacker, nobody wanted to risk that it might be possible.

"So, you gonna let me in on this big secret, or you gonna keep being all weird and cryptic?" Austin asked, more curious than fearful.

"It's haunted," Kurt blurted out. And then took a drink and pretended to watch the TV on the wall in front of them.

Austin stared at the side of Kurt's face.

"What?" Kurt turned around and said.

"What do you mean, 'What?' You're just gonna throw some off the wall crap like that out there and expect me not to call you on it?"

"Trust me. I know how it sounds. But it's true."

"So that's supposed to be why everybody moved out; because the house at the end-a-the block is haunted?" Austin asked with a cynical glint in his eyes.

Kurt nodded, "Yes," and then said, "It started with the neighbors nearest to 612, because of all the noise…and the ghosts or spirits or whatever were always taunting their kids from the windows while they played in the street. From there it was like a domino effect. Colin Sachs is the only one who…"

Kurt suddenly stopped talking and put his finger to his mouth and whispered, "Shhhhh." Just then the bartender walked by, pointed at their glasses, and queried with his eyes.

"I'm good," said Austin.

Kurt almost asked the bartender to make him another screwdriver, but then he thought about how he would have to explain to Nancy why he had gotten drunk on a Friday afternoon when he was supposed to be working.

"I'm done. Thanks," he said.

They sat there watching TV until the bartender walked back down to the other end of the bar, and then Austin grilled Kurt some more about the neighborhood secret. After a while Kurt became annoyed with Austin's persistent skepticism. To shut him up, he told his new neighbor everything that he knew about the house at the end of the block. He told him about the people who had lived there.

"There were four families in the span of five years," Kurt said. "All nice people. Good people. That's how they started out anyway. By the time they left, though…"

"You can never really know people, Kurt," Austin replied. "Ordinary people are into all kinds of crazy shit behind closed doors. Families, too. I hear about it all the time in my line of work."

"Not these people. One thing you'll learn is that everybody knows everybody's business at the Estates. Between the Meet and Greets, the community meetings, and functions, and the busy-body's yapping at the gym."

"This place just gets better and better," Austin sighed.

"I knew these people, Austin. I saw how that house changed them. They weren't the same by the time they left. Escaped is more like it."

"You escape from jail…or from a third-world country. Not from a house."

"From this house you escape…if you're lucky."

"So what, exactly was it that chased them all away?" Austin asked. "Or what did they claim it was, I should say?"

"They would tell us things at the community meetings. We didn't believe them at first. I've actually been in the house. Most of us have. And I'll admit. There is…*something* going on there. It's a feeling—like a sense of dread. It makes you want to get outta there as fast as possible. We all felt it. I don't know how those families stayed as long as they did based on that feeling alone. But, you see…none of us ever *saw* or *heard* anything at the time. And these weren't your garden variety 'bump-in-the-night' ghost stories they were telling us. We're talking phantom laughter, disembodied eyes in the darkness, voices hurling vulgar remarks, indoor lightning. They had names for some of the things. The mud dog. The baby in the walls. The stripper."

"What's so scary about a stripper?" Austin scoffed. "She fat or something?"

Kurt hesitated, and then said, "Supposedly she lures men in and then ties them down...or tricks them into thinking they're tied down and makes them watch her strip."

"Again. Is she fat or deformed or something?"

"She doesn't strip outta her clothes."

"Then what does she..." Austin started to say, and then his eyes grew wide and the muscles in his face relaxed.

Kurt nodded at Austin's sudden epiphany, and then he finished the thought for him, "Her skin."

Austin felt the hairs on his arms rise.

"They say she screams in pain the whole time, but she still keeps on dancing. Pretty fucked up, huh? The media came around after the first few incidents. This was back in '08...'09. Of course, that brought out the whackos. It was just awful. Nobody wants that again, so everybody acts like the place doesn't exist."

"The big white elephant on the block, huh?"

"Exactly. We took the developer to court to get him to tear the place down. But you know how slow the legal process can be."

Kurt told Austin the theory shared by most of the neighbors, that the hauntings had something to do with the recycled building materials used to construct the house. In fact, the entire cookie-cutter community was constructed from recycled building materials. Maybe the specific materials for 612 had come from someplace or places where terrible things had happened.

Austin kept coming back to the "stripper." He told Kurt that he might have seen her standing in the bedroom window one of those times when he walked around the neighborhood to get a vibe for the area.

"Really?" Kurt replied with alarm. "She's one of the rarer ones from what I've heard. The two guys who've seen her...

one of them had a heart attack and he's never been right since. The other one—a contractor—committed suicide a few days later. "You see her face?"

"No. I only saw her from the chest down."

"Be thankful that you didn't. They say that's how she gets you; like she's so beautiful that you can't resist her."

"What are you thinking?" Kurt asked Austin following a quiet span.

Austin thought for a moment, and then he smiled and said, "I think the nutjobs in the city don't have a thing on you suburbanites."

Kurt was just drunk enough that he found humor in Austin's remark.

"You might just be right about that, my friend."

Austin finished his drink a few minutes later and then he shimmied off of the barstool. He flashed a mischievous smile and said, "Come on. Let's go over there now."

***

Austin closed the South Street facility at nine pm and raced home on his motorcycle with ghosts and haunted houses on the mind. The old *Unsolved Mysteries* theme ran through his head.

"I'll get it." Nancy Sadler yelled when the doorbell rang.

Kurt was too lazy to get up from his comfy chair in the den. If he reclined it all the way, he could see into the next room, where the front door was. So that's what he did.

He watched his wife turn on the smiles and bat her eyelashes when she answered the door and saw Austin standing there.

She reeled it in when Kurt came into the room trying to act like he had been busy doing something productive when he was only watching television.

"Austinnn." Kurt sang nervously. He hadn't told Nancy that he had left work early this afternoon and stopped at Cavanaugh's for a drink. Now he would likely have to deal with having kept it from her as well.

"I'll have your old man here looking so buff that you won't be able to keep your hands off him," Austin said to Nancy.

Standing there, all loose and welcoming, when before she had been closed and lethargic, Nancy Sadler laughed like a school-girl.

"Old man?" Kurt playfully challenged.

"Ohhhh…He was only joking," Nancy scolded.

Kurt felt a twinge of jealous anger. The dynamic with Austin was different in the presence of a female. He exuded an animal magnetism that left Kurt feeling emasculated. Kurt wanted to run over and put his arm around Nancy, but that would be inappropriate. Besides, the guy he bonded with over drinks earlier wouldn't do anything to jeopardize his marriage. And Nancy might stray in her head, but that's as far as she would go.

"No. I was serious," Austin joked. "Actually, I came by to drop off a few vouchers for free training sessions at my place, Human Power."

"Aweee…That was so nice of youuu," Nancy purred.

"It's no big deal. We talked about it this afternoon."

"This afternoon?" Nancy said, confused. She looked over at Kurt who was standing there, oddly tense. He had been signaling for Austin to 'shut the hell up,' until Nancy's eyes fell upon him.

Kurt broke under Nancy's questioning glare. "I ran into Austin in the street this afternoon. We stopped for a drink at Cavanaugh's."

"That's interesting," Nancy said.

Kurt translated her tone to mean there would be hell to pay later on.

"Those vouchers are good for two guests," Austin said, attempting to counteract the sudden tension. "You could go together." And then he isolated Nancy and added, "Not that you need it."

Nancy smiled.

"Oh please," she said. "I'mma mess."

Austin looked her over, eyes widening in approval. "I don't think so."

Under different circumstances, Kurt would've warned Austin for stepping over the line.

"Oh. Well…thank you, Austin."

Austin worked his magic and charmed Nancy into a pleasant mood again. Afterward, he worked on Kurt for 30 minutes before he finally agreed to join him for a walk over to 612 Huntsacker. One of Kurt's stipulations was that his trainer for the free sessions be a hot chick; "like the ones from the infomercials," he specifically stated.

Austin recommended Christie. She was a former NFL Cheerleader.

At 10:27pm, Huntsacker Lane was like a narrow corridor walled in by square and rectangular patches of light with human silhouettes moving back and forth behind them. A skylight of blue-black watercolor hung overhead. Streetlamps, like anglerfish illicium with glowing lure attached, jutted up from the pavement at the beginning and middle of the block and cut triangles of light into the dark cloak that lay over the present. There were two streetlamps at the back of the cul de sac that didn't work. In fact they never worked.

"So why stay if it's so bad around here?" Austin asked Kurt as they walked up Huntsacker toward the house at the peak of the cul de sac curve like two young boys embarking on an adventure into the unknown.

"Not everyone can afford to just pack up and move, Austin. I certainly can't. And with the economy the way it is, selling the house is next to impossible. Some folks, like Colin Sachs, were just too damn proud to give in to ghosts. You probably saw him. Big guy…Kind of unkempt looking... He lived right next door to 612 until a few days ago."

"Yeah. I know who you're talking about."

"I was surprised that he finally gave in after everything he's been through. Him and his wife, Nadia were like the 'it' couple on the block. But then that place…That house… It changed him. It changed both of them—but Colin mostly. Nadia begged him to move the family outta there, but he refused. Said he wasn't going to be chased out of their dream house. Nadia eventually got tired of it, and took the kids and left. That was what…just over a year ago, I think?"

They were close enough that they could see 612 Huntsacker looming on the cul de sac curve. It was quieter at this end of the block and swirling with emptiness as if even the crickets and the bats had moved out. The moon had disappeared behind the watercolor clouds.

"That's Colin's place on the right," Kurt discreetly pointed. "The one with the big fence."

"Yeah. I was wondering about that thing."

"Ugly, isn't it. He built it to block his view of 612."

Austin walked out of the corridor and into the open circle where three houses faced him from the outward arching curve of pavement. Kurt was a few steps behind. It was dark back there and he was looking around like a nervous gazelle scanning for predators.

612 Huntsacker sat at the apex of the curve. The house to the left of it was vacant and looked as if it had been for a long time. Colin Sachs' place was on the right. It was the only house in the area with security bars over the windows and a 20-foot wooden fence. The fence looked unstable and, as with the security bars, completely out of place.

The place looked innocent enough. Aside from the awnings over the windows and the bowed outer wall on the first floor, it was identical to Austin's house. Kurt's house had a more conservative, "boxie" design, but appeared of the same family.

The front lawn was in need of a manicure, but not desperately so. The landscapers cut the lawn only when it was in dire need. And when they did, they worked with haste.

Austin came to a line of stenciled yellow letters painted in the street. The letters spelled out a warning. "DO NOT PASS!" Beyond the stenciled letters a 30-foot hot zone extended outward from 612's innocuous facade.

"Pretty sure Colin Sachs put that there," Kurt spoke quietly as he walked up beside Austin, who stared quizzically at the warning.

Following the trajectory of the yellow letters, Austin

traced an invisible line up to the shoulder of Colin Sachs' giant, ugly fence.

"So what happens if I cross it?"

"How bout we don't find out."

Austin shot a surprised look at Kurt and said, "You really are scared-a-this place; huh? Have you ever even seen one-a-these…ghosts?…with your own eyes, I mean?"

"No," Kurt replied as if he didn't want to admit it. "But I've seen the looks on the faces of some of the people who fled. And I've talked to them. These ain't flaky people, you know. Yet they were shaken to the core. I mean literally terrified. I've never seen somebody so scared. It scared *me*."

Austin was busy drinking in the place and only half-heard what Kurt had said. He didn't get a "haunted" vibe from the infamous house. In fact, Colin Sachs' home with its bars and fence looked more suited to a spooky occurrence or two.

"Come on. It's getting late," Kurt said.

"What? You wanna leave already?"

"I agreed to come up here with you so you could see the place. Well. There it is. See? Now let's go."

Kurt turned to leave with or without Austin.

Austin threw his hands up in protest. His eyes happened past the house and spied an open window on the second floor.

"Kurt! Look!" he said, suddenly excited.

Kurt flinched at the unexpected rise in Austin's tone. He spun around and admonished Austin with a "Shhhhhh!"

Austin was pointing at the window.

"Somebody musta just opened it!" he quietly exclaimed.

Austin's hip pocket started ringing. Startled by the noise, he fished out his phone and checked the display.

UNKNOWN flashed across the tiny screen.

He held the phone up to his ear and said, "Hello?"

He could hear breathing on the other end. There were hints of movement. And then…

"Come closerrrrrr…Pretty boyyyy," said a soft, playful voice.

Kurt, who was analyzing Austin's expression, saw his eyes shoot wide open.

"What? Who is it?"

Austin held the phone away from his face and put it on speaker.

Kurt leaned forward and listened, but nothing happened. He made a face at Austin, who responded by shrugging his shoulders. There was a click...and then a dial tone played over an incredulous moment.

Seconds later someone screamed. It confused the men as it came from somewhere behind them.

"Sounds like the Mifflin's house," Kurt thought out loud.

Austin took off running toward the screams.

Kurt had to dig deep to keep up with Austin, who ran like a cheetah. The screaming had stopped by the time they arrived at 618 Huntsacker.

Steve and Laura Mifflin lived at 618. Steve was a brainiac who worked in Pharmaceutical Research. Laura was a veterinarian who might've been pretty if she put on a little makeup and stopped dressing like a Quaker. Their respective careers kept them so busy that they were virtual strangers to their neighbors and to their seven-year-old daughter, Kelsey.

Kurt and Austin stood at the foot of the Mifflin's lawn waiting to hear...something. The light was on in the large living room window, but the curtains were closed.

Seconds passed in silence. And then a woman screamed. A loud crash followed. It sounded like someone or something had been thrown into a heavy piece of furniture, which then slammed into a wall. The woman cried out in pain. An aggressive, masculine sound, like a grunting growl or a growling grunt, came next. The woman screamed again, and then she started yelling for someone to "Get him off me!"

"That sounds like Laura," Kurt said to Austin.

And then a male voice yelled, "Stop running so I can help you!"

"That's definitely Steve."

"Get away from me!" shrieked a terrified Laura. "No! Don't touch me! Don't touch me!"

"Stay still, dammit! Stop running from me!"

An undulating silhouette with flailing arms and thrashing

hair passed, shrieking and growling, in front of the window. And then it was gone. The noise, however, persisted.

Austin bolted for the front door and rammed it with his shoulder. It didn't budge. Kurt thought that maybe he should help, but he was afraid. Austin kept trying. He finally broke the door in and fell inside.

Standing there, scared and uncertain, Kurt heard Austin yell, "Hey!" And then the violent noise amplified. A scuffle ensued.

"What are you doing?!" Laura yelled. "No! Don't hurt him! You're hurting him!"

There was a loud thud. Laura screamed. And then it got very quiet.

Kurt aimed his ear at the front doorway of 618 and listened intently. The door was wide open and leaning from the frame. The top hinge had been torn away leaving an angry wound. Someone was sobbing and whimpering inside. Based on the timbre of the voice, it was either Laura or Kelsey Mifflin.

Some of the neighbors ran up and hurled a thousand questions at Kurt, but he barely heard them. He was too busy imagining the worse for Austin, whose voice he should've heard by now. Before Kurt knew it, his feet were moving and the open doorway of 618 was rapidly bouncing closer.

Kurt ran in and stopped dead. A few of the neighbors followed him inside. They heard Kelsey Mifflin crying hysterically upstairs and saw overturned furniture and broken glass spread across the living room. They saw Steve Mifflin lying on his back in the middle of the floor. A wooden coffee-table leg, painted red, protruded from his chest. He was facing the doorway with wide, awestruck eyes that never closed.

A few feet away, Austin climbed to his knees in a daze having just woken up from a forced nap. Rubbing the back of his head, he sat back on his heels and looked around. A small handgun holstered against his ankle was clearly visible. He saw Steve Mifflin impaled on a coffee-table leg and gasped, and then he saw Kurt and a small group of his neighbors crowding the doorway.

Ted Woodruff ran in like he was angry that he hadn't

arrived first. He surveyed the scene and began delegating tasks.

"Somebody check on the girl?"

One of the men ran upstairs.

"It was an accident!" Austin yelled at his neighbors. "He had the stick…He was beating her with it…I was trying to stop him!"

Laura Mifflin was slumped, naked in the corner by the large front window clutching the curtain that she had pulled down with her when she fell. Her arms, shoulders, and chest were covered in welts and bleeding lacerations that were thin and deep, like giant paper cuts. Blood drained from her nose. More blood filled her iris. The puffy skin around it was damp from perpetual tearshed. The skin surrounding her eye socket was horribly inflamed and colored black and blue. She was stonefaced, in shock.

"Let's get her covered up," Ted commanded. He ran over and did it himself when no one volunteered.

Laura looked around the room with dead eyes as Ted wrapped the curtain around her. She looked right past the crowd of stunned and confused neighbors. She rolled her eyes the other way and cried out. Her face twisted and tightened and she began to bawl. She lifted her hand and pointed. She could have been pointing at Austin, who was sitting on his heels projecting remorse back at her. Or she could have been pointing at the bouncy ball with the ugly, warped face painted on top, which lay face-up in the next room.

***

The ambulance came and took Laura Mifflin to the hospital as the entire neighborhood watched. Another one took Steve Mifflin's body away. The police questioned Kurt, Ted, and the other men who had witnessed the scene inside 618 Huntsacker, and took their statements. Someone had warned the police about the gun hidden under Austin's pantleg. They surrounded him at gunpoint and made him lie down on his stomach in the Mifflin's front lawn. Most of the neighbors thought the cops had crossed the line when it took three officers to restrain and then cuff him. They manhandled him into the backseat of a squad car.

Austin was questioned and then released a few hours later without so much as an apology.

MONTGOMERY COUNTY POLICE DEPARTMENT
VICTIM-WITNESS STATEMENT FORM

Name: *Laura Jean Mifflin*
Address: *Utopia Springs Estates, 618 Huntsacker Lane*

Please understand. This is as difficult for me to write as it will be for you to digest. Know that I am a good, upstanding citizen of sound mind, not the crazy person that the events in this statement might seem to suggest.

I was toweling off after taking a shower when I was attacked. I still had soap in my eyes so I wasn't able to see who or what it was at first, but it felt like I had been slapped across the front of my body with a damp rubber mat that then vacuum-sealed itself to me and wouldn't let go. The thing was suffocating me. I panicked and managed to peel it off of my face. It cried out like a person when I dug my nails into it so I squeezed as hard as I could and it eventually let go.

I hold the thing out in front of me. It looked like the character painted on the bouncy ball that my daughter Kelsey borrowed from her friend Sue Ellen Woodruff. The best way to describe the thing is...it's a teenager. Male. Maybe 17 or 18 years old. And literally as flat as a pancake. It has a homely, sort of pitiful-looking face with sad eyes. I think they were brown, but I'm not sure.

It looked frightened at first, while I was holding it there, and then it flew into a rage. It lunged at me and I screamed. Then it wrapped itself around my head and started to suffocate me again. I was running out of air, and I knew that my screams were muffled by the thing's body, so I told myself to calm down.

"Now you're gonna do exactly what I say or I'm gonna kill you! Then, I'm gonna kill your husband! Then, I'm gonna kill your little Kelsey!" the thing said in a weird, tinny voice that reminded me of AM radio.

"Please don't hurt my family," I say. It tells me to "Shut the F up!"

I stand there frozen, fearing for me life while the thing unravels from around my head and moves down my body like a snake. The edges of its hands were sharp. I can still feel them groping me. I can still hear it moaning in my ear like it was enjoying the whole thing.

I couldn't take it anymore. I tried to pull it off, but it was stronger than you'd think for a person as flat as a pancake. This made it angry. It wrapped itself around my body and squeezed. Then it put its hand over my nose and mouth and said something about me having made a "BIIIG" mistake. I was able to pinch its hand away from my face long enough to get a few more seconds of air. I ran screaming from the bathroom with the thing wrapped around my body, trying to squeeze the life out of me.

My husband, Steve came running out of his office. Kelsey was crying in her room. Steve tried to pull the thing off, but it won't budge.

"Gonna kill you all!" it's yelling at us, but it sounds more frightened than angry.

I was getting lightheaded from its hand over my nose and mouth, but I tried to hold on. The last thing I remember is Steve whacking, and poking the thing, and trying to pry it off of me with an umbrella. He was being too careful not to hurt me, so I yelled something like, "Hit it harder! Kill the damn thing!" And then I must have passed out.

After weeks of coddling and dancing around the truth, a doctor informed Laura Mifflin that her story was most likely the product of denial.

"I believe that your mind just isn't ready to accept that your husband of 12 years would try to harm you, that he experienced some sort of breakdown, probably from stress, and attacked you in a rage," he said to her.

Laura became so upset that the orderlies had to come and restrain her. The doctors diagnosed her with Severe Depression and PTSDS. With her family's blessing, they admitted Laura to the Psych Ward for further evaluation. Kelsey was placed with Steve's parents in the interim. The public never found out about her "Third man" story.

Some people in the community blamed Austin for Steve Mifflin's death. In trying to subdue Steve, he had gone too far. The busybodies made a hobby out of second-guessing his actions.

"He didn't have to kill him."

"Couldn't he have warned him?"

"Couldn't he have pushed Steve out of the way when he saw where he was gonna fall? Couldn't he have held Steve down until the police arrived? He's supposed to be some kind of fitness expert. What, he's not strong enough to handle a scrawny thing like Steve? And what's he got that gun for? He's not a cop."

"Austin says he saw Steve Mifflin beating Laura with a wooden leg from the overturned coffee table," Kurt lamented to the bartender at Cavanaugh's Pub as the man restocked liquor bottles—mostly top shelf stuff—only half-listening until the story picked up. "He shoved Steve after wrestling the table-leg away from him. Steve stumbled backward and fell on top of one of the coffee table-legs that were still attached."

It was Monday at 10 am. Cavanaugh's was empty save for a sweaty man delivering boxes of frozen food on a handtruck. There was no music, no eye-candy, and two alpha-male wannabees wrapped in designer suits talked sports news on the television. Kurt was never much of a sports fan.

He should have been at work, but his head was swimming with violent images that he hoped a little liquid therapy would assuage. To hell with the repercussions once Nancy found out. Kurt made it a point to remind himself of that fact.

"Steve was lying there, dead, with the thing sticking out of his chest when I ran in," Kurt remembered. He was looking off as if the scene played out in the air in front of him. "Laura's curled up in a ball in the corner, buck naked. She's got these...*cuts* all over her body." He shuddered at the image and then said, "It's not every day you see something like that."

"I'll say," the bartender replied. "Austin the guy you were in here with before? The pretty boy?"

"Yeah," Kurt replied and then he downed the last swig of his drink (a screwdriver) and slid the empty glass forward on the bar.

"Another one?" The bartender asked.

Kurt thought for a moment, and then said, "I'm gonna go for it, Regis."

The bartender gave him a look.

"What? You never watched *Millionaire*?"

"Zat some kinda game show?"

Kurt started to respond, but then said, "Nevermind. Yeah. I'll have another."

The bartender took Kurt's empty glass and made him another drink—a double.

"Compliments of the house," the man said as set the new drink on top of a clean napkin.

"You don't have to do that," Kurt whined.

"Nah. You've earned it."

Kurt made a face at the size of the glass. "I might have to take the rest of the day off after this one."

"You strike me as the kind of guy who could afford it."

"Financially maybe," Kurt smirked. "The wife'll have a lot of questions, though."

"She got you on a short leash, huh?"

"I guess you could say that. Lately anyway. I've been keeping myself busy since it happened. Staying late at work. Coming home dead tired. Falling asleep while she's unloading her fears and concerns. I'm just trying to keep my head together. You know? She says I'm being selfish. That she and my daughter Lili are dealing with it, too. That I should be there with them. And she's got a point. But she wasn't there, at the Mifflin's, that night. She didn't see Steve lying there with his eyes wide open, the thing sticking through his chest.

All the blood…This was a guy I had just seen alive on my way to work that morning."

"Y'ever try talking to her about it; telling her what you just told me?"

"Nah…That never works out as smoothly as it should."

"Yeah. They certainly don't think like us, do they?" The bartender quipped.

Kurt smiled and raised his glass at the bartender's gesture. "Much obliged," he said and then he took a drink. He curled his lips, showing teeth in reaction to the vodka's burning aftertaste.

"Pleasure's all mine," the bartender said, "I haven't heard a story like yours in a good minute. And I hear 'em all damn day."

Kurt set the glass down and took a moment to gauge his drunkenness. Currently he was around 4 on a scale of 10. He caught himself revisiting the images again and frowned them away. The bartender had just unpacked the last bottle of Absolute Citrone and was breaking down the box.

Kurt waited until the man was finished, and then he said, "When I analyze the whole thing in my head, it had to have happened like Austin said."

The bartender moved on to the next box.

"Is there some debate?" he asked as he slid a utility knife from his hip pocket and used it to cut the box open.

"Not really, just a couple instigators tossing out theories. I guess carrying a gun makes Austin suspect in their eyes, even though he has a Concealed Carry Permit for it. Austin's pissed at me right now, by the way. He thinks I told the cops about his gun since I was the only one who knew about it."

The bartender paused, a bottle of top shelf Tequila in each hand. "Really?"

"I didn't though!" Kurt blurted, as if to thwart any suggestion of his disloyalty. "The gun was clearly visible strapped to his ankle that night. I told him so. Then he says I could've spoke up in his defense when the police were giving him shit about it. Frankly, I was in shock."

The bartender continued restocking.

"So, lemme get this straight," he said. "You said the two of you arrived at the scene together after you heard the wife screaming?"

"Yep. Austin ran in about 30 seconds before I did. Seemed like forever, though. I think I kinda panicked for a second."

"Well that's silly then," the bartender said. "Obviously something was going on *before* you guys arrived. And even if it wasn't, based on your description of the scene inside the house, there's no way anyone coulda done all that in 30 seconds?"

"Exactly," Kurt said, feeling validated by the bartender's assertion. "It's just a few busybodies spreadin' that horseshit. The general consensus is that Austin did the right thing. Ted loves the guy all of a sudden. Ted's the kind of asshole who can't stand being upstaged. Knowing him, he probably cozied up to Austin so he could feel like a badass by association."

"This Ted sounds like a real piece-a-work."

Kurt raised his glass, and said, "I'll drink to that." He took a sip and swished the liquid around his mouth before swallowing. His actions were slightly affected, although not to the extent that he noticed. "Freakin' Guardians...Sons-a-bitches are all working out at Austin's place now. They've even invited him out to the shooting range with 'em."

"Feeling left out, huh?"

"Disappointed is more like it," Kurt said. "I'da thought Austin would be above the Guardians and all their nonsense. But then, who the hell am I? Right? Still, I'm thinking about going to the next meeting, just to sorta make amends with Austin and reconnect with Ted and guys—as painful a notion as that sounds."

"When's the next meeting?"

"7 pm tomorrow. Why? You wanna come?"

"Noooo *thanks*," the bartender laughed.

The phone rang. Kurt nursed his double and tried not to eavesdrop on the bartender's conversation—something about reserving the bar for a party. On the TV a montage of sports highlights. The bartender returned a short while later looking as if he just remembered something.

97

"You never did tell me what the official ruling was," he said to Kurt.

"That Steve had some kind of stress breakdown and went postal on Laura."

"Yeah," the bartender chuckled. "They'll do that to ya if you let 'em."

"Hey! Steve was a friend of mine..." Kurt snapped. "Well, sort of."

"My apologies, man," the bartender said. "I didn't mean any disrespect."

"Ehhh...Don't mind me. I'm just a little tightly wound at the moment," Kurt said, flagging a hand at the man's apology.

He took another drink and became suddenly pensive. Seconds later, thoughts came pouring out of his mouth.

"You know. To be completely honest...Laura *is* a bit of a nag," Kurt said. "I guess that could've played a part."

"I'm just going on what you're telling me," the bartender began. "From what I've heard so far, I'd say it definitely plays a part. Nothing against women, but some of them have a way of slowly breaking a man. Problem is there're a lotta guys out there who'll put up with that shit. It goes on like that for years, and then one day, the poor bastard just snaps."

Kurt thought of Nancy, and felt a rare swell of appreciation that she was not one of those women. He was the type who would have put up with it.

"Steve was a good guy," Kurt remembered with a smile. "A little uptight, but a good guy nonetheless."

"It seems pretty cut and dry to me," the bartender said.

"Yeah, but you're forgetting where I live."

"Good point. No offense, but I never understood the appeal of those places. Everybody up in your business."

"It's definitely not for everyone."

Kurt didn't account for how mentally exhausted he would be when he drove into the front gates Tuesday evening. He had driven home from work on autopilot while he worried about 100 things at once, most of them work-related.

He dragged himself from the car and trudged up the driveway with heavy legs. Stress pressed his shoulders downward. He walked inside and stumbled over the bouncy ball, which Lili had apparently left in the vestibule. Normally that would have pissed him off, but Kurt was too tired to get pissed. He opened the door and tossed the ball onto the front lawn, where it belonged.

The neighborhood rugrats had gotten hold of the bouncy ball before the adults could dispose of it, as they had discussed, and now they didn't have the heart to take it away from them. There was nothing really wrong with the thing aside from the fact that it was present that night at the Mifflins', and thus tainted somehow.

Nancy gave Kurt the silent treatment all night. She was still angry about his trip to Cavanaugh's yesterday morning when he should have been working. It made him want to be as far away from her as possible.

There was still time to make the meeting. Kurt told himself that he would decide one way or the other after sitting with Lili for a while. He had a talk with her about responsibility. She apologized, in tears, for leaving the ball inside, and promised never to do it again. He felt guilty for making his little girl cry and cradled her until they both fell asleep.

Kurt woke up a half-an-hour later and watched a little TV in the living room. During that time, he decided that he would rather speak to Austin in private, and he would do just that tomorrow. Reconnecting with the Guardians could wait.

***

Nancy was in a much better mood when Kurt got home from work the next night. She had suddenly decided that the kitchen needed a makeover and spent the day painting the walls a rust color. Her hair was pulled back and she was covered in paint. Kurt thought she never looked prettier. He heard muffled barking coming from behind the closed basement door and was pleasantly surprised to find that Nancy had locked Rucksack in the basement because she wouldn't stop barking and jumping all over her as she tried to paint.

Lili had left the bouncy ball inside again, but surprisingly, Kurt wasn't all that bothered by it. Nancy's appearance had something to do with that.

"Lili's staying the night at her classmate Stephanie's," Nancy told Kurt when he asked where she was. And then she went about touching up the baseboards with paint.

"Again?"

"Yep. They're getting really close, those two."

"I don't know how I feel about that," Kurt replied. In fact, he felt jealous, and slightly annoyed that Nancy hadn't consulted with him before allowing Lili to stay with her friend. Suddenly, the bouncy ball reemerged as a point of contention.

"She left that damn ball inside again...after she promised me she wouldn't," Kurt instigated.

"That was my fault," Nancy replied as if it was nothing. She didn't even stop painting or turn around to face her husband. She appeared too focused on doing a good job to be lured into an argument. Or maybe she was just ignoring Kurt's ire for the greater good. "I told Lili I'd take it out, but I forgot. She was in such a hurry to be with her *Stephanie*. You know how she gets."

All Kurt could think about was how Lili used to get that way about him.

"And I wanted us to have some time to ourselves," Nancy purred in a sexy voice. She stopped painting and gave her husband a look that he hadn't seen in months.

Kurt's anger dissipated as he watched Nancy paint. She was on her knees and leaning forward so that the waist of her sweatpants slid down and revealed the top third of her ass. She arched her back, and swayed her hips back and forth, and sat down on her heels to give her butt cheeks a nice spread. Before long Kurt forgot what he was angry about. They had the entire house to themselves for the night. The thought gave him goosebumps.

Kurt opened several windows to dispel the strong odor of paint fumes, and then they ordered Chinese and ate it by the fireplace while Rucksack whimpered and whined and clawed at the basement door. Nancy wanted to let the little shit out. Kurt told her that they desperately needed the time to themselves. Nancy agreed, but complained about her appearance.

"Just gimme a half hour to shower and change," she begged.

But Kurt convinced her that she never looked more beautiful. The remark set her face aglow.

"You haven't spoken to me like that in months," she replied.

After dinner Kurt dug a quilted comforter from the linen closet and laid it out on the floor in front of the fireplace and they made love on top of it while the bouncy ball with the ugly, warped face watched from the vestibule. When they were finished Nancy went upstairs and took a shower while Kurt lay there naked, half-conscious, and spent. The showerhead made a powerful hiss that Kurt was tuned in to as he faded in and out of sleep on the quilted comforter.

"What the…! Nice one, Kurt!" he heard Nancy yell from the bathroom. It sounded like she had stumbled or slipped.

Kurt figured it was probably one of his shoes that he had neglected to put on the rack. Nancy was always complaining about that. There was a silent pause, and then she began to laugh. Kurt didn't realize how tense his body had become in those few moments.

"Stupid. Ugly. Thing," Nancy chided in a lowered voice and then there was a sound, like a rubber ball smacked or kicked against the wall.

Kurt wasn't sure to what Nancy was referring; only that she was still in a good mood. In his drowsy, post-orgasmic state, that was all that mattered. Soon he was chasing sleep again.

Kurt's eyes fluttered open at the sound of a struggle. It was coming from upstairs, in the bathroom. He listened, groggily, half-awake, thinking it was a dream until he heard Nancy cry out in a distressed voice, "Kurt! Help me!"

Kurt leapt into his pants and exploded up the steps afraid of what he might find in the bathroom—the groper perhaps.

"That's not possible. You can't be—" Nancy screamed before her voice was cut off. A loud thump followed.

Kurt found Nancy lying facedown on the bathroom floor clothed in a pair of panties.

"Honey!" he yelled as he ran up, crouched over her, and shook her repeatedly. "What happened? What's wrong?"

Kurt turned Nancy on her back when she didn't respond. His feet slipped out from under him and he fell on his ass and scooted away from the hang-jawed, sleepy-eyed expression on Nancy's face. There was a lump the size of a golf ball over her right eye. Her face, chest, and arms were covered with thin lacerations that cut deep. Some were short and some were long. It was obvious that she had fallen, or had been thrown, and that she had hit her head on the floor. She lay there with her eyes half open, unresponsive. Either she was in shock or she was...

Kurt crawled over to his wife, took her head in both hands, and lifted her face close to his. A droplet of blood rolled out of her right nostril, and over her lip, and into her mouth.

"Nancy! Honey!" he peered into her eyes and yelled. "Please answer me!"

Kurt tried everything to wake Nancy from the sleepy-eyed trance, but she never even flinched. He put his cheek to her mouth to see if he could feel her breath. He could not.

"Oh my God!" Kurt cried out. "Nancy!"

A suspicious noise came from Lili's room.

Kurt ran into Lili's room, turned on the light, and was instantly overwhelmed by pink. He looked around, sweating and breathing heavily, and then ran over to the closet on the other side of Lili's canopy bed and yanked it open expecting to find the groper hiding inside. A row of tiny outfits swathed mostly in pink with frills and hearts and animals dancing whimsically on them were suspended from hangers. Kurt shoved the clothing aside and looked behind them. Nothing... He shoved them back the other way. Still nothing...

Kurt backed out of the closet and closed the door. His eyes darted around the room. Something wasn't right. He could feel it. Yet the room looked the same way Lili had left it this morning. Her bed was made. The floor was picked up. Dolls were put away.

The walls were a collage of floral-themed sketches done in crayon, and pages and centerfolds torn neatly from kiddie magazines. There was *Spongebob* and *Hannah Montana* and *Wall-E* and *Phineas and Ferb*. There was the huge poster of Gru and his minions from *Despicable Me,* right next to a life-sized cardboard standee of a homely boy with a terrified expression. He was frozen in a non-pose as if he had been caught unprepared. Kurt might have found that strange had he been thinking straight.

Kurt thought of the bouncy ball and wondered where it was. He looked around the room, but didn't see it. He grabbed a lamp from Lili's dresser, snatched off the shade, turned the wide wooden base upside down, and gave it a shake to test its weight. Then he skulked toward the door with the weapon cocked back.

Kurt happened by the 32" flatscreen TV that Nancy had bought Lili for her sixth birthday, against his wishes. A heavily shaded doppelganger of Lili's room was cast on the screen. He noticed an empty space on the back wall that had previously been occupied by the life-sized standee. He suddenly realized that the homely boy was the same character from the bouncy ball and it scared him. He didn't know why.

Kurt turned and scanned the area where he guessed that the standee would have landed, face-down, if it had fallen. There was nothing there. And then, as if from thin air, a disembodied face materialized a few feet in front of him. It was the homely boy. His face was literally flat and looked as if it had been stretched from the sides. It was hovering about five feet, four inches from the floor.

The boy, whose name was Louis (aka Louie 2D) looked at Kurt as if he was shocked to have been spotted. He gasped, and then turned sideways and seemed to disappear.

Kurt stumbled backward into the wall. He hit the TV with the back of his head and nearly cracked the screen. He stood there, trembling and unable to think. His heart thumped like a bass drum. His mouth was dry. He stared at the area where the face had been, thinking that maybe it would appear again, but it didn't. Then he stuck his arm out in front of him and leaned forward. His fingers probed and searched the air like insect antenna. His feet followed. He half-hoped that he wouldn't find anything.

Kurt saw a flash of movement at waist level and then felt something tighten around his wrist. He flinched and tried to pull his arm back but it wouldn't budge. The homely boy named Louis whipped his flat head around and yelled in Kurt's face. He had been standing there, turned sideways, the whole time.

"LEAVE ME ALONE!"

Kurt squeezed his eyes shut, turned away, and screamed like a girl.

Louie coiled his flat, wide arm tighter around Kurt's wrist. He slapped his other arm around the thick, wooden canopy post of Lili's bed, snaked it tight, and grunted as he flung Kurt to the floor.

Kurt felt something on him as he thrust to his feet. It was nearly weightless with a damp, rubbery texture. It ascended his legs like a snake threading its flat, wide body between them and up under Kurt's groin and around his stomach and ribs, and then it squeezed all the air from his lungs. A hand slapped over Kurt's nose and mouth and prevented him from inhaling more air. The hand was flat as a pancake yet deceptively strong.

Kurt ran out into the hallway screaming into the flat, rubbery barrier.

Louie constricted his body every time Kurt exhaled.

Kurt's fingers probed frantically looking for some slack in the strange rubber flesh where he could dig his fingertips in and pull the thing off, but there was no such spot that he could find.

Kurt heard, then felt his ribs crack. His legs became like distant appendages underneath a foreign body. A white haze blurred the edges of his sight and began to close inward.

Kurt was aware that none of this made sense, that he was being attacked by something that couldn't possibly exist, that this physical impossibility had left Nancy to die on the cold, hard bathroom floor, and it was probably going to kill him too if he didn't get it off of him.

He started biting at the rubbery muzzle, but his teeth kept sliding against the smooth, damp texture. And then with what seemed like his last breath, he inhaled and bit down hard.

Louie cried out and unraveled from around Kurt's body. Kurt doubled over and began gasping for air. The boy was holding his wounded hand as he worked his flat, wobbly body upright and erect. It took about 30 seconds.

"YOU HURT ME!" Louie cried out like a scared mama's boy. And then he held his hand up to show off the wound. "SEE WHAT YOU DID!"

Kurt could see the other side of the hallway through the garish hole in Louie's hand.

Louie charged at Kurt growling through clenched teeth. Kurt responded with a barrage of flailing fists. The boy dodged each blow like an invertebrate boxer. He leaned away from a wild punch and into a backbend with his hands planted on the floor. He kicked his legs up, wrapped them around Kurt's body, and slithered tight.

Kurt coughed and grunted at the same time. He was frustrated to have landed in the thing's grasp again.

Louie snatched his torso up from the floor and was face-to-face with Kurt. Kurt threw his arms up in front of his face and turned away. The boy whipped his arms out to his sides. They became stiff below the elbows. Holding his hands like blades, Louie slashed at Kurt repeatedly, tearing into his arms. Kurt lowered his guard for a second. Seizing an opportunity, the boy wrapped himself around Kurt's head and slithered to an airtight seal.

Kurt panicked and ran blind. He slammed into a wall or two and then went over the railing. The steps bit into his back when he landed on them. He yelped at the pain. It was such that he considered staying down, however his feet had already planted beneath him and launched his body forward.

He stumbled down the remaining steps pulling on and clawing at the rubbery mask that covered his head. The boy's legs were still wrapped around Kurt's torso and constricting tighter with each expelled breath. In the background, Rucksack barked, and growled, and whined as she tried desperately to claw her way through the basement door and help her master.

Kurt came running out the front door of his house and down the walkway toward his car. His cries for help were muffled by the damp, rubbery mask. He felt himself starting to slide into catatonia. This time the symptoms were much more pervasive. The sensation of floating disembodied...The hazy white blur closing in from the edges of his vision...

Kurt struggled for air but there was none to be had. His muscles began to give out and he buckled and nearly collapsed next to his car.

Sensing that Kurt was on the verge of passing out, Louie suddenly unraveled from around his head, and slithered down his body. He wrapped both arms around Kurt's legs, and squeezed, forcing them close together, and then he yanked Kurt's feet out from underneath him. It was a move that he had utilized many times before. Louie was used to tussling with women, however, so he was thrown off by Kurt's strength and tenacity. As a result of this miscalculation, the boy wound up underneath Kurt's body when he hit the ground, and was knocked dizzy.

Austin Wallace turned onto Huntsacker Lane on his motorcycle and drove up the block. He cranked the throttle when he saw Kurt lying facedown in the grass next to his car and rocketed towards him.

The bike fishtailed to a stop. Austin set the kickstand with his foot, pulled his helmet off, and hopped off of the bike. He paused, and then ran over, and crouched beside Kurt's body.

"Kurt! What happened, buddy! You okay!"

Kurt didn't answer.

Austin scanned the immediate area and saw nothing to suggest foul play. He rolled Kurt over and prepared to perform CPR.

Kurt moaned and began to squirm as if he was having a bad dream.

"Thank God!" Austin exhaled. "Kurt! It's me! Austin!

What's the matter, buddy?! What happened to—"

Austin saw a single eye staring up at him from the ground next to Kurt's head. The eye blinked. Startled, Austin leaned away.

Louie lay on his back pinned halfway beneath Kurt's body. It had been his experience that most people needed at least a minute to come to some form of understanding upon seeing him for the first time. It took Austin half that before he reached down and snatched his gun from the ankle holster.

At the same time, Louie yanked his free arm straight below the elbow like a switchblade, and then slashed upward. He coiled his arm around Austin's ankle right after and used his weight to try to pull his stuck half from underneath Kurt's body.

Austin squeezed the trigger unintentionally and fired the gun into the grass. He reached up and slapped a hand over his throat. Fear washed over his face as his fingers probed a linear wound. The wound was deep and ugly and it appeared to nip at his fingers.

Austin gasped and stumbled backward. The wound in his throat sneezed a bloody mist. Louie was still holding onto Austin's ankle and was yanked from underneath Kurt, who was lying on his back moaning, and squirming, and creeping drunkenly toward consciousness.

Louie slithered up Austin's back as he staggered over to Kurt's car and leaned on it coughing, and gasping, and choking on his own blood. A spray of blood painted the fender red with each attempted exhale.

Louie lay flat against Austin's back with his legs wrapped around his waist like he was riding piggyback. Austin was hunched over the hood of Kurt's car with his head down. Blood poured from the wound in his throat and from his mouth.

Louie reached up and was about to snap Austin's neck and finish him off when he heard a number of people approaching from behind. He whipped his head around 180 degrees.

The Guardians were armed with handguns. Ted Woodruff was in the lead, his handgun holstered at his leg, a hunting rifle held across his body in both hands.

"Who is that?!" he yelled at the unfamiliar man hunched over Kurt Sadler's car.

"He's trying to steal Kurt's car!" Someone said.

"Shit! He's got a gun!"

Ted lifted his rifle and fired once at the unfamiliar man.

Louie was able to spin Austin around at the last minute. Ted reacted with confusion at the sudden appearance of Austin's face, but it was too late.

The bullet punched Austin in the upper chest and spun him around like a ragdoll. He slammed, face-first, into the side of Kurt's car, and dented the passenger-side door, and was dead before he hit the ground.

Luckily for Louie, Austin landed on his side and then rolled onto his back. He used the seconds between impact and final rest to unwrap his legs from around Austin's waist and slither underneath Kurt's car.

"Oh shit! Issat...Austin?" a horrified voice wondered aloud.

Realizing who he had shot, Ted lowered his rifle and turned white as a ghost. The other men hurried over to Kurt, who was stirring, half-awake. Ron Stanky was the first to arrive at his side.

"What happened?! Are you hurt?" he asked Kurt.

Kurt looked up at Ron Stanky, Jim Sigworth, and Burt Murphy as if he didn't know them. His eyes were glazed and reddened and floating lazily beneath heavy lids that played at closing.

"Can you hear me, Kurt?! What happened?!"

"Maybe we should call an ambulance?" Jim Sigworth suggested.

"It's already on the way," replied Burt Murphy, who was standing over them holding a cell phone to his ear. He closed the phone, put it in his pocket and glanced over at Ted, who still hadn't moved. "Christ almighty! This is bad."

"Nancy!" Kurt cried out and tried to sit up. His muscles weren't ready to support him and he fell backward.

Ron and Jim reached out and grabbed hold of him.

"No! Nancy! I gotta check on Nancy!" Kurt snatched his arms away from them and growled with passionate determination. And then he tried to stand. It was a futile effort.

Kurt tried to stand several more times before his neighbors convinced him that he was in no condition to move, let alone get up and walk. Ron assured him that someone would go check on Nancy for him.

Kurt lay there on his back staring up at the sky while Burt Murphy went inside to check on his wife. More people were filing cautiously toward the scene from the surrounding neighborhoods. Ted had made his way over to Austin's corpse and was standing over it with heavy shoulders.

Kurt let his head roll to the side. This put Austin's corpse directly in his line of sight. He saw Ted Woodruff standing at Austin's feet wallowing in guilt and dismay and he wasn't quite sure what to make of it. And then his eyes suddenly widened. Kurt lifted his arm and pointed at the space beneath his car, where he had spied a familiar shape undulating in the grass.

To everyone else it looked like he was pointing at Austin.

"He's dead, Kurt," said Ron with a heavy-hearted tone. "Ted shot him."

"I didn't...I mean...He had a gun!" Ted clumsily stated in his defense.

"It's okay Ted. We were there," said Ron attempting to calm him down.

"No it's not! It's not okay!" Ted yelled.

Kurt was still pointing at the space beneath his car. His eyes were wide as half-dollars and set amongst features distorted in terror.

"I know. I know," Ron consoled Kurt. "Try not to get yourself worked up. There's an ambulance on the way."

Kurt mumbled something in response. Ron pointed his ear down and listened.

"Th...tha...gr-o-per..." Kurt stammered and then he fell unconscious.

Ron sat back on his heels radiating shock. He looked over at Austin.

"What did he say?" Ted demanded to know.

Ron hesitated, and then he said as if he didn't believe the words that came out of his mouth, "I think he said that Austin was the groper."

At that very moment, Burt Murphy appeared at the front door of Kurt's house looking like he had just seen a ghost. He announced that Nancy Sadler was lying on the floor of the upstairs bathroom, apparently dead.

The news gave pause to everyone within earshot.

Standing over Austin's body, Ted cast knowing eyes down at his neighbor. He was shaking his head. "Sneaky son-of-a-bitch. I knew it all along," he muttered under his breath.

"What was that?!" Burt Murphy yelled and ran around to the far side of Kurt's car.

He startled, raised his gun.

"What's wrong?" Ted wanted to know.

"I saw something move," Burt whispered, still searching down the barrel of his gun.

But it was only the bouncy ball with the ugly, warped face resting against the front wheel where someone had apparently left it. Burt lowered his gun.

"Fucking *thing*," he said as he kicked the ball up the street and watched it roll into the heavy shadows that lived on the vacant side of Huntsacker Lane.

A short time later an ambulance arrived with a police escort. Huntsacker Lane had become crowded with nosey residents of the Utopia Springs Estates.

***

The bouncy ball named Louie had rolled further away and was watching from a safe distance and under the cover of heavy shadows. It was darker on this end of the block, but darkness suited Louie just fine. The congestion in front of Kurt Sadler's house was as good a sign as any that it was time to move on from this place. But the limbo between haunts was the most agonizing part of being alone. Appeasing his lecherous proclivities was becoming secondary to finding a permanent haunt or, dare he dream, legitimate acceptance. Louie had become familiar with the people here at the Utopia Springs Estates, and didn't want to leave. Theirs were the kinds of painfully regular lives that he often fantasized about and that he sought out in part to experience vicariously as he haunted their homes. He was addicted to the sense of belonging that he hadn't felt since his early days at the Toxic Brothers Traveling Carnival.

There had been a number of close calls, though. Too many. Tonight being the closest so far. Louie was lucky to have gotten away. Luck was a common theme in his life post Toxic Brothers. Just that he had survived the tornado that decimated the carnival was a miracle in itself.

Eventually the police left and the crowd on Huntsacker dispersed to their homes. Louie rolled up the street toward the cul de sac curve pondering his dilemma. He sulked and felt sorry for himself. He came to a line of stenciled letters in the street, stopped, and glanced down at them curiously. Then he looked up and saw a lit window in an upstairs room of the house at the peak of the cul de sac curve. The address was 612. He would have ducked into the shadows had he not already been lurking there in the darkest part.

Feeling uneasy, Louie watched and waited.

A naked woman appeared in the window and lingered there. Her shoulders and head were cut off by the half-raised blinds. The windowsill cut off her legs just below the succulent, meaty curve of her hips. She had breasts the size of grapefruits, a flat stomach, and what his old friend Harpo Ton disparagingly referred to as winter bush. But it was all good to Louie. Hers was the kind of body that he had only seen in adult magazines from the 70s.

One for the road, Louie salivated as he sized up that naked woman in the window, and then when she walked away, he rolled up to the front door of 612 Huntsacker Lane, unfurled his body, and slithered underneath it.

TECHNICOLOR TERRORISTS

"If I never see another clown it'll be too soon," the young rookie told the sergeant between shortening breaths. Tears streamed from his reddened eyes. He placed a hand over his nose and mouth to keep the combined odor of gasoline and spilled blood from his lungs. The odor was so strong that it made his eyes water. He suddenly felt like he was going to be sick.

"There's a trash can over there," the sergeant pointed.

But the rookie was already running for the front door. He was hunched over and belching bitter fumes. "Don't go out there!" the sergeant yelled after him.

Bainbridge Street was crowded with nosey spectators and press and the sergeant didn't want them to see that one of his officers couldn't handle the pressures of the job. Little things like that helped to erode the public's trust in the police department. The 27th Precinct was already skating on thin ice in that regard.

The rookie hurried out the door and vomited all over the steps. Then he crept to a full stand, unsure. With his eyes squeezed shut, he wiped his mouth with his sleeve and took slow, deep breaths until the dizziness subsided. He opened his eyes and saw that he was the center of attention. He froze, hypnotized by the ambush of faces and camera flashes.

Over his shoulder the front door swung open. The sergeant's beefy arm reached out and snatched the rookie inside.

Another squad car pulled up to the curb and a thick-bodied Homicide Detective named Mars Kersey leapt out of the passenger side. Mars was a sometimes quiet and introverted, sometimes crazy and intense, but altogether likeable guy who spoke to most people in single word responses.

Physically, he was nothing special. Neither short nor tall, handsome nor ugly. His facial structure was unremarkable with features that aligned in a way that suited his strangely beguiling personality. He was sturdily built and compact without being muscular. He wore a bullet proof vest over a black sweater, jeans, and a pair of knock-off Timberland boots.

A uniformed officer stepped out on the driver's side and trailed behind Mars, who approached the house with an aggressive stride.

Mars walked in the door and instantly recoiled from the smell. He squinted his eyes at the burning sensation and cupped his hand over his nose and mouth as he surveyed the scene. The uniformed officer did similar.

The scene as described by dispatch didn't prepare them for what they witnessed.

"This ain't no random home invasion," Mars thought out loud.

They could see two bodies from where they stood—a husband and a wife. Caucasian. Mid 30s, as far as Mars could tell. The husband was wedged between the chunky arm of a couch and a blood-smeared wall. His wife was lying face-down in the middle of the living room. Both of them had met a violent and messy end, and both wore clown face-paint. The husband had a red, felt ball stuck to the tip of his nose. The assailant or assailants had written "SELLOUTS" on the wall in blood that most likely belonged to one or both of the victims.

Mars walked into the room fanning away the fumes and scanned, through watery eyes, for the ranking officer. He bristled at the sight of two dead dogs—pitbulls with clown faces—lying in pools of blood. A passing officer commented on Mars' dismay.

"The childhood this sicko musta had, huh?"

Mars didn't respond. He went into the next room and found the sergeant in a corner giving the riot act to his nauseous rookie. He walked over and flashed his badge. The sergeant glanced and nodded, sent the rookie on his way, and then turned back to Mars.

He shook his head. "Gaddam rookie," he muttered under his breath.

Mars answered with a nod.

"The Gleasons...Paul and Jessica..." the sarge began. "Neighbors say they were a happy couple, married for 14 years, the kinda folks you couldn't help but like."

"*Well, some*body didn't like them very much."

"Apparently that somebody meant to burn the place down. Whole place has been doused with gasoline."

"Wonder why they didn't?" Mars said, speaking through his hand.

"Change of heart?" the sarge suggested.

"I'm thinking maybe he or they were interrupted."

"Maybe. The couple's 12-year-old son called it in on the mother's cell phone. Name's Bradley. Apparently he was hiding in the closet when it all went down."

"Has he said anything about what happened?"

"Poor kid probably saw or heard his whole family being murdered. I don't think he's in any condition to talk."

"Dispatch mentioned *three* bodies," Mars stated.

"Mother-in-law's in the kitchen..."

Mars' eyes shifted to the doorway that led to the kitchen. Just then an officer walked out looking thoroughly befuddled.

"...and the breakfast room."

Mars walked into the kitchen and saw two teary-eyed officers standing in front of a pair of chubby legs protruding from the wall just above the sink. Judging by the housedress, the ankle-high stockings, the slithering stampede of varicose veins, and the granny-panties, the legs belonged to an older woman— no doubt the mother-in-law. The sink, and the area around it, was hidden beneath a layer of plaster-dust and little bits of broken tile. Mars spotted one of those Don Bodeel Magic Ashtrays crushed beneath the debris.

Don Bodeel was the current king of TV pitchmen, a fish-faced older man with a chewed head who stamped his name on hundreds of questionable inventions and then hocked them via cheaply produced infomercials.

The mother-in-law's slippers lay on the floor where they had apparently fallen off her feet when she became lodged in the wall—however the hell that had happened.

"Rest of her's in here," one of the officers said to Mars as he pinched his nostrils shut.

Mars stared at him for a moment, as if to validate that this wasn't some kind of joke. The officer gave no indication of such, so Mars walked across the kitchen and stopped in front of the door across the room. He examined the legs from this new angle. Then, with his feet planted in the kitchen, leaned through the doorway and saw the woman's upper-half protruding from the other side of the wall that both rooms shared. His eyes grazed her face and caught hints of an ashen white base with bright red licks about the mouth and cheekbones. Mars leaned back out of the room and exhaled.

Clearly it required a second, more thorough look. So, Mars counted to three before leaning through the doorway again.

The impact with the wall had crushed the woman's nose and cracked her ocular cavity on the left side. Blood had drained into her eyes and given them a demonic glow. Her jaw had been shattered. Mars wouldn't have known all this had he not inspected her closely, as the assassin had left her with a clown-face frozen in cross-eyed, slapstick shock.

The next morning Mars received a phone call from the director of Atwater House, where they were keeping 12-year-old Bradley Gleason until his next of kin could be located. He told Mars that the boy had suffered a "hellish" night, and that their facility wasn't equipped to deal with someone with such…"demanding needs." Mars was scheduled to speak with Bradley later in the afternoon, but after the call from the director, he decided to drive out sooner.

The staff set them up in the Therapy Suite. Bradley Gleason was stretched out on the couch like a patient. The therapist's chair was a big, wooden thing that was hard to move, so Mars grabbed a simple plastic fold-up from the hallway, turned it backwards, and sat down in front of the couch.

"So, Bradley—"

"Call me Brad."

"Okay…Brad. The staff tells me that you had a rough night."

"They won't leave me alone," Brad whined.

"Who won't leave you alone?"

"The clowns!"

Last night

Boys aged 9-to-13 were housed on the third floor of the main building. Each dorm room slept 20 to a room, 10 beds per side. Bradley Gleason was in room 316. His bed was located on the wall side, which put him directly in the path of the moon's beaming salutation as it shined through windows across the room that were much taller than they were wide.

Lights out was at 9:30pm sharp. Brad spent some time afterward getting to know his dorm-mates via whispered conversations in the dark.

"The first night always sucks," one boy warned. "But you'll get through it."

But Brad didn't want to get through it. He wanted to feel the security of his father's presence, the contentment of his mother's, and the esteem that came with belonging. He wanted to be in his room, sitting on his bed and watching *The Fresh Prince of Bel Air* reruns.

Brad wanted to be anywhere but this juvenile detention center masquerading as a foster care facility, and he made repeated tearful declarations of that fact.

"Either keep it to yourself or go somewhere else so the rest of us can get some sleep," an older boy scolded.

"Cut him some slack, dude! It's his first night," another, older boy said.

"I don't care. At least he *had* parents."

"Dude, you're an asshole."

"Your mom's an asshole."

Eventually sleep came for everyone except Brad, who lay there trying to make as little noise as possible as he cried at the ceiling. The darkness was populated by snores and groans and sleepy verbal spillage that was half-coherent at best. Bedsprings and frames balked as sleeping bodies shifted.

Brad tossed and turned to escape the lunar spotlight from the tall, wide window closest to his bed. He squeezed his eyes shut and imagined utter blackness, and still the moonlight made it through.

The window had been left open slightly and as the night

went on, a breeze riled up and chased Brad further underneath the covers. After a while, the chill reached Brad through the thin white material. He wanted to get up and close the window, but felt that it wasn't his place to do so.

Maybe it was meant to be left open. Either way, Brad didn't want to risk ruffling any feathers should someone prefer the breeze. So, he pictured someplace warm and ventured there mentally. His parents were with him. The family dogs—Ghost and Leopold— were there, too.

Brad startled awake unaware that he had dozed off, and then lay there afterward wishing for sleep to reclaim him and free his mind from the deluge of pessimism. He heard men's voices—two of them. He followed the voices over to the window across the room.

Security guards, Brad presumed. They must have been sitting on one of the benches down in the courtyard. They were talking about some girl they wanted to bone; some brunette with "a rack that you can bury your face in" and "an ass that won't quit." Apparently she worked in the kitchen.

"Mannn, what I wouldn't give for a shot at that."

"You ain't lying, bro. You know Stan hit that."

Or maybe it was Dan, or Jan. Brad couldn't tell.

The two men talked and laughed for a while and then it was quiet. Sleep crept up on Brad like a thief in the night. His eyes parted as if by a sliding switch. And then he was awake again. There was activity down in the courtyard. It seemed like seconds since his last waking memory, but Brad knew that probably wasn't the case. He lay there listening over the litany of nocturnal offenders.

"It's this one, right here…316," he heard someone say.

"You sure? Cause that's what you said the last time."

These voices were vastly different from the ones he heard earlier. They didn't sound real. Like the voices you'd hear on cartoons.

"What the hella you doin'?'"

"I'm makin' sure. Now, get offa my back."

A metal bedframe cried out. Without moving, Brad looked to see what it was. A boy whom he knew only by his face was sitting up in his bed. The boy's bed was situated way at the other end of the room, where it was darkest. This kept the details a mystery, like whether his eyes were opened or closed. Brad assumed from the boy's slumped shoulders and head that they were closed and that the boy was dreaming.

But then the boy raised his head. His torso inflated. His back straightened. His shoulders lifted. He craned his neck, and leaned, and tilted his head. He was clearly searching for something, or someone.

Afterward the boy returned to an upright seated position, and then he plunked down onto his back like someone had snatched away his soul.

Another boy sat up in bed. His name was Colin or Connor. His bed was closer to Brad's than the first boy's, but far enough that he couldn't quite see his eyes either through the multiple layers of darkness. Colin or Connor had the same lethargic posture, and slumped head.

Feigning sleep, Brad watched the boy lift his head and look left and right, craning and tilting. He stopped with his face pointing in Brad's direction and lingered there for a short time, and then he plunked down onto his back and was out like a light.

The bed frame next to Brad cried out, but it was only David Foster rolling onto his back. David had been pretty cool to Brad. The other boys were afraid of David because he had allegedly taken a baseball bat to his alcoholic stepfather's kneecaps. Based on Brad's observation of David thus far, he didn't seem like the volatile head case that everyone made him out to be.

David shifted beneath the covers and Brad flinched. Then, out of the blue, he sat straight up just like the other boys had done. He turned toward Brad, moving with a mechanical cadence. His mouth was open, but he was still snoring.

David's arms flexed and then lifted as if tethered to invisible strings. He reached up and pinched his eyelids between his index fingers and thumbs, and peeled them up to reveal his eyes, moving rapidly, rolling up into his head. Finally they stopped rolling, locking onto Brad.

"There you arrrre!" The voice that came from David's mouth was not David's but something resembling a cartoon character...or a clown.

Brad was instantly transported back to the closet. He relived the same paralyzing fear that had gripped him the previous night while listening to his parents being killed. He'd heard every twisted word of their tormentors. David's new voice was from the same place.

Brad screamed.

David's muscles became liquid and he plummeted to the floor.

Brad scrabbled backward and off of the bed.

David cried out in pain, and then seemed to awake. He was full of questions as he picked himself up from the floor, "What thaaa fuck?! How the fuck did I..?" He froze when he saw Brad, the new kid, standing there in the shadows, looking suspicious.

Brad leaned toward the other boy, still unsure, and asked, "That you, David?"

"Tha fuck else you think it is?" He suddenly recoiled. "Wait, you ain't no faggot, are you?"

Voices jumped out of the darkness.

"Shut tha fuck up, yo!"

"No shit, man!"

"Who-a-faggot?"

The lights came on.

"Turn them fuckin' lights off!" somebody yelled. More voices joined in the protest.

An older man wearing a robe over sweats, a pair of flip flops, and a furious scowl stormed in and stood in the middle of the room. Technically, his name was Mr. Wade, but he insisted that everyone just call him Wade. He was the houseparent on duty that night.

Wade followed the roomful of sleepy-eyed glares over to David and Brad, who were both standing. Then he looked at his watch and groaned, "One-a-you boys wanna tell me why I'm in here dealing with this foolishness at 1:25 in the ayem?"

Nobody spoke.

"Okay. Then maybe I should make everybody stand at the foot of their beds until—"

"No. It was me," Brad confessed. "I…had a nightmare."

"And you?" Wade said to David.

"He scared me, man!"

Wade instructed everyone to "Go back-ta-sleep," and then he escorted Brad out into the hall, turning off the lights on the way.

Brad was expecting a full-on reprimand, some "over-the-top" example to establish a tone for the possible wrath that awaits any precocious, trouble-making new kid who thinks he's above the rules. But Wade sat the boy down and got all Dr. Phil on his ass. He asked uncomfortable questions that encouraged Brad to confront the sounds and images that filled his brain.

"Kids get jumped, or shanked …or raped in places like this," he cried.

Wade assured the boy that that would never happen here, especially not on his watch.

Brad wept for his parents and confessed how he missed them so bad it hurt, and how he couldn't bare the thought of never seeing them again. When the subject of the clowns arose, Wade suggested he consider that they weren't real.

"What you heard through the closet door was just very bad people—sick and twisted as all hell—but flesh-and-blood people just the same, who did a very, very bad thing."

"But I saw one of 'em," Brad replied. "A fat one with blue dreadlocks. He opened the door before I could grab the knob. I thought he was gonna kill me, but he just put his finger to his lips, like 'Shhhhh,' ya know, and then he closed the door. Then I heard him tell the others that there was nobody in there."

Wade took in the information with a compassionate grimace that said, "This boy is fucked beyond my pay-grade." He gave Brad some stock advice on getting back to sleep followed by a nod and a disarming smile.

"You can close the window if you'd like," Wade whispered as he left.

Brad slinked over to the window on his tippie-toes. He

inched it closed careful not to make any noise, and then he tip-toed over to his bed and slid between the sheets.

David was asleep. Thank God.

Relieved, Bradley closed his eyes.

"Yo... You wasn't tryin' nothing, was you?" It was David's voice. His real voice. "On the real, though…"

"No, man!" Brad whispered, nervously. "You musta been sleep-walking or something."

David continued to stare.

"Dude! I'm not gay!"

A few moments passed.

"Do you remember what you were dreaming about?" Brad inquired. "Cause they say that you're actually, like, acting out your dream or something when you sleep-walk."

A pensive David shook his head, "No. I just remember hearing you scream…then I was on the floor."

They talked for a while longer. Brad was in the middle of a story about his dogs, Ghost and Leopold when he noticed that David had fallen asleep, and he was once again alone in the dark with his thoughts. The moon had moved on from the windows so the room was much darker.

He became reacquainted with the milieu of snores, and groans, and sleepy verbal spillage, and squeaky bedsprings and frames. Then Brad heard something from the window, sort of a springy-bounce and hollow metal sliding and creaking.

He heard the noise again. It seemed to be coming from the courtyard. He knew that sound. Sounded like someone on a swing…no, a trampoline. His neighbor owned a trampoline that he would sometimes use when his mother wasn't around.

But it was 3:25am; hardly the time to be jumping on a trampoline. And the courtyard with its cherub and angel statues, benches every ten feet and grassy areas wrapped in iron fencing with spiked tips, was hardly the place.

The noise persisted. It became so loud that the boys sleeping closest to the window should have woken up. But no one had flinched. Brad moved closer to the window and watched.

Several bounces later a pair of eyes, attached to a clown face, broke the surface of the windowsill. They hovered there peering through the window, into the darkened room. They rolled knowingly toward Bradley, and then gravity snatched them down.

Bradley tried to scream when the clown-eyes returned, following another bounce, but he had no voice. He wanted to jump out of bed and run for the door, but the clown-face had triggered a relapse of neuro-muscular paralysis rendering him motionless as well as speechless. He remained stalactite-still by the window. The clown gazed at him menacingly.

Brad closed his eyes and concentrated on his limbs, attempting to summon the strength to carry him out of this room. Finally, he managed to pull away from the clown, rolling himself onto his stomach where he lay face down in the pillow. He willed his muscles to move, slowly gathering the strength to try again in a minute or so.

The bouncing had suddenly stopped. And then, out of the brief silence that followed came a tapping of fingernails against glass.

Tap. Tap. Tap.

Brad ignored the sound hoping that this whole thing was just some terrible dream, that he would wake any minute.

Tap. Tap. Tap.

An icy chill ran through Brad's veins. He was so scared that he almost forgot to breathe.

Tap. Tap. Tap.

"We know you're awake in there," said one of his roommates, a boy who was fast asleep and speaking in a voice that was not his own, the same cartoonish voice that David had used before.

The boy's words found their way beneath Brad's trembling flesh and gave rise to goosebumps.

"How could anyone expect you to sleep after what you've been through…" The voice was the same but spoken through a different messenger this time, a boy on the other side of the dorm, who was also fast asleep.

Brad screamed into his pillow, but his voice was restricted to the confines of his head.

"Your parents…GONE!"
Please go away?!
"Life as you know it…OVER!"
Please just GO AWAY?
"And now you're allllll alone in this shit-hole."
Please?!
"I don't need to tell *you* what happens to nice boys like you in places like this, Bradley."

The voice poured from the mouth of a third sleeping roommate…

"All these lost souls hurtin' for mommy and daddy's love. All that misguided rage swimming in raw, unchecked testosterone. Nuthin' but time for it to fester into somethin' cruel and nasty."

…and a fourth.

"You wanna be that guy, Bradley? Cause that's what's gonna happen if you don't come wit us."

***

Mars had given Brad Gleason his word that he would do what he could to get him out of Atwater House, when the truth was that what he could do was Jack-shit. Mars felt a sense of connection with the boy, with the entire case, in fact. He had lost his parents at a young age, too. The drunk driver who swerved into their lane and hit them head-on just happened to be a clown on his way to a birthday gig. Hence Mars had a "thing" about clowns.

By all accounts, Brad seemed like an intelligent, thoughtful, and well-spoken, human being likely to succeed in life if given the opportunity. It would take some serious therapy to get him back on track, though. And that was something else that Mars knew first hand.

He made a note to check up on the boy tomorrow, but it was the hottest summer on record, and the heat had a way of stirring up anger in individuals with little hope and too much time on their hands. Thus Mars was busy playing good guy to the random thugs and miscreants who turned inner city neighborhoods into urban warzones.

A few days passed. Mars' cell phone rang while he was working another crime scene, yet more violence between individuals with automatic weapons and zero concern for life. The call was from a "267" number that he didn't recognize—most likely one of his street informants with a piece of info concerning one of the many cases he was working. He hit "ignore," and let his voicemail take the call. He waited for a "message" chime that never came. Instead the phone rang again. He hit ignore. No message.

Ten seconds later, the phone rang yet again. The other officers at the scene were becoming annoyed with him.

Mars snatched the cell phone from his pocket. *This'd better be important.* He stepped back and turned away from the sheet-covered corpses and the annoyed police officers, so he'd have a little privacy, and then lifted the phone to his ear.

Before Mars could get a word out, a high-pitched voice lunged at him from the other end of the line. The caller was speaking so fast that Mars couldn't understand what he was saying, but he recognized the voice right away.

"Brad?"

"You have to get me outta here! They're gonna kill me if you don't!"

"Who's gonna kill you?"

Don't say the clowns...Don't say the clowns...Don't say—

"The clowns."

Ahhh fuck!

"Wait-a-minute, Brad! Sloooow down...Now, first things first; where are you?"

"They locked me in the penalty room."

"Who did?"

"Security."

"What'd you do?"

"Didn't you hear me?! I said they're trying to kill me!"

"The security guards are trying to kill you?"

"Noooo! You're not even listening! I thought you cared, but you're just like everybody else!"

"That's not true, Brad. But you have to understand. I'm

127

a cop. I can't just drop everything and come running every time you think you see a clown. Now, I know that you believe they're after you, but—and I'm not, in any way, trying to downplay what you went through—you have to understand that it's probably just—"

Click!

Mars snatched his head away from the sudden dial-tone in his ear and swore loudly. He turned around and met with a number of quizzical eyes on him from the officers standing nearby. Rather than offer an explanation, Mars walked further away and pressed "redial."

Brad made Mars wait before answering the phone.

"Don't hang up!"

"You think I'm crazy," Brad whimpered.

"I don't think you're crazy, Brad." *Well, maybe a little crazy.* "And I want to apologize for what I said before. I didn't mean for it to come out like that."

"I'm scared, Officer Kersey. What am I gonna do?"

"You said they put you in the penalty room?"

"This morning."

"I'm not judging you or anything, but what did you do?"

Brad hesitated, and then he said in a shameful voice, "I stabbed one of the house-parents with a fork from the cafeteria."

"Dammit, kid!" Mars lamented.

"It was an accident! I thought he was one-a-them. They came for me again last night. I ran and ran, but they were everywhere. Sometimes I would just see their feet sticking out from behind a wall, or an eye watching me from around a corner, like they were messin' with me or something. I made it down to the lobby when one of the house-parents came outta nowhere and tackled me."

"Let me speak to the house-parent in charge," Mars demanded after a moment of thought.

"I can't."

"Why not?"

"They don't know I have this phone. I…took it outta that same house-parent's pocket."

***

Mars drove to Atwater House the next morning and was shocked to find out that Brad Gleason had been released to the custody of a police officer named Hank Stryker.

"What? When the hell did this happen?!"

"Earlier this morning. Why?" asked the wide lady behind the front desk. According to the name tag, her name was Lorraine.

"Why the hell wasn't I notified?"

"Well, I wasn't aware that—"

"I gave specific instructions that I be notified if there were any developments with the boy...."

Lorraine was at a loss for words.

"What did you say this officer's name was? Stryker?"

"Yes, sir. Hank Stryker."

The name sounded like an alias, and a very bad one. Something was up here.

"Did he say where he was taking him?"

"I'm not sure, sir. I didn't speak with him directly about that."

"Well, who did then?!"

"That would be Mr. Halifax."

"Get him out here!"

The secretary made a call and out walked a petite man with pointy shoulders and sensitive eyes magnified by thick lenses encased in wiry frames. Halifax didn't look anything like he sounded over the phone. Mars had imagined a stodgy, older man of generous girth. What he saw was a bleeding heart-type who was too smart for his own good.

Mars rejected the man's extended hand and tore into him proper. Halifax took the verbal beat-down with the high-minded aplomb of a Vulcan, and then calmly retorted that he and his staff had no reason to doubt the other officer.

"Hank Stryker?" Mars said in a tone meant to highlight the name's implausible sound.

"Yes. He showed his badge to me and to Lorraine, here."

The woman behind the desk nodded and said, "He

produced the proper release forms, too."

"I'm sorry that no one called you, Detective, but we get very busy here at Atwater House. Besides, the officer mentioned that he was taking the boy down to the station to look over some photographs. I figured you would've known about the whole thing"

"What station? The 27th?" Mars inquired.

"All he said was that he was taking the boy 'down to the station,'" Halifax said. "He didn't say which one, and, quite frankly, I didn't think to ask."

***

The Homicide Unit went full gusto on the Gleason Case. Just as Mars suspected, there was no Hank Stryker working for the Philadelphia Police Department. Was this Stryker connected with the Gleasons' murder, or was this a separate case of child abduction? If the latter was true, and the abductor was some kind of pedophile, then the opportunity for a lifetime's worth of deep, mental scars was presented with every passing second that Brad was in his custody—hypothetically speaking, of course. Mars almost always assumed the worst.

Weeks passed with no leads whatsoever. Mars and his team scoured the police database for any cases involving clowns.

Three came up.

Case 8621436: New York -A clown performer who was robbed on his way home from a gig. The perp was caught a few blocks away. Case Closed.

Case 7298773: Maryland -A circus clown was killed in an accident with a canon apparatus that was supposed to shoot him into a net 50-feet away. It was later determined that the canon was rigged to over-shoot the net. A female contortionist, who was also the clown performer's ex-lover, was arrested for the crime. Case closed.

Case 7583629: New Jersey -A string of nighttime burglaries in affluent communities throughout the state. In several of the cases residents have described one or more of the assailants as looking like a clown. While the others made no such mention, it became obvious to police that the same person or persons had committed each crime.

Cherry Hill PD eventually arrested several employees of Burke's Clown Services, when it was learned that clowns from their company had been hired out to perform at each of the burglarized houses prior to the night of the burglary. The men were cleared when the investigation uncovered that a third party had been hacking into Burke's Clown Services' phone line and intercepting incoming calls from potential customers. It became clear that this third party or parties were portraying themselves as performers from Burke's, and returning later to rob the customers. The identity of said third party or parties is still a mystery.

Cherry Hill PD had also questioned a man named Sebastian Storm during the investigation into the string of burglaries. Storm was that joker-faced illusionist who worked the Atlantic City Casinos. He used to be on all the billboards you see while driving on I-95. Storm had been spotted in the vicinity of two separate burglaries, first in Spring Lake, and later in Cherry Hill. The police didn't have enough evidence to hold him, so they let him go. The case-file contained a more recent Daily News article with a headline that read, **Clown Prince of Illusion Gone Missing. Friends/Loved Ones Suspect Foul Play.**

Following his instinct, Mars dug deeper into Case 7583629 and learned that the police never found Storm's body or any sign that a violent act had ever been committed. That Storm had met with foul play was pure conjecture floated by his family and the media.

A search of Storm's home revealed evidence that the illusionist was obsessed with clowns. But there was nothing else of merit.

Mars put the word out to his street informants. But there was no information to be had.

And then the bodies of Paul and Jessica Gleason disappeared from the morgue a few days later. It was as if they had just gotten up and walked out on their own. No one could explain it.

131

"You almost killed him, Mars!" Captain Malek scolded as he paced behind his desk. His nostrils were flared. He was frowning like a man in love with anger. The captain was normally such a subdued man.

Squeezed uncomfortably into a small chair Mars felt like a child being reprimanded by his teacher. His crime: going ballistic on a perp in the interrogation room. It happened yesterday, on a completely unrelated case.

"Fucking slimeball deserved it," Mars said.

"We're cops, Mars. Most of the people we deal with 'deserve it,' but we can't just go around kicking ass in the name of the law. We've got enough problems as it is."

"It's this damn case!" Mars asserted.

"I know it is," Captain Malek replied in a sympathetic tone. "And I know you feel responsible for whoever took the Gleason's bodies."

"Stoddard is one of the best ME's in the country, if not *the* best. He didn't deserve to lose his job over this. Let alone that the whole thing makes us look like a bunch of dummies."

Zach Stoddard was the Chief Medical Examiner. He and his staff were let go following the disappearance of the Gleason's bodies.

"Exactly my point, Mars," the Captain said. "And you go and make it worse with this shit. And the fact of the matter is that Stoddard and his team dropped the ball, big time. Maybe I wouldn't have fired him, but it wasn't my call."

"He's got a wife and kids, though!"

"That's not mine or your problem, Mars. What you need to be focused on is what you're going to do to rectify the situation with this perp. I got this asshole's attorney breathing down my neck about pressing charges. I got the press blowing up my phone for an official statement from the department?"

"Ohhh... It wasn't that bad," Mars flagged.

"Not that bad? Really?" The Captain snatched a piece of paper from his desk—a Victim Statement Form, and begin to read from it. 'Without warning, Officer Kersey leapt onto the table and kicked me in the face, knocking me out of my chair. When I woke up on the floor a few seconds later, Officer

Kersey was sitting on my chest punching me repeatedly in the face. If it wasn't for the two officers that ran in and pulled him off of me—"

"Okay! Okay! You made your point," Mars conceded. "I lost it. Alright. I'm sorry. It won't happen again."

"You bet your ass it won't."

"I suppose you want me to make a public apology."

"For starters. In the meantime, I'm ordering you to take a few days to get your head together while I figure out what to do about this."

Mars shot forward and blurted, "But the case…"

"What part of 'I'm ordering you,' don't you understand?"

Mars didn't respond, looking down to conceal his fluster.

"If it makes any difference, it was the Commissioner's call. Not mine," the Captain said. "Detective Shields will run point on your case-load in the meantime."

Shields, whom Mars affectionately referred to as Shieldzie, was his number two.

"And you'd better pray that I can talk that piece-a-shit out of pressing charges."

Before he left the station, Mars filled a flash drive with the info he had found on Case 7583629. He took a hardcopy of the Gleason File, too. On his way out, he pulled Shieldzie aside and informed her about Case 7583629.

"The answer is somewhere in *this* case," he told her. He was tense, on edge, with a slightly crazed twinkle in his eyes. "I want you and the boys to make it a priority. I'm gonna do the same on my end."

Mars spent his time off obsessing over the case. He spoke with people from the Cherry Hill, Atlantic County, and Spring Lake Police Departments regarding the burglaries. There were no new leads.

He called Shieldzie three, sometimes four-times-a-day for updates, pretending not to hear the annoyance in her voice after his repeated calls.

The next day Mars rolled up on some drama at a red light. A crowd had formed in front of Marcelo's Corner Grocery where an old Latino man wearing an apron was yelling and pointing down the street. Mars rolled the window down and listened.

"Thief! Thief! Somebody stop him!" the man yelled in a thick Puerto Rican accent.

Mars looked up the street and spotted a stocky man in a hoodie and track pants darting in and out of the heavy flow of nine-to-fivers and shoulder-checking people who didn't move out of his way quick enough as he ran away from the scene. He had a duffel-bag cradled in his arm like a football, and if Mars saw correctly, a gun in his right hand.

Mars stomped on the gas and caught up to the perp. He drove alongside him for half-a-block, eagle-eyeing the man through his passenger side window. Then he sped up, swerved hard-right at the next corner and stomped the brakes.

The perp slammed into Mars' right fender and went flying over the hood. He landed in the street on the other side of the car and lay there, reeling from the collision.

Mars jumped out of the car and ran to the felled perp.

"Don't you fucking move!" he instructed, gun thrust downward.

The perp was seeing stars and of little threat. Mars holstered his gun, pinned the perp down with his knee, and cuffed the man's hands behind his back.

"Guess you picked the wrong day," Mars said, swollen with adrenaline.

People clapped and cheered. Sirens wailed in the distance.

Mars checked the man's pockets and fished out a wallet full of fake IDs. One of the IDs was for an Officer Hank Stryker. Mars nearly fainted when he saw the thing. But then he got to thinking. He was still forbidden from working the case, which meant that once the blue-and-whites got a hold of Stryker, or whatever his name was, he would officially be off-limits.

"What's your name?!" Mars barked down at the side of the perp's face. The man was coming to and starting to wriggle. "Your real name!"

"Fuck you, man!"

The sirens were only a few blocks away. Mars ordered

the perp to his feet and into the backseat of his car. The man was hesitant. Something about Mars made him nervous. He looked off in the direction of the sirens as if he preferred to go with them.

"Hey, man… You sure you're-a-cop?"

"I said, get in the car! Now!"

Mars helped the perp into the back seat and slammed the door. He drove towards the docks, and found a spot where the hookers like to take their Johns. He turned off the engine, and shoved his gun in the perp's face.

"You're gonna tell me where that boy is or I swear I will end your miserable life right here."

Their eyes were locked in battle. The perp's defiance turned to fear.

"You can't just kill me. You're a cop."

Mars thought it through, and then he lowered his gun and slid it back into its holster while the perp watched, grinning at the small victory. Mars leaned across the front seats and retrieved something from the glove compartment. Then he turned back around and faced the perp.

"Where's the boy?"

"What boy?"

"His name is Brad Gleason. A week ago you impersonated a police officer and kidnapped him from Atwater House."

"Sorry man. You got the wrong guy."

Then, without warning, Mars reached over the seat-back and thrust his arm at the perp, who pushed off with his legs in retreat and banged the back of his head against the rear window. He yelped at the sharp pain that radiated out from his ribs and caused his entire body to contract painfully. He thought he was being stabbed until Mars pulled back and the perp spied an object in his hand that was roughly the size and shape of a television remote control. It was a stun gun.

"Aye! What tha fuck! That's police brutality, man! I want my lawyer!"

"The boy…" Mars said, calm and threatening.

The perp hesitated. And then he said, "I don't know what cher talking about."

That moment's hesitation was all the verification that Mars needed. Not that there was any doubt to begin with. He reached over the seat and punched the stun gun into the perp's chest.

"You FUCK!" the perp groaned through the electric daggers that pierced his chest and through the prickly surge that tuned every nerve it encountered to its full capacity.

Mars held the stun gun there. At some point the perp's screams turned feminine.

"Okay! Stop! I'll talk!" he pleaded. "Ahhhhhh! Stop!Stop!Stop!Stop!Stop!"

Mars pulled back and sat there waiting for the perp to come to his senses. The perp was taking too long, obviously stalling. Mars held up the stun gun and thumbed the button. Electric light danced with spastic grace between metal prods.

Alright! Just back off with that thing, the perp said with his body.

"My job was to spring the kid and deliver 'em to the Regent Motel on Essington. And that's it."

"Deliver to who?"

"A couple-ah clowns…"

Mars' expression dropped.

"I mean literally, clowns," he said in reaction to Mars' drastic emotional shift.

Mars sat there staring out the window for more than a minute. His guilt had been amplified triple-fold by the perp's mention of clowns. He pictured the look on Brad Gleason's face as he shot down the boy's claims about the clowns and it was too much to bear.

"What did they want with him?"

"They didn't say and I didn't ask."

"And you were okay with that? You were okay with handing off an innocent 12-year-old boy to a couple of guys you don't know, who happen to dress like clowns?"

"As long as I gets paid, man. Sides, we ain't talkin' bout a little tyke or nothing. Kid's 12-years-old. Hell, I was on my own by then."

Mars squinted angrily as he listened.

"I will tell ya, though…" the perp added, "them dudes, they wasn't just dressed like clowns…Damn fools gave me the creeps."

They gave Mars the creeps, too, and he had never even seen them.

"What if they're pedophiles?! I mean, didn't you ever stop to think?! Are you really that fucking dense?!"

"Didn't even cross my mind."

Mars was blown away by the perp's apathy. Even with all the low-lives he'd encountered in his line of work, it was rare to find people who were truly cold-hearted. This guy was one of them. It deserved another round with the stun gun, so Mars reached over the seat and gave it to the heartless perp. He was so enraged that he blacked out from the high of inflicting pain on this man and was eventually dragged awake by a pair of police officers.

Fighting against their grasp, Mars looked up and saw two squad cars parked in front of his own car. Another one was parked behind it.

A third police officer helped the perp from the backseat of Mars' car. The man was yelling "Police brutality!" in Mars' direction.

Mars was suspended without pay while the department investigated Hank Stryker's claims of police brutality. Hank was really Shawn Riley, a mostly small-time repeat-offender.

"I don't know nothing about no clowns or no missing 12-year-old," Riley told the interrogator. "That crazy-ass cop tortured me into confessing to something I didn't do. If I'm guilty of anything, it's shoplifting," he said as if shoplifting was an honorable thing. "I'll cop to that. But that other shit…I don't know nothin' about nothin'."

Riley played the victim for the cameras while the ambulance-chasing TV lawyer he hired looked for dirt on Detective Mars Kersey. He dug up the murder suspect who Mars had recently assaulted in the interrogation room, and convinced the man to go to the press with his story.

"The media's calling me a rogue cop," Mars complained to Sheildzie via telephone.

"You need help, Mars," Sheildzie replied after a long pause. "I don't want to see you throw your career away."

"So now you're turning on me, too?!"

"Nobody's turning on you, Mars," she defended. "Not me. Not the Captain—"

"Speak for yourself."

"What's that supposed to mean?"

"Cap'n Malek told me point blank that I probably ended my career as a police officer."

"He also persuaded the press not to air your photo," she quickly retorted.

"Really?"

"Ya. Really. They were gonna air it on the Evening News."

"Shit," Mars said to himself, reflecting on the implications of his identity being revealed. As an undercover cop, he coveted his privacy.

"This case has got you all twisted, Mars. You just can't see it."

"I can see just fine," he said, and then he started rambling on about the perp's mention of clowns.

"As much as I love you, Mars…Please don't contact me or the rest of the team until you've dealt with your issues," Shieldzie replied, holding back emotion and speaking as if she was repeating an order handed down by Captain Malek. "All I want…All any of us wants is for you to get better. I hope you realize that."

Mars silently stewed, and then, in a calm, deliberate tone said, "I never thought you, of all people, would betray me, Shieldzie."

"I'm going to hang up the phone now, Mars," she replied.

"I've saved your life, Goddammit!" he yelled at her.

"And I've saved yours!"

CLICK...

Mars got drunk off his ass that night. A case of Pabst Blue Ribbon and shots of Jim Beam were the offenders. He awoke the next morning to a spinning room and a pressurized throbbing in his head. He squeezed his eyes shut and clutched the sheets to keep from being thrown from the bed. The ride lasted 20 minutes. Afterward, Mars lay there on his back basking in the stillness and meditating on current events.

It's the kid's parents' fault for getting mixed up in whatever it was that got them killed, he told himself. *It's the staff at Atwater House's fault for not pressing Stryker for more information before releasing the boy in his custody. But it ain't YOUR fault. It ain't YOUR fault that you couldn't do more to protect the boy. What were you supposed to do; adopt him? There weren't any clues that this was anything more than a murder. A weird, fucked up murder, but a murder just the same. It ain't your fault that you felt something for the boy. That's called a heart. Even hardened homicide dicks like you have one.*

***

Mars spent the bulk of his day seated in front of his laptop. The Gleason File lay open, next to it, on the kitchen counter. The computer screen was hard on his eyes and the kitchen barstool that he sat on had no back support, so he was constantly rubbing his eyes and arching and twisting his torso to work out the tension in his back. Whenever he felt like he needed a break, Mars reminded himself of the potential rewards to come should he solve the case, and of the folly of wasting time.

Solve the case and maybe you save the boy.

Solve the case and, in some round-about way, you'll send this latest wave of issues with your folks' deaths into remission. Mars had already accepted that he would never be rid of them completely.

Solve the case and maybe you'll get your job back.

Mars compiled a list of facts pertaining to the case and burned it into his retinas.

—Paul and Jessica Gleason found murdered. Bodies dressed up and painted like clowns.

—Brad Gleason claims clowns "coming for him" at Atwater House.

—Gleason's bodies disappear from morgue.

—Hank Stryker/Shawn Riley kidnaps Brad / drop-off at

Regent Motel on Essington. Stryker/Riley hired by clowns. Stryker/Riley: "they wasn't just dressed like clowns…Damn fools gave me the creeps."

—Case 7583629's clowns somehow related.

Clowns…They were the one common denominator. Mars drew a blank when confronted with the thought of finding one. Clowns performed in carnivals and circuses. As far as he knew there were no carnivals or circuses in town.

He found more than he wished to know about them on the Internet. There were venues and services to suit the most ardent of clown enthusiasts. There was clown porn, clown personals, clothing-optional clown fetish-parties, a clown maid service, clown limo drivers, clown-escorts, clown bodyguards.

Mars compiled a list of six clown-for-hire businesses located in the Philadelphia area. One-by-one, he paid them a visit.

Ton Brothers Clown Co.,—#3 on his list— was located in an old storefront. Mars walked in the door and was greeted by the sound of maniacal laughter. He looked up, startled. The laughter had come from a speaker above the door. This was their version of jangling bells to indicate that someone had entered.

That figures, he mused.

Inside, a long counter cordoned off a small, rectangular area between it and the front window for the customers to stand. There was a clown behind the counter. He wore a Ramones T-shirt under a military jacket with "S. Ton," stenciled over the breast pocket, black leather pants, combat boots, and a bottle-red Mohawk. He was talking on the phone and playing solitaire. The cards had clown faces printed on them.

S. Ton smiled big and mouthed an apology to Mars for the phone call. He gestured that he'd only be a minute and then stammered a while longer with the call. Seemed like his attempts to wrap up the conversation were being cock-blocked and redirected by whoever was on the other end of the line.

S. Ton made faces at the phone and Mars smirked.

He glanced past the clown and saw a few old desks, an ancient-looking metal file cabinet with three long drawers, and a water cooler. Way in the back, a thrown-together lounge area made up of an old couch and folding chairs and a clunky television. There was no one in the lounge area, but the TV was turned on and tuned to an infomercial for the Podeel Pocket Breast Pump.

Dirty blinds hung from the windowpanes and sliced the sun into rectangular slivers of light. A few doors on each side—a couple offices, a bathroom, maybe a modest kitchenette, and a closet, Mars guessed.

The atmosphere wasn't exactly indicative of a clown depot. The floor was in need of sweeping. The desks were full of clutter. The other clown businesses had cheerful banners and framed photos of clowns hanging from brightly colored walls. There were balloons, and clown paraphernalia, clown books and instructional videos on clowning under glass countertops.

This place was nothing like that. The Online Ad stated that Ton Brothers Clown Co. hired out clowns as well as renting and selling costumes and related paraphernalia. If not for the clown with the bottle-red Mohawk behind the counter, one would never guess that this place had anything to do with clowns.

The clown on the phone finally ended his call, hung up the phone and introduced himself. The 'S' stood for 'Spiro'.

Mars stiffened at the look of recognition that suddenly came over Spiro's face. Fighting back a wave of uneasiness in the clown's presence, he turned and glanced behind him, thinking that maybe the look was intended for someone else. It wasn't.

"I know you from somewhere?" Mars queried.

"Not likely." Spiro spoke with a weird, slapstick accent and a sly, sideways cadence as he collected upturned cards from the counter, slid them into the deck in his hand and began to shuffle, all without taking his eyes off Mars. "You're a flatfoot, ain't cha?"

The archaic vernacular was part of the clown's schtick, as Mars saw it. He was surprised, however, to have been made so quickly. Mars was under the impression that he didn't dress like a cop.

Another clown leaned out from behind a fake Rhapis Palm Tree that stood beside one of the desks and asked, "What's a flatfoot?" The second clown's upper-body was the epitome of broad and it was readily obvious to Mars that the Rhapis' trunk was too skinny to conceal the man's girth.

"A gum-shoe," Spiro replied.

The second clown stared blankly.

"Bacon," Spiro said.

Blank stare.

"A cop! You shithead! Sheesh, Bully, whasthematter with you?"

"A COP?!" Bully said as if the word caused him pain.

A door swung open on the right side and a different clown-face oozed over the edge of the door. He looked into the main office area, broadcasting shock. This one was portly with a round face and a big, downward-pointing smile painted over his real mouth. Blue dreadlocks dangled from beneath a slightly oversized top-hat perched at a tilt on his head.

"A COP?!" the dreadlocked clown said, echoing the previous clown's sentiment.

A groaning swell of bubbles led Mars' eyes over to the water cooler standing against the left wall. A warped grin stared back at him through the dissipating bubbles and the listing water that stretched and widened the smiling, painted visage.

"A COP?!"

But the clown who spoke this time was crouching on the other side of the water cooler and not submerged in the tank as his voice and the bubbles had suggested.

Something jostled behind the counter. Seconds later a clown crawled out from underneath one of the desks. He was wearing a white shirt, untucked, with a black tie and black slacks with dirt marks on the knees. His hair was a shoulders' length of greasy, black tendrils. His face-paint was dark and foreboding in a way that was also comical. His name tag read Vigo Ton.

Vigo straightened the lapels of his shirt, patted dirt from his knees, and then stuffed his hands deep into his pockets. He walked toward one of the doors in the back of the office, whistling some nonchalant melody in a deliberately corny attempt to feign innocence. He disappeared into one of the back rooms.

Presto, Bully, and Whacko Ton stepped out from their respective hiding places, dug their hands deep into their pockets, and mimicked Vigo's corny performance. They left the room through separate doors.

There was a commotion inside the metal file cabinet; the one with the three, long drawers. The top drawer slid open and a jumble of limbs appeared over the lip. A lanky, anonymous clown climbed out and mimicked the other clowns.

Soon they were coming out of the woodwork like roaches, crawling out of every conceivable space that would hide something about the size of a man, and some that would not. They whistled and strolled nonchalant with their hands dug deep into their pockets making a spectacle out of trying to appear inconspicuous.

Doors swung open and slammed shut as the clowns walked into back rooms one after the other. The collective din of their whistling reached a pitch that tickled, and then hurt Mars' ears.

The last clown walked into a back room and slammed the door behind him and the main area became relatively quiet again. The television was still on and tuned to the same infomercial. Outside, traffic rumbled and hummed passed the storefront window behind Mars.

Mars was feeling overwhelmed, but he held it together for the sake of the case.

"Bacon?" he complained to the Mohawked clown.

"No offense, chum. But I'm a clown. I gotta go for the funny," Spiro Ton confessed.

"I didn't find that funny."

Spiro stopped shuffling the cards.

"No? Well, that's too bad. We'll have-ta work harder to meet your...*elevated* standards."

Mars smirked at the sarcasm in the clown's response.

"How many people you got back there anyway?"

"Just a few."

"A few? There musta been 20 clowns just now."

"Tricks of tha trade, mi amigo," Spiro boasted. "So...to what do we owe the pleasure of your visit? Oh-fficial business?"

"Why? You do something wrong?"

The clown playfully bristled and replied, "Not that you know of..."

Touche, Mars nodded, smiling slightly.

"Actually, I'm here as a customer. It's my kid er...my son's birthday next week and I wanna do something special for the little rugrat. So, I'd like some info on your services?!"

Spiro's face lit up.

"Our services! Our services! Why didn't ya just say that in the foiyst place?!"

The room went dark. A spotlight burst into existence and shined on the clown who had somehow changed into a black tuxedo. A piano intro played out of thin air. A gloved hand reached up from below the counter and handed Spiro a top hat, which he flipped and set atop his head. And then he backed away from the counter and broke into song. To Mars the clown appeared to glide on air.

Spiro Ton gave a detailed rundown of the Ton Brothers Clown Co's services in the form of a surreal song and dance number. The performance enjoyed full musical accompaniment despite there being no instruments in sight.

Mars heard doors opening and closing, and the shuffling of feet in the darkness over the clown's shoulder. A few seconds later, another, wider spotlight, born of darkness, set its roving glance on a roomful of clowns dancing, and singing, and tumbling, and juggling, and stomping on all kinds of physical laws in the service of a living commercial.

Spiro threw glitter at Mars at the end of the number. Some got in Mars' mouth and he spit it out, smiling in awe. He had seen things that he couldn't explain and he was thoroughly impressed, and slightly intimidated by the Ton brothers' almost supernatural abilities.

"How'd you do that...with the guy on the tricycle?"

One of the clowns had ridden a tricycle up a wall and onto the ceiling where he then dangled from the handlebars of the upside down trike.

"Like I said before, chum. Tricks of the trade."

"That was really somethin' else, man. You guys should be on TV with-those tricks."

"TV?" Spiro coughed the word out and made a face like he had eaten something bitter. "You think this is some kinda novelty act?"

"Scuse me?"

"What we do here...You think it's all about fame or money?"

Expecting a punchline or another song and dance number, Mars just smiled and played along.

An arm crept up over Spiro Ton's shoulder as he continued to rant, a gloved hand at the end. Chubby fingers flexed and spread apart.

"This is a way-a-life, chum. You see this, here?" Spiro pinched a section of his cheek.

The disembodied arm cranked back and...

"This ain't just grease-paint, ya know...This is—"

...smacked Spiro Ton in the back of his head, instantly silencing him. Comical surprise froze on his face.

Mars didn't get the joke, but he continued to smile out of courtesy.

Spiro's face melted calm. He reached beneath the counter and handed Mars several pamphlets to look over at his own leisure.

Mars told the clown that he liked what he saw here, and that he would get back to them in a day or two regarding the party for his "son." He asked a few more questions about how they did "this" or "that." Spiro said the same thing every time.

"Tricks of the trade."

Mars left the Ton Brothers Clown Co., mystified by the unusual experience and feeling strangely euphoric.

***

In the five hours after he left the Ton Brothers' Clown Co., Mars Kersey, the sometimes quiet and introverted, sometimes crazy and intense, but altogether likeable guy who spoke to most people in single word responses, had become a social butterfly. He had drunkenly stated, "I love you, man," to complete strangers about 10 times. He had been the life of the party at two separate bars packed with Friday night crowds. And he even managed to score a threesome with a pair of bubble-headed college chicks looking to expand their sexual horizons.

They wound up in a room at the Holiday Inn on Walnut Street near Broad. The action was hot-and-heavy until one of the girls—the hotter one—kept bitching about condoms. Mars couldn't give a rat's ass about condoms. His dick was so hard that it had siphoned all the blood from his brain to maintain its consistency, which was that of bedrock. He had no concerns beyond appeasing the rigid beast. He blew the girl off, until she turned ice cold and covered those nice, perky, young breasts of hers with a shirt.

In the store Mars ran into a man he recognized, but whose name he couldn't instantly recall. The man read Mars' expression and started to introduce himself.

"Gavin—"

"—Rossi," Mars interrupted, finishing the man's sentence. "That's right."

Gavin Rossi was the former Medical Examiner's assistant. Before his suspension, Mars had planned to question Gavin and his former boss Zach Stoddard regarding the Gleason's disappearance. At the moment, however, he couldn't care less. He was high on some unknown substance and fiendin' for some hot, young, way out-of-his-league, college-girl, threesome pussy.

Mars' face was set in a subtle perma-grin that lived just beneath the surface. His eyes, though floating beneath a glassy sheen, were welcoming. His posture was loose and unguarded.

Gavin furrowed his brow at the alien in Mars Kersey's body. The man he knew was much more reserved and inaccessible and he was too mindful of his persona to ever allow himself to be seen in this blissfully drunken state. The man he knew would have had the decency to at least try to hide that huge erection threatening to tear through his pants and attack someone.

They traded awkward small-talk and then Mars headed toward the bank of cashiers up front.

"Those bodies... You know. The Gleasons..." Gavin said after him.

When the words finally reached him, Mars was stunned. He turned and focused a sober gaze on Gavin, who appeared nervous, and when their eyes locked, momentarily hesitant, as if he was afraid that he had said too much.

"Yeah...?" Mars replied anticipating something big.

"Their skin... It wasn't paint. That was their real pigment. I don't know how to explain it. We couldn't prove it 'cause the bodies went missing. So we kept quiet."

It was as if giant, unseen hands had reached through the layer upon layer of intoxication, stunned Mars with their icy, sobering touch, and then dragged him back through the last five hours in a matter of seconds.

***

Mars never made it back to the hotel room. After speaking with Gavin Rossi he drove home and spent the rest of the night with his ass stuck to the barstool staring at a collage of files, and handwritten notes, and crime scene photographs, and ads for clown services torn from the Yellow Pages spread out on the kitchen counter. His laptop was like a lopsided centerpiece. Though open and awaiting his instructions, it was pushed aside.

A steaming hot mug of coffee kept him company as Mars scanned the collage with panoramic vision, waiting for something to jump out at him and say, "Here I am! The clue you've been looking for!"

147

Mars simultaneously reviewed his visit to the Ton Brothers' Clown Co. He saw things, in retrospect, that he had missed before, things he should have noticed, things that any rookie would have caught.

That clown...Spiro...He must've slipped me something.

It was the only way to explain his monumental lapse in scrutiny and attentiveness. It would certainly explain all the crazy shit he witnessed. The clown he saw riding up the wall. The big, broad clown who came out from behind the fake tree. All those clowns who sprung up out of nowhere. Spiro Ton's quick change and his little song and dance number.

Maybe it happened when that bastard threw the glitter at him. Mars remembered that some of it had gone in his mouth. And he had been wiping the stuff from his clothing all night. He looked down and noticed a few flecks right now.

Coulda been doused in LSD or somethin', he thought as he pinched a tiny fleck from his sleeve and held it up to his nose. It didn't smell like anything. He was about to taste it, but then thought, *What if it IS, LSD?*

It couldn't have been the glitter, though, because a good bit of impossible weirdness had gone down before the song and dance number. Spiro had thrown the glitter at him afterward.

Previously discarded details were resurrected and examined with fresh eyes and a mind open to a wider array of possibilities. He thought of that perp, Hank Stryker/Shawn Riley's claim that the clowns who hired him were more than just working stiffs hiding under greasepaint to make a living. He thought of Brad Gleason's accounts of the clowns haunting the dorms and hallways of Atwater House.

After several hours a theory began to germinate.

Our perps (the Ton Brothers) drug their vics first. Perps then take pleasure in taunting and harassing vics, who, under the effects of the as-yet-unknown drug, are wracked with vivid hallucinations, which ultimately incapacitate vics. But why murder? Why kidnapping?

Mars' hunch said that the answers lay back at the offices of the Ton Brothers' Clown Co. He would find his redemption there, too. But first he needed some sleep.

***

Mars parked on Riddendale Boulevard, across the street from the Ton Brothers' offices and shut off the engine. He checked his watch. It was 12:45am on a Saturday. The neighborhood was slightly north of rundown, but with a certain kitsch. There was an antique shop, a thrift store that celebrated quirkiness, and a pizza place among the abandoned storefronts. Nearby, an apartment building filled with grad students and young professionals on their way up the ladder. A brigade of street lamps kept the area well-lit.

Riddendale was a large street that saw a fair amount of traffic even at this hour of the night. The pedestrian traffic was minimal. A few vagrants, and drunken grads, and upwardly mobile stiffs stumbling home from the row of bars a few blocks away. The hoodrats often targeted them for mugging.

There was too much activity on the boulevard, so Mars reclined his seat, and watched the place through the driver-side window, waiting for the flow to subside. The sight of the unassuming building brought back memories of being inside, of Spiro Ton with his bottle-red Mohawk, and of all the impossible shit that went down.

Mars ran down his checklist of supplies partly to circumvent the ambush of recent memories.

Flashlight...Check.

Lock-picking kit... Check.

Nightvision goggles... Check.

Gun (just it case)...Check.

Cell phone switched to 'Vibrate...' Check.

He glanced down and reviewed his attire.

Black pants.

Black hoodie.

Black gloves.

Black sneaker-shoe hybrid.

Good to go...

Mars visualized the layout of the office and mapped out the most efficient course, which depended on where he was able to gain access. He wondered if there was an alarm. A good cop would have noticed that earlier. He mused about what the alarm would sound like. Would it be the standard ringing or buzzing, or something more clown-centric? He tried not to dwell on what might happen if he got caught. His career was already in the shitter.

Mars broke in through a side window. He was able to pry it open rather easily. The wooden frame was so corroded that the latch peeled away as if it was nailed into Playdough. Thankfully, there was no alarm.

Inside it was pitch dark. Mars could tell by the way the sound of his feet hitting the tile floor echoed, that the room was small, tiny, in fact—probably a bathroom. Crouching beneath the forced-open window, Mars slid the night-vision goggles down over his eyes and surveyed his immediate surroundings. A murky green film overlay his altered vision.

As he had guessed, he was in a bathroom. Scanning right to left, Mars noticed a few balled up tissues or paper at the bottom of a wire-mesh waste-basket, but saw nothing of significance. The door had been left open revealing a swatch of the main office area that he remembered. The place appeared empty, but appearances were often deceiving, so he used the utmost caution as he slinked up to the doorway and peeked into the main area.

It looked the same as before. He saw the fake Rhapis Palm and the water-cooler and caught a chill in remembrance. There was one more door on his side of the main area and two on the other. He checked the door on his side first.

The small, windowless room was completely empty. The rooms on the other side were the same. He walked out into the main area and checked the area behind the water-cooler, and then behind the fake Rhapis Palm. Maybe there was a trap door or a fake wall or something. He had to know. There wasn't.

Incredulous, Mars moved on to the file cabinet. He slid the top drawer open and...

Chubby snakes made of fabric leapt out at him. A compressed hissing sound accompanied the assault. Mars sidestepped the lunging fabric and pulled his gun. He tracked the snakes with his aim, following them to the ground where they bounced and then lay still. He leaned over for a closer look and then rolled his eyes when he realized what they were. The old snakes-in-a-can gag.

How original.

With his heart beating a-mile-a-minute, Mars shook his head and muttered, "Fucking clowns... Crazy bastards probably spend all day pranking each other."

Inside the top drawer Mars found one accordion folder full of contracts and invoice forms dating back to April 2010, and that was it. He opened the second drawer.

More snakes.

Mars cursed his startled reaction. The drawer was otherwise empty. The third drawer was the same. This time he expected the snakes, though.

Mars was reluctant when he came to the desks. There were three of them, with four drawers each. Now what were the chances that they'd be booby-trapped?

The desks did indeed contain more snakes, however they were randomly placed, which resulted in Mars being startled again. Inside the drawers he found clown routines written out on paper, informational pamphlets, blank applications, and invoice forms, and contracts, and elaborate doodles drawn in crayon. Some of the doodles depicted violent acts.

Disappointed, Mars plopped down at one of the desks and lamented in the dark. Could he have been wrong? He took the goggles off and used the butt of his palms to rub away a dry itching in his eyes, and then stretched them wide open, trying to adjust to the darkness. He flexed and relaxed the sides of his face to alleviate the tightness where the goggles' straps dug into his skin. Those damn things came in handy, but wearing them too long always gave him a headache.

Mars remembered the wire-mesh waste basket in the bathroom, the one with the balled up paper inside. He had dismissed it at the time, thinking that there would be so much more to find in the back rooms and out in the main area. But now that he was desperate...

Holding the goggles to his eyes, Mars walked into the bathroom and emptied the contents of the waste basket onto the floor. There were three balled-up pieces of paper amongst the used tissues. One contained a number of handwritten jokes—bad ones. The other contained a partial clown routine that had been crossed out in ink.

Mars unraveled the third piece of paper expecting to find the same. There was an address written at the top—371 Ramstein Way.

***

Mars skulked down Ramstein Way on foot. The area was stocked with large, opulent houses with luxury cars parked in the driveways. There was no street parking, so Mars left his car a quarter-mile up the road in the parking lot of an all-night supermarket rather than stand out like a sore thumb. The street, itself, was darker than hell and so quiet that Mars could hear himself thinking. He referred to that as "country quiet." The houses were guarded by lamps on fancy iron posts, usually standing on either side of the front doorway.

Mars emerged from a wall of shrubs and crouched at the base of a slender driveway with a large, Art Deco-style house perched at the top. There were two cars parked at the foot of the house; a minivan covered in ultra-liberal bumper stickers and an expensive-looking sedan.

Mars heard the hum of an engine coming toward him down Ramstein and froze. The passing car's headlights illuminated a shadow looming over Mars' right shoulder. He gasped and spun around, but it was only the mailbox. White numbers emblazoned on the side read, 371.

The house at the top of the driveway was constructed of wood and windows arranged in a way that called too much attention to itself. The curtains were drawn and the lights were out. Mars didn't really have a plan, only a thirst to know how this place related to the clowns. Maybe the owners were former or prospective clients.

Mars sneaked up the driveway as a basic plan came together in his head. He crouched behind the minivan and zoomed in on the wooden structure for possible points of access. There were two, short, rectangular windows in the base of the house on the side that he faced. He slinked over to the windows and peered inside.

A neon Budweiser sign set the room aglow with the suggestion of red. He saw a bar, a pool table, and a projection-screen TV on the wall. The walls were covered with long swirly-que strokes of the brightest red and green paint on top of a yellow base, and floating circular shapes with thin, serpentine tails. Were they supposed to be balloons? There were four, free-standing video game machines lined up against the back wall. One of the games was called Joust. Mars used to sneak out of Sunday School to play that very game in the corner store across the street from his church when he was a tween. To the games' immediate right, there was a dimly lit doorway and an ascending staircase.

Mars tried the window. He had no intention of entering the place, but he was curious to see. The window was locked. He tried the next window. It was locked, too.

On the other side of the house Mars spotted broken glass lying in the grassy area below the basement windows, and moved closer to inspect. The window had been shattered and then pulled open—probably from the outside. Suspicion washed over his features as he stared at the broken window wondering, and then hoping that the clowns were to blame.

He heard a sound not unlike a scream. It had come from inside the house. Mars turned his ear to the broken window. He didn't have to listen long before he heard the sound again. Only this time it was much louder and more intense.

Mars determined that the sound was most likely that of someone groaning through a gag over their mouth. It was a sound that he had heard before in his line of work.

Mars squeezed through the opened window and lowered himself into the basement. He worried that he had been too loud, until he realized that any sound he had made was drowned out by the noise from the floor above. It sounded like someone stumbling drunkenly, barefoot, followed by a brief struggle, followed by more stumbling.

He heard the groaning sound again. Now that it was

trapped within the confines of the house, there were nuances that he hadn't noticed before. The grunting was actually comprised of several voices. Mars counted three...maybe four.

He already had his hand on his gun, so he completed the motion and snatched it from the holster. He crept quietly, foot-over-foot toward the staircase in the back, ready to turn his gun on some unlucky bastard. The room stunk of new carpet and cedar so much so that Mars wondered how the homeowners could stand being down there.

He passed a closet door, the kind that slid open and closed on a track, and noticed that it wasn't fully closed. There was an inch-wide sliver of darkness between the closet doors. Mars peeked inside and saw a pair of eyes bugging out at him. He backed away from the door and took aim. The eyes were still visible, floating in the darkness inside the closet. Since they hadn't moved, Mars thought that maybe it was some kind of prop, or a poster of some sort.

He reached out with one hand and slid the door open enough to see a woman inside. Her clothing, and body-type, said pampered housewife, however her face said that she was a clown beneath the surface. Half her face was torn away, like a mask, revealing a layer of true white-skin with constantly-shifting flourishes of black and red around her eye and the corner of her mouth respectively. Or maybe the clown side was her real face and the slightly-above-average-looking middle-aged woman who wore too much make-up-face on the other side was the mask. The woman's hair was dirty blond and bone straight on one side, wildly arranged and green on the other.

Shaken by the ghastly blend of faces, Mars nearly fired on the woman.

"Who are you?! Do you live here?!" he demanded to know. He kept his voice at a whisper lest he alert whomever was upstairs.

"Are you one of *them*?" the woman looked Mars over as she whimpered. He didn't seem to fit the bill.

"I'm a cop."

"You have to do something or…or they'll kill us all!"

"Who are they?"

"They're fucking terrorists! That's who they are! They did this to meeee!"

"Shhhhh!" Mars scolded.

"What gives them the right to decide how we should live our lives?! What gives them the right?!"

"How many of them are there?"

"I don't know…four, I think. They've got my husband, and my sister and brother-in-law. They're tied up in the living room."

Mars guided the clown-housewife back into the closet.

"Stay here, and don't make a sound."

The woman protested, citing that there were too many of them for Mars to handle alone. Mars put his finger to his lips and shushed her, but she kept on talking, so he slid the door closed on her rambling pessimism and headed for the staircase ready to kick some ass.

"It's too late for that now," came Spiro Ton's slapstick voice from the living room. "Didn't you people read the letters?"

"They ain't read 'em," quipped Presto Ton.

"Shoulda read the letters, folks," said Bully.

"Yeah…you think we're doin' this for our health?" Vigo chimed in.

Mars counted four voices in total, all familiar. He remembered their names from the clown shop.

"We told ya what was gonna happen if you didn't listen?" Spiro warned.

The wall that ran along the staircase was topped with a wooden railing held up by a row of stout, vertical pillars spaced a foot apart. Mars could see through the railing into the living room of the house, however his view was obstructed by a large loveseat. He saw two people slumped against a wall with their hands tied behind their backs. Ball-gags strapped to their heads forced their jaws apart. Flecks of glitter decorated their clothing, the wall behind them, and the carpeted floor beneath their outstretched legs.

155

There was a youngish woman (maybe in her early 30s) and an older man (late-40s) leaning on each other for support. Their faces were a map of bruises and lacerations that revealed hints of true white skin, similar to the clown-housewife from earlier. They groaned and writhed in reaction to the same naked, stumbling footsteps that Mars had heard previously.

Mars dropped down to his belly and ascended the remaining stairs like a lizard. He peered around the railing and saw the four clowns from the Ton Brothers' Co. standing in a circle playing keep-away with a severed human head. The owner of the head, a half-naked young man wearing tightie-whities and a garish stump on his shoulders that spewed blood like a fleshy volcano, stumbled and flailed in pursuit.

Mars concluded that the headless man was the clown-housewife's brother-in-law, which meant that the 30-something woman slumped against the wall was most likely her sister and the older man was her husband.

The flailing brother-in-law fell into one of the clowns, who shoved him away, laughing at the poor man's peril. Despite his head being separated from his body, the man appeared cognizant of what was happening. His eyes constantly darted, reorienting after every toss, and attempting to locate his body to guide it in the right direction.

But that's not possible. Not even remotely possible.

The clown-housewife's sister spotted Mars peeking around the railing. The look on her face gave him the chills.

Operating on instinct, Mars jumped up and took aim at the clown closest to him, a portly thing with blue dreads and a top hat.

"FREEEEZE!"

Mars suddenly became the center of attention. The clowns stopped tossing the severed head around, instead jockeying gazes between big brother Vigo and Mars. It was then that Mars noticed that the clownish flourishes painted over the white base of their faces were moving like liquid underneath a clear surface. Currently the flourishes were set to 'Anger,' and floating on top of frowns. And there was glitter in the air.

The bound victims were yelling at Mars through their

ball-gags, trying to communicate something to him, but it all just sounded like passionate gobbledygook. The severed head was saying something, too. And he was looking at Mars. The whole scene spooked the hell out of Mars, but he fought to remain focused. Regardless of what else was going on here, he was in the presence of thrill killers. Experience had taught him that they were especially unpredictable.

Presto Ton stepped forward projecting confusion. He spread his arms and shrugged his shoulders and said to Mars in a familiar accent, "What? Doncha know?"

"I said FREEZE!"

"Yer only dreaming, friend."

"Yeeee-ah. Dreamin'. I like that," another clown chuckled.

Big brother Vigo reached over and smacked that clown upside his head.

Mars ordered Vigo to, "Drop the...head." As he edited on the fly, the words fell clumsily from his mouth. The unedited version—*Give the man his head back*—sounded too unbelievable to utter.

Vigo let go of the severed head and raised his hands in mock surrender. The head made a loud crack when it hit the floor and cried out in pain.

"Didn't ya hear me, friend? I said yer dreaming."

"I fucking heard you! Now shut the fuck up and don't come any closer!"

"Right now you're sleepin' like a baby in your own bed, nestled niiice and cozy underneath the sheets while your brain reviews the day's events."

What if all of it *was* a dream? The visit to the Ton Brothers' office... The exuberant high that turned him into a temporary celebrity for a night... The threesome... This...

"If you weren't dreaming, could I do this?" Presto said as he flipped the top hat off his head, reached inside, and pulled out a woman—the clown-housewife—up to the shoulders, her arms pinned against her sides by the small circumference of the hat.

Presto Ton had the woman by a clutch of her hair as she screamed and wriggled violently. And then he stuffed her back into the hat and flipped it onto his head.

Mars was in shock. His arms suddenly felt heavy. He labored to hold them up.

"Or this…" Vigo Ton said, and then kicked the severed head at Mars, who leaned out of the way.

The severed head was screaming as it sailed over Mars. It hit the ground somewhere behind him and cried out in pain.

Mars looked round just in time to see the flailing, headless body chasing after its own head. And he just happened to be in the way. There was no time to move, so Mars fired two shots that did nothing to slow its charge, and then he braced for impact.

***

The smell of smoke was heavy in the air. Mars sucked it into his lungs and began coughing violently. Flames cackled and snapped in the background. They were close enough that Mars was sweating from the intense heat. His eyes fluttered and then shot wide open and were instantly stung by heat vapors and smoke. As the mental fog cleared, Mars remembered the clowns…and the headless body charging at him.

But first things first…

Through a veil of rapid blinking, he saw a wall of fire in the next room. Fingering out like tentacles, the flames spread along the carpeted floor. Furniture, drapes, appliances were all seized upon and devoured. An entertainment console fizzed and popped, raining down sparks that grew into new fires wherever they landed. The fire would reach Mars in a matter of minutes.

Between Mars and the flaming tentacles, a long, wooden dining-room table extended away from him. He was sitting in a chair at the head of the table. There were other people there with him. Clowns. Dead ones. There was one with a half-normal face—a middle-aged woman—sitting at the other end of the table. Mars remembered her from the closet at the foot of the stairs.

Oh, wait…Didn't one-a-those fuckers pull her out of a hat?

158

He recognized the face beneath the clownish surface of the man sitting directly to his left. It belonged to clown housewife's husband. All of the victims were here, in fact, even the headless brother-in-law. His severed head had been placed, upright, on a dinner plate set on the table in front of his seated body. His face had been turned clownish like the others.

Mars fought to plant his feet and remove himself from the macabre dinner-party, but something held him to the chair. His eyes crept south, squinting through the heat and smoke reluctantly, knowing what he might find.

His wrists were tied, with multi-colored jump-ropes, to the arms of a sturdy wooden chair. The same rope secured his ankles to the legs of the chair.

Growling like a trapped beast, Mars tugged, and yanked, and twisted attempting to free himself, with no success. His lungs tired quickly from the excessive amounts of smoke he had inhaled and he succumbed to another coughing fit.

Looking through reddened, watery eyes, Mars watched the fire ebb closer.

On one pass, he glanced a quarter-inch-thick jagged ridge running along the clown housewife's husband's hair and jawline, and looked closer. It looked like the man was wearing a full-head mask of his normal, human face, which had been torn or hastily cut out revealing a clown-face underneath. The other victims had similar ridges running along the border of their faces. The jagged patterns differed from each victim.

Mars thought of the Gleason family and suddenly Gavin Rossi's voice materialized in his thoughtstream...

"Their skin... It wasn't paint...That was their real pigment."

The flames had reached the table and were chowing down on the clown housewife at the other end. Mars could hear their joyous snap, crackle and pop as they ate through her pants and feasted on the flesh, and fat, and muscle of her sausage legs. Pungent smoke billowed from singed fabric and cooked meat. The flames' ferocity amplified with every searing bite until their cackling became a roar. A sudden whoosh of hot wind gave her blouse a rise when the flames ignited the glossy fabric and, in an instant, her entire torso was engulfed. Her face began to blister and swell from the heat. The flames climbed up her neck and licked her face. Her flesh boiled and began melting away in layers.

Mars heard a moist pop and watched the housewife's eyelids deflate. Milky white froth poured from between them and sizzled under high heat as it oozed over the garish, rigid texture of burnt flesh. The housewife's body slumped forward wearing a suit of flames. Her forehead met the table with a thud and ignited the lacy, white tablecloth on top.

Mars tore his eyes away, horrified. He shuddered, speculating what a death like that would feel like and how long he would suffer. If he didn't get himself out of this chair, he was going to find out pretty damn soon.

The heat from the encroaching flames nipped at his face and singed his eyebrows and lashes. Mars recoiled from the angry vapors, squeezed his eyes closed, and scrunched up his face. The air was getting thicker and harder to filter through his stinging lungs. As much as he wanted to panic, and to scream, and to cry like a baby, Mars knew that a level-head was key to his survival. He kept telling himself that as the flames advanced.

Let's see how calm your ass is when you're getting fried, the cynic in him commented.

Mars gathered his waning strength and unleashed a short burst of intense struggling before his muscles gave out on him and his lungs begged for mercy. He stopped to recover, and then repeated the process. He did this several times and was eventually able to work the rope loose on his left wrist. He pulled and then snatched his arm free and stared at it like he had never seen an arm before.

Relief washed over him, intoxicating, briefly sedating him against the heat and the fear of burning to death. Seconds later, when the buzz wore off, he looked up and saw three of the dinner guests wearing suits of fire. The flames were only a few feet away and approaching fast. The heat was unbearable. He could feel the side of his face tightening and beginning to cook.

Wearing a painful grimace, Mars fanned the flames with his free arm. He lifted the table-cloth and yanked it downward hoping that the cresting fabric would somehow chase the flames away.

Mars reached over and dug his fingers underneath the rope around his right wrist and pulled until his fingers were numb. He heard a gasp from his left and whipped his head around.

It was the clown-housewife's husband. Apparently he wasn't dead. The flames had just riled him from his unconscious state. Or maybe the pain was such that it woke him from the dead.

"It hu…hurts," he groaned, deep-throated, through gnashing teeth and bulging eyes filled with fear. "Please help me. I c…can't move."

Mars thrust himself away from the man and inhaled a massive breath of dense, smoldering air. He coughed and choked as the chair tilted and toppled over sideways.

Mars fell hard to the wooden floor, fought to remain conscious. The room was spinning above him. He focused through blurred, tripled-vision on the groaning, gurgling, thrashing man made of flames in the chair to the left of where he formerly sat.

There were only seconds left to save himself from the flames' juggernaut approach, but frankly he felt like sleeping. He no longer had the strength to fight the creeping lethargy filling his mind. So he closed his eyes and let his head fall to the side.

Suddenly…

The front door burst in. The noise was loud enough that Mars heard it over the flames' cackling roar, over the burning furniture and the crumbling infrastructure that rained down in chunks. He recognized the sound and was granted a brief respite from forfeiture. He tuned his damaged hearing to it. His mind offered suggestions.

Was it God coming to whisk him away to Heaven?

Was it the Devil coming to drag him to Hell?

Or was it the Philadelphia Fire Department coming to rescue him?

A shadow darkened his space. Mars looked up and saw three men cloaked in shadows standing over him. As he focused and his vision began to clear, the three men became one shadowy figure, reaching towards him. And then he passed out.

***

A late-model Cadillac that was as big as a house floated on plump whitewalls down an industrial corridor. Looming structures made of pipes the size of mutant anacondas, and ladders, and platforms with high railings looked down on a jumble of warehouses, and parking lots, and forklifts, and delivery trucks of varying shapes and sizes.

The Caddy stopped in front of a warehouse marked 47E and honked its horn twice. A heavy door slid open. There was a man named DeFlorio on the other side struggling to move the thing. He was skinny with long arms and blonde hair styled in some forgettable way. He wore a tee shirt with some loud, irreverent, retro bullshit printed on the front, and a pair of black track-pants. A machine gun rode slanted on his back.

The Caddy drove in and two sketchy-looking men stepped out. The driver, a short man lost in an oversized suit, went by the name Soza. The other man wore a black sweater/slacks ensemble that made him look like a cat-burglar. His name was Rickson.

Soza and Rickson waited until the skinny man closed the door and then approached him, smiling.

"Quite a workout there, huh, DeFlorio?" Soza joked.

The skinny man glared at Soza, exasperated.

"Relax. It was a joke."

DeFlorio looked away, annoyed and said to Rickson, "He's in the car?"

"Back seat." Rickson replied.

"You make sure he's unarmed?"

"No!" Rickson said, sarcastically. "Whadda *YOU* think?"

DeFlorio didn't rise.

"C'mon. Boss is waiting," he said, stepping backwards

162

and eyeing the back door of the Caddy.

Soza and Rickson lifted an unconscious Mars Kersey out of the backseat of the Caddy. His head was slumped and hidden beneath a burlap sack that his captors had put on him to conceal the location of the warehouse. His wrists were bound in front of him with a plastic handcuff. Struggling with the sleeping weight, the two men held Mars up by the armpits as they followed DeFlorio through a maze of boxes and packing crates and out along the border of rows upon rows of the same stacked on wooden slats.

A walkway wrapped around the interior of the warehouse 25-feet up. Some kind of office set in the southwest corner of the walkway. The lights were on and there were people inside. A long staircase ran diagonal along the wall from behind the office down to the warehouse floor.

The men came to a clearing in the back. There were two forklifts parked side-by-side. Empty slats were stacked nearby. Boxes full of packing Styrofoam waiting to be fed whatever merchandise this place sold or purported to sell. A giant industrial fan stood dormant by a nearby support column.

Further back, a small gathering of dangerous men waited for them near a cluster of chairs arranged as if for a class of some sort. The empty chairs faced a humorless-looking gentleman in a high-end, off-the-rack suit standing by a large packing crate whose purpose it was to hold up his piping hot cup of tea. He stood apart from the other men and was seemingly immune to the anxiety that infected the two most vocal members of the group, who spoke amongst each other, sharing suspicions. A third, rather insignificant-looking man, listened, but offered no opinion of his own.

"Who'se the chump?" Quipped Freddie "Six-Toes" Figueroa when Soza and Rickson walked up with the unconscious man with a burlap sack for a head held between them and placed him in one of the chairs.

Freddie was stick-thin with greased-back hair and a mouthful of long, coffee-stained teeth that he constantly picked with his pinky fingernail.

Soza started to answer, but the humorless gentleman shushed him and commandeered the conversation.

"He's clean?" Humorless addressed DeFlorio, who passed it on to Rickson, whom he knew would take offense.

"He's clean! Alright! In case anybody else is wondering..."

"Might wanna do something about that temper 'for you sling nat shit at the wrong muthafucka," suggested one of the vocal members of the group; a dark-skinned man with a baby face and a large, disarming smile that often fooled people into thinking he was harmless. His real name was Quincy Marshall, but no one ever called him that. Not if they valued their life. In the street he was known as Big Sleep.

Big Sleep's eyes turned cold. Rickson couldn't handle the icy gaze and looked away.

DeFlorio walked over and stood guard next to a narrow, heavily-shadowed corridor between stacked boxes approximately 10-feet behind the humorless gentleman.

"Yo! Who...da FUCK...is dis?!" Six-Toes split his ire between Soza, Rickson, DeFlorio, and the humorless gentleman while pointing at Mars' slumped body. "You take all our weapons and expect us to just sit on our fuc-kin' thumbs while you start bringin' in surprise guests?"

"Calm down Mr. Figueroa. I assure you that—"

"I assure *YOU* that my people ain't gonna be happy when they hear about this. This was supposed to be a closed meeting."

"If your...*people* have a problem with it, then they can see me personally," said a gravely voice situated deep within the narrow, heavily-shadowed corridor that DeFlorio guarded. "Now sit down! And shut your mouth!"

The gravely voice belonged to Ugly Frankie, the Don of Dons. Frankie was so ugly that he chose to live in the shadows never revealing his face to anyone. One look could kill a man, was the joke.

Six-Toes begrudgingly slid a chair underneath him and planted his narrow ass in it.

The other men followed suit.

Glowing embers ascended within the shadowed corridor

as Frankie puffed his cigar and exhaled.

"Now that I have your attention..." he began. "I've called you boys here as a favor to a close personal frienda mine. He needs help to...scratch an itch he's been having, so to speak. This itch, if left unscratched, could be a problem for all of us in the long run, so it behooves you all to give serious consideration to my good friend's proposal."

"Behooves?" Six-Toes whispered and received a round of shrugs from the other men.

"Regarding our mystery guest...He's was a last minute addition to my list, and one that came quite unexpected," Frankie said. "He's someone that you all know; some of you more intimately than others. For the sake of our current endeavor..."

"Endeavor?" Six-Toes whispered.

"I think he means the job he wants us for," Big Sleep leaned over and quietly replied.

"I'd advise that those of you with an axe to grind put that shit behind you for now, and think of the bigger picture. Is that understood?"

Six-Toes was the only one among the men who didn't nod right away.

"Mr. Figueroa..." Frankie said.

Six-Toes nodded and Frankie instructed Soza to remove the sack from Mars' head.

Big reactions all around. Six-Toes' was the most flamboyant.

"Holy Fuck!" he jumped out of his seat and said. "You brought a *PIG* in here?"

Six-Toes reached for his pistol before realizing that he had given it to DeFlorio when he first arrived.

"Whathafuckisthis...somekinna set-up?"

"SIT! DOWN!" Frankie demanded. "Or so help me I'll disappear your jumpy little ass before you finish your next thought!"

Six Toes' eyes tracked down and saw a cluster of red dots floating over his heart. The other men saw it, too. He followed the connecting beams up to the walkway and saw a sniper posted at each corner.

"Sit cho silly-ass down," Big Sleep whispered through his teeth.

Someone coughed. Startled heads whipped toward the sound of Mars Kersey coming to.

Consciousness was met with a splitting head-ache and a painful cramp in the back of his neck. Mars cricked his neck from side-to-side and then a wallop of recent memories flooded his mind and he shot fully awake. Mars jumped out of his seat when he saw the gallery of miscreants seated all around him.

"What the fuck!" he yelped with wide, crazy eyes.

He realized that his hands were tied when he reached for his gun, which was no longer in the holster, and flew into a panic. It took both Soza and Rickson to contain Mars, and force him back into his seat.

"Looks like that plan-a-yours is really workin' out well," Six Toes quipped at the shadow that hid Ugly Frankie.

Frankie took a deep puff from his cigar, but gave no reply.

"Relax, Detective," he said to Mars. "Today you're among friends."

"Friends?" Mars growled. "All I see is a bunch of scumbag murderers."

"Hey! Fuck you, man," said Six Toes.

"I'da thought you'd be more grateful to the man who saved your life, Detective. Perhaps I should've instructed Mr. Soza here to let you burn along with that poor family."

Mars felt a swell of anxiety over the remembrance of this latest near death experience. There had been at least three over the course of his career, but none this close. He could still hear the flames' cackling roar. He could still smell the fragrant aroma that seasoned the smoke when the fire tore into the bodies seated at the table. He could still see their flesh melting and sliding from their faces. And now he was surrounded by the city's most revered ice men, unarmed, with his hands tied together. Mars felt too vulnerable to even consider relaxing. Instead he kept reminding himself of each man's reputation.

—**Freddie Six Toes** was known for his berserker modus operandi, which included biting off the noses and ears of his victims in a wild murderous frenzy. He was wanted for at least a dozen homicides.

—**Big Sleep** was good for eight or nine murders that Mars knew of, plus a slew of strong-arm robberies, home invasions, and carjackings.

—**Some painfully insignificant guy whom Mars had never seen before...**

—**Soza and Rickson** smelled like Feds on the take to Mars. He could feel it in his gut.

Mars' gut had become a great purveyor of suspicion over the years. That suspicion usually led to an arrest. He called it a sixth-sense, a gift that separated good cops from the adequate ones.

—**Ugly Frankie Esposito,** the Don of Don's who was not above whacking cops. Allegedly.

—**DeFlorio,** Ugly Frankie's personal bodyguard.

"How did you find me? How did you know?" queried an incredulous Mars.

"*YOU* found *US* when you stumbled onto our... 'investigation,'" replied Ugly Frankie. "We've had eyes on the clowns for over a month. And here you come, Mr. Disgraced Police Man, gonna save the day *AND* his tarnished reputation in one fell swoop. Didn't expect to find what you found, eh?"

"Who are they?"

Frankie took a puff from his cigar, exhaled and then said, "Better to let my good friend explain it to yoos all."

Frankie spoke into some kind of walkie talkie and seconds later a heavy door opened and closed somewhere above the men. Multiple footsteps descended the metal staircase. The bottom was located back behind the stacks. The metal "Clank" was replaced by a flat "Click-clack" sound when the footsteps reached the warehouse floor and approached the gathering of dangerous men.

Don Podeel walked out from between stacks flanked by stoic bodyguards. He wore his usual attire (a white dress shirt

167

unbuttoned at the neck, and khakis) underneath a black blazer, that usual opportunistic glow on his narrow, squinty-eyed, fish-face, and an expensive leather briefcase in his hand.

Podeel nodded at the shadow where Ugly Frankie stood puffing from his stogie and walked up to the crate. The humorless gentleman took his cup of tea and stepped aside giving Podeel the floor.

Podeel set the briefcase down on top of the crate and thumbed the gold latches open. Ever the showman, he was cognizant of the suspense that gripped the room as he peeled the lid open.

There was an audible reaction to the stacks of crisp, clean hundred-dollar-bills inside. He closed it after a few seconds.

"That's five hundred-thousand," he said as if he was pitching one of his products. "Should you choose to accept my offer...and survive, you'll get another five-hundred thou' upon completion. And there's more..."

"Whaddaya want us ta whack your competition," Six-Toes joked. "Whatsiz name...Billy Mays...or the Sham Wow guy?"

"Show some respect!" Ugly Frankie scolded from the shadows. "This is a close, personal frienda mine you're talkin' too."

"It's okay," Podeel smiled.

To Six Toes he said, "Billy Mays is dead. And Vince..."

A quizzical frown from Six Toes. *Who's Vince?*

"...the Sham Wow guy. He's one-ah *them.*"

"One-ah them?" shrugged the insignificant man, who spoke with the soft tone and the placid delivery of a kindergarten teacher addressing a roomful of students on their first day of school.

"He means a clown. Right?" Mars looked to Podeel.

Podeel glanced in Mars' direction, and then looked away without responding. Mars took that as a "Yes."

"This city has a virus," Podeel began. "...a virus that has been spreading across this planet over the past few years."

He explained that the 'clown' persona was just one of several they used to blend into human society, that their true nature was much more sinister. He called them tricksters, tormentors, and 'painted devils'.

"They are the things assigned to populate the dreams and hallucinations of mad men," he said.

He cited demonic possession as another example of their wickedly playful nature.

"Sometime back when the Earth was still flat, a group of them fled their vile, pitiless realm with visions of starting life anew amongst the humans, whom they envied for their freedom to choose their own destiny."

The Earth was never flat! Six Toes thought out loud

"It's a figure of speech, you dipshit," Mars responded.

Six Toes glared.

"These...dissenters hid their true identities beneath suits of living flesh and struggled to suppress their wicked impulses. To this day, most of them still can't quite get it right. You can usually spot them if you know what to look for. Others have become so good at hiding that even other clowns can't tell. You've all passed them in the street, or sat beside them on the bus, or taken them home from a bar. They are your friends...Your neighbors...Some of you even have some in your family. There have always been extremists among them, who detest the idea of living as a human."

Podeel looked directly at Mars and said, "Your clowns—the Ton Brothers—are part of a growing trend of neo-extremists who have taken to violence to further their cause. Until a year ago, the Tons were just another family of clown grifters performing tricks and picking pockets on the circus and carnival circuits."

Ugly Frankie interrupted... "They first came on the radar with us when they started pulling robberies in one-a-my areas. They would intercept calls to other clown agencies, and then show up at the client's house and case the place while they performed."

...and then he passed it back to Podeel.

"And they have no qualms about killing whomever gets in their way. So don't be fooled by their jovial demeanor. Now, somewhere along the way the Tons got political. The Gleasons and the Wiszniaks—that's the family whose burning home you were rescued from, Detective—were targeted by the Tons. The campaign starts with notes mailed anonymously to the victims. The notes contain cryptic messages made up of letters cut out from magazines.

'We know who you are.'

'Stop living the lie or else.'

'We're watching you.'

The messages become more threatening as the notes continue. If the victim doesn't capitulate to their threats, then they are murdered in cold blood."

"So let's say I believe all that horse-shit you just told us—"

"Aye!" scolded Ugly Frankie. "You're pushin' it, Figueroa!"

"It's not horseshit," Mars added. "It's true. I know how ridiculous it sounds. I was where you all are until yesterday."

His eyes lingered on the gallery of murderers, none of whom had anything to say, except for Six Toes, whose face communicated frustration at being muzzled by Ugly Frankie.

"What about the Gleason boy? Brad?" Mars asked Podeel.

"The children of their victims are sent to camps to be reeducated. These camps operate under the auspices of clown training schools. But you won't find them in any phone book."

Six-Toes raised his hand. He looked like he was going to burst.

"Whadda you fucking retah-ded?" Frankie scolded.

"It's just a simple question," Six Toes whined in his defense.

"Go ahead," said Podeel.

"I don't mean no disrespect, but ah…Why do *you* care? Even if all that, what choo said, is true, what does it have to do wid you? I mean…a million bucks is a lotta dough, but I ain't putting my ass on the line for no amount a money until I know the whole story. Capiche?"

"I heard THAT," Big Sleep commented.

"Personal reasons," Podeel responded to Six-Toes and Big Sleep's disappointment.

"What? That's not good enough for yoos?" An annoyed Frankie interrupted again. "How bout cause these fuck-in scumbags took from people in my area? That's reason enough right there!"

"How do we know that our...friend-for-the-day over there ain't gonna turn around and try to rat us out to his buddies the first chance he gets?" asked the insignificant man.

"Oh, I wouldn't worry about that."

"Why not?" Big Sleep asked.

"The detective and I have a mutual friend."

Mars was confused.

"Unfortunately, this friend has got nothing but bad things to say about you, Detective. And he's been telling everybody who'll listen about all the horrible things you did to him the last time you two saw each other. In fact, I hear he's scheduled to meet with the District Attorney at the end of this week so he can tell her all about it, too. I might even have a few suggestions for him to ah...spruce up his story so that they put you away for a long time. And once you're inside there's no Segregation Unit that'll keep you safe from me. *Or*...I could just as easily see to it that our mutual friend never makes it to the DA's office. That's entirely up to you, Detective."

This was usually the point in an undercover investigation when Mars had to decide whether the case was worth another man's life, even a lowlife, recidivist piece of shit like Hank Stryker.

Having weighed his options under duress, Mars decided to play along until he could get his hands on a phone and get word to Shieldzie and Captain Malek, and coordinate a plan to rain down Holy Hell on the whole lot of these fuckers— the clowns, the hitsquad, Ugly Frankie and Don Podeel— with the full force of the Philadelphia Police Department. He knew they'd be watching him the entire time, and that they'd probably keep Stryker alive as insurance until the job was done.

"I want these clowns as badly as you do," Mars said to Frankie. And he meant it.

***

The Goldman was a failed movie theater in a failed stripmall out by the Philadelphia International Airport. It was built as the centerpiece to the Goldman Plaza, shades of old Hollywood grandeur in its design. Old signage loomed pitifully over the row of lifeless storefronts extending out from the theater on the left and right, like arms made of darkened windows with faded posters for outdated promotions peering out. Weeds pushed through cracks in the barren parking lot and, over time, made the cracks larger. Miscellaneous trash formed clusters in random spots.

Traffic zoomed by on Island Avenue, a busy thoroughfare that ran parallel to the stripmall. The plaza's back was to the overgrown swampland that converged with the Tinicum Nature Preserve about a quarter of a mile away.

Two trails cut through the thicket that blanketed the swampland and spit out two teams of well armed men at the rear of the plaza.

Mars Kersey ran with Team A along with Big Sleep, who kept bragging about how he was going to show everyone how they handle shit in the 'hood, and Soza, who ran point. Ugly Frankie had instructed Soza to "Take the pig out if he tries anything funny."

Rickson was heading up Team B, which consisted of Freddie Six-Toes, and the painfully insignificant man, who told everyone to call him Sig.

Ugly Frankie had armed all the men from his arsenal of pilfered munitions. They were each supplied with a Podeel Pocket Assassin—which were only available on the black market—donated by the man himself. Soza wore Mars' nightvision goggles on top of his head and a headset microphone.

The teams communicated via hand-signals and then separated.

Team A moved off toward the Goldman's back door in a single-file crouch-run.

Team B quietly scaled a thick drainage pipe and moved

along the connected rooftops toward the Goldman in a similar fashion.

The Tons made their base in the old theater. Ugly Frankie had lost a few good men acquiring that information. The plan was to place surveillance on the Goldman from a safe distance until the clowns left, at which time they would break into the place, take up position, and sit tight. They would take the clowns by surprise upon their return, attacking them from high and low. Poor bastards wouldn't know what hit them.

Soza was unaware that Mars had borrowed his cell phone, sent an anonymous text to 911, and replaced it as he napped in the backseat of the car right next to Mars, whose shoulder he unknowingly used as a pillow. He finally woke up when Mars shoved his head away.

Mars had originally planned to text Shieldzie and the Captain directly, and to reveal his identity, but reconsidered, fearing that they might not take him seriously. In the meantime, he tried to buy some time by fumbling with his equipment, and by signaling the team to "stop," every five feet, because he thought he heard something.

It took three of them to lift and pull the old, rusted backdoor open quietly after Soza picked the lock. A rush of musty air came at them from the darkened innards of the grandiose structure.

Soza slid the nightvision goggles down over his eyes and peered inside.

"Some kinda stock room," he said scanning right to left. "C'mon."

Team A filed into the vertical rectangle of darkness, following Soza, who stopped once they were all inside and pressed the earpiece to his ear. With the door left wide open, dusk eavesdropped on the stockroom and provided ample light. They saw boxes coated in dust both stacked and strewn about. Some appeared unopened. Tubes for shipping large posters leaned against the walls and lay on the floor. A few theater chairs, and outdated promotion items.

"We're in!" Soza whispered into the tiny microphone floating in front of his mouth.

Mars picked up on a distant sound and threw his hand up to alert the others.

"Listen…" he whispered. "You hear that?"

By now the men were visibly annoyed with Mars' overzealous caution, except for Soza, who had heard the noise, too.

The hodgepodge of sound was difficult to identify. There was commotion, voices, even music, all amplified to a seismic level. It sounded like a movie playing in one of the theaters.

"I thought there was only five of 'em. We saw five leave, right?" asked a worried Soza. He leaned toward Mars and whispered. "Whadayou make-ah that?"

Concentrating on the sound, Mars shrugged his shoulders and shook his head, *I dunno*.

"Sounds like we missed the previews," quipped Big Sleep.

"This ain't no joke, son." Soza warned Big Sleep. "I suggest you remember that."

Big Sleep sucked his teeth. He was unimpressed with Soza, and with the clowns' reputation.

Soza reached out to Team B again.

"Rickson. You there?" he said into the microphone. "We got something down here. Sounds like it's comin' from one of the theaters."

No response.

"Rickson! Get yer head outta yer ass and respond!"

He did not.

"Fuck!" Soza said in a harsh whisper and then he muttered to no one in particular, "Piece-a-shit headset!"

"It ain't the headset," Mars responded. He said the rest with his eyes. *It's those fucking clowns*!

"How do you know?" Big Sleep scoffed.

"Because I've dealt with these bastards before. It's them. Trust me. I can feel it." He chin-pointed at Soza. "He knows it, too. Doncha, Fed?"

Soza glared at Mars.

"Tha hell are we standin' around for then? Let's go get them muthafuckahs!" said an eager Big Sleep.

Skulking in single file, Team A slinked through the

stockroom doorway and down a murky, red-orange corridor that reeked of old. The deep red carpet was stained from a half-decade-worth of soles tracking in dirt from outside and worn from their constant trampling. The walls were a few shades lighter, with hints of orange. Fancy light fixtures coated in dust and cobwebs were mounted on the walls every 20 feet.

The team came to a set of double doors marked Theater 1. Circular windows in the doors revealed complete darkness inside. The muffled noise was indeed coming from one of the theaters, but not this one.

Moving on, they came to the lobby. The murky, red-orange atmosphere infected this area as well. The refreshments counter was still intact. A sticky, dusty layer made it difficult to see the mummified refreshments on display inside the glass counter/display case. There was a dead popcorn machine at the end of the counter. A bank of old video game units stood against a wall; archaic titles like, Zookeeper, Rastan, and Space Harrier. Old couches wrapping around pillars were surprisingly well-preserved. Posters for the last films shown here (*Rumble in the Bronx, Welcome to the Dollhouse*, and *Trainspotting*) encased in oblong boxes hung from the walls. Cardboard standees for upcoming films circa 1996 looked as though they had been used as a dartboard.

Doorways marked Theaters 1 through 4 led off to their respective screening rooms. The sound was coming from the doorway marked Theater 3. They could all hear it now. It was definitely a movie; horror, from the sound of it.

Soza made eye-contact with the team and pointed at the doorway and received a bunch of "No shit," expressions in return.

They crept down another dark, red-orange hallway, and stopped in front of Theater 3, tension mounting as the sound grew in volume. Dancing patterns of light shone through the circular hole in the double-doors. The hallway was colored with luminescent shades of blue/grey.

Soza signaled for the men to "Hold tight," and then he ordered Mars Kersey to look through the circular window.

The film playing was shot with a home video camera —
Mars absolutely hated that art house shit. He saw a woman
kneeling over an unconscious or dead man. She wore a ball-
gag around her neck like a necklace. The man had blood all
over his chest. A thick flap of skin flayed away from his cheek
and dangled there, a smooth, white surface underneath. The
woman was crying as she shook the man and yelled for him
to "Wake up!" Behind her, five pairs of legs materialized
from the darkness, or so it seemed. Although they were only
visible from the waist, down, Mars recognized their clothing.
It was the Ton Brothers.

He recognized the woman, too, and the man lying
unconscious or dead on the floor. He even recognized the
house in which the video was shot. He had just been there,
tied to a chair as flames threatened to eat him alive.

Apparently the Tons had filmed the whole thing. He didn't
remember seeing any cameras. And he didn't remember the
scene that he was watching. It must have happened while he
was unconscious.

He saw someone sitting in the third row of the theater,
fourth seat in from the aisle — a woman, judging by the shape
of her head and shoulders. She had an ugly, asymmetrical
hairstyle.

"What is it? Whaddayou see?" Soza asked.

Mars returned to the group and told them what he saw.

"There's a woman in there, too," he said. "Knowing these
bastards, it's some kinda dummy; probably booby-trapped.
I'm gonna check it out. You guys watch my back."

"Since when did you start giving the orders?" Soza
complained.

Mars responded by raising his gun to a ready position
next to his face. Without a word, he tip-toed up to the door.
The other men followed.

Mars pushed the door open enough to squeeze through.
He held it open for Big Sleep, who then did the same for
Soza.

Mars stood nearly upright at the top of the aisle and
scanned the room. Aside from the woman, the room appeared

to be empty. He still couldn't tell if she was real or fake. He looked back and nodded at the rest of the team, and then he approached the woman with his gun held out in front.

"You there!" he said, calling on his authoritative police persona to hide the fact that he was nervous. "Put your hands where I can see them!"

The woman didn't move.

He tried not to look at the screen despite the pull of familiar voices as he approached the woman from behind.

"I know you heard me, lady!"

No response.

She didn't as much as flinch when Mars accidentally stepped on an empty bag of pretzels and winced at the sound it made.

A sudden ambush of transistor noise distracted him away from the woman. The men covered their ears and doubled over from the noise. The movie screen was awash with vertical bar interference, then horizontal, then vertical again over a backdrop of heavy static.

The static began to settle. The bar interference widened into a new image, shot on video just like the previous one. On the screen they saw Rickson standing in the middle of a dark room with his gun drawn, squinty-eyed as he struggled to see in the dark, and scared shitless. He whipped his head around and spun to follow as if he thought someone was attempting to sneak up on him.

"Rickson!" Soza called out.

"Awe shit! You dead now!" the woman in the third row yelled at the screen.

Mars flinched at the sound of her voice.

"Get your hands where I can see 'em, lady! NOW!"

The woman acted as if she didn't hear him, which was impossible considering that he was only about 10-feet behind her.

Mars tossed a quizzical glance at the other men. They were equally baffled.

Over Rickson's shoulder, a door at the far end of the hallway began to open by itself.

"What's that?" Soza said, pointing at the screen. Mars looked at the screen and focused on the blanket of pitch black beyond the fully opened doorway over Rickson's shoulder.

A bell jingled.

Rickson whipped around and pointed his gun at the dark doorway. A confusing shape shot from the darkness like a locomotive exiting a tunnel.

By the time his mind acclimated to the sight (a clown with a bottle-red Mohawk riding a child's tricycle), the uncanny thing was halfway down the hall and coming fast. The clown was hunched over the handlebars, pedaling hard and smiling like he reveled in his mission. The clownish flourishes around his eyes and mouth moved like liquid, finally settling into a devilish grimace.

Rickson squeezed off round after round, but Spiro Ton maneuvered out of the way of every bullet, like some extreme trike phenom. He rode up onto the wall, and then the ceiling, and down the opposite wall, and finally skidded to a stop when his wheels touched down on the floor.

"Looks like you're *ALL* outta bullets, chum," Spiro quipped.

Rickson *was* outta bullets, and feeling completely vulnerable.

"Get outta there, man!" Soza yelled at the screen.

"I know that's right," said the woman in Row 3.

Mars looked down as if he forgot the woman was there. He had unknowingly lowered his aim as he watched the events onscreen. He started to lift his gun, but found himself transfixed to the screen once again.

"Goddammit, Rickson! Do something!" Soza yelled. He paused, frustrated, and then said to the rest of the team. "We gotta do something!"

On the screen, Rickson reached for another clip.

"Aunh. Aunh. Auuunh…." Spiro warned as he cupped his hand around the bulbous end of a small horn attached to the trike's handlebars.

Rickson scoffed at the thing... *That's all you got!*…and went for the clip.

Spiro squeezed the horn. It made a terrible sound, like a ghost ship sounding off as it drifted along in some eerie oceanic nightscape. A wind made of sound waves lifted Rickson off his feet and hurled him backward into a wall. He bounced off and fell hard. He landed on his belly and lay there dazed and confused.

"Too slow," Spiro quipped. He pulled back on the handlebars and the trike roared like a Harley. He revved the engine several times and pulled himself into a wheelie. Six inch metal spikes pushed through the front tire until they covered the entire circumference. Spiro lowered the front of the trike and it sped forward kicking up old, rotten wood, and shredded carpet fibers.

Then the screen switched to the POV of the spiked wheel racing toward Rickson's face. The thing was right on him. He only had time to scream.

The screen went black and left Theater 3 several shades darker than before. It took Mars and the rest of the team a moment to adjust to the darkness and several more to come down from the sensory rush of the events they had just witnessed.

"Tha fuck was that?! Tha fuck is going on?! Was that real?!" Big Sleep yelled. Fear in his tone.

Mars switched his focus to the woman in Row 3. "Goddammit, Lady, Get cher fuckin' hands where I—"

Tears broke from Soza's face. He rushed angrily past Mars and charged toward the woman.

"You fucking Bitch! I'm gonna kill every last ona you!"

"Soza, wait!" Mars yelled as Soza grabbed the woman by her hair, and shoved his gun into the side of her face.

The woman's head popped off of her shoulders as if made for such a purpose.

"Oh She-yit!" Big Sleep said.

Startled, Soza looked down at the head in his hands. It was made of plastic and was rather unconvincing up close. A jumble of wires dangled from its neck. A small digital timer was attached to one of the wires. It was counting down from seven...six...five...

"A bomb!" Mars yelled as he ran back up the aisle, shoving Big Sleep aside, and dove for the double-doors just as the plastic head detonated in Soza's hands.

***

Mars jolted awake to a whiney female voice buzzing in his ear like a gnat on crank. He was sitting in a crowded movie theater. His head hurt and his right arm felt numb and dead like he had been resting his weight on it too long. His right leg was sore, too.

The girl sitting next to him was talking like she was some authority on the movie-watching experience. She scolded him for falling asleep.

"Plus it's like you're wasting your own money," she added.

Somebody shushed the girl and she shrunk into her seat, embarrassed. Mars looked around, seeing only the backs of people's heads and shoulders. He looked behind him and saw rows upon rows of faces transfixed and dowsed in blue light from the movie screen. There wasn't an empty seat in the house.

The girl seemed vaguely familiar. Her name was Charlotte or Cheryl and Mars reckoned they had briefly dated when he was in his twenties. That is if he took the dream as reality and the present as a dream. As of yet, he still hadn't decided.

Mars performed all the prerequisite tests. He pinched himself. He squeezed his eyes shut and opened them again. He gave himself a light smack across the cheek, which prompted a dissatisfied frown from Charlotte or Cheryl.

Something was still not right. His gut told him so. Until the shellshock from the dream settled, Mars attributed it to just that.

Mars flexed his arm to work out the numbness. His limbs felt heavy when he adjusted his seated posture.

Man, I musta really been out, he thought as he sat back and reflected on the dream. He gave reverence to his minds' ability to produce such a vivid, intense and realistic depiction of his future. He discreetly dug his wallet from his back pocket, opened it, and looked at the driver's license. The photo was of a 23-year-old Mars Kersey. He was still just a beat-cop then.

"Would you stop fidgeting," complained Charlotte or Cheryl.

"How long was I asleep?" Mars asked.

"I don't know. A few minutes..."

The funny thing was that Mars remembered how this date turned out. It was their first. He remembered that his dick was sore for days afterward thanks to Charlotte or Cheryl's big teeth getting in the way when she blew him. She had informed Mars that they couldn't have intercourse that night because she was on the rag. She actually used words like 'intercourse' and 'fellatio.' That bugged him.

Mars even remembered the movie they saw on their date; some art-house crap about a dysfunctional family dealing with divorce. He didn't recall having ever seen a movie in which clowns portrayed Mafia goons, yet the presence of clowns lent further credence to his dream. And when he thought of the unfathomable things they had done in the dream, it made more sense that the Ton Brothers were the product of a sleeping mind.

On the screen...

"Freddie. Freddie. Freddie...I always knew you wasn't too smart, but I didn't think you was a complete dumbass," said the clown-Mafia Don to the skinny, terrified husk of a man who stood with his hands tied behind his back in front of a five-man crew of clown-goons.

The man had been stripped naked save for a loincloth made of raw beef that was held together by strings.

The clown-goons bore a striking resemblance to the Ton Brothers from Mars' dream, only they were wearing expensive suits. Vigo Ton played the Mafia Don. He wore his long black hair greased back. His slapstick accent was replaced by a forced rasp, like a bad actor channeling Marlon Brando in *The Godfather*.

181

The terrified man was a spitting image of Freddie Six-toes.

"If you let me go, I promise I won't say a word," Freddie begged.

"Freddie here says we should let him go," said Don Vigo to his crew of clown-goons. "Whaddayou boyz think? Should we let him go?"

The clown-goons sniggered and chortled as if Freddie's life was worth nothing to them.

I don't know," goon-Spiro responded indecisively.

"I say we whack his ass right here," said goon-Bully. "We let him go and he'll bring his people back here. Or worse yet, the cops."

"No! I swear. I won't say anything. Please?"

A silent moment, and then...

Goon-Bully had a sudden change of heart. "Okay," he said. "That's good enough for me. Let's cut him loose."

Though he suspected that the goon was fucking with him, Freddie wanted more than anything to live, thus he reacted with a hopeful lift in his posture, and a gleam of anticipation in his glazed eyes.

The clown goons were grinning and eying him up like they were in on a private joke that he wasn't privy to, one that he was the butt of.

Don Vigo mockingly pondered, and then said, "Okay. You can go. But on one condition."

"Anything..."

Don Vigo nodded to goon-Spiro, who then disappeared into a door in the back of the room.

He returned moments later holding a leash with two of the meanest, ugliest Rottweilers Freddie had ever seen attached to the other end. They were snarling and frothing at the mouth and violently tugging at the leash with Freddie locked in their sights.

Freddie panicked when he saw the dogs. Two goons grabbed him and held him still.

"No! Please! Not like this!" Freddie pleaded.

"Fred-deeeee...Where's your sense of adventure?" Don

Vigo teased. "All you have to do is make it to that door."

He was talking about the door across the room, some 15-feet away. Might as well have been 100-feet.

Freddie's face settled into the realization that he didn't have a chance. He became nauseous. He tried to find the right words to make the goon take mercy on him even though he already knew that mercy probably didn't exist in this guy's mind. It didn't exist in his when he was set to whack someone.

Out of the corner of his eyes, Freddie saw the lead goon nod at the clowns that held him still.

Freddie took off running the instant they let go of him. He heard the dog's claws scrape against the ground as they pushed forward and started after him. Seconds later he felt their teeth clamp onto his legs and sink in. He yelped and screamed like a girl.

The dogs were big, maybe 70-pounds each and their combined weight made it difficult for Freddie to maintain his balance, let alone to move forward. There was still about five feet to go before he reached the door. A voice in his head told him that this was as far as he would get.

* * *

"I can't watch," Charlotte or Cheryl whined with her face buried in Mars' shoulder.

Mars barely noticed as he was too focused on the events unfolding on the screen. The length of Freddie's suffering disturbed him. There were still signs of life after the dogs had eaten through the raw-meat loin-cloth and feasted on Freddie's genitals, and much of his inner thighs. His throat had been torn away, yet he was still struggling to breathe. Mars could tell by the rise and fall of mangled viscera and the bubbling suds that spilled from the wound onto the cement floor. His body twitched when teeth made contact as the larger of the two dogs nipped at random spots on his naked body. The other dog moved back and forth from his ravaged throat to his mangled groin feverishly lapping up blood and tugging on loose meat.

"Is it over?"

When Mars finally looked down to address Charlotte or Cheryl, he saw a black man's face wearing her blond hair and make-up. It was Big Sleep.

Mars gasped and moved to lean away, but found himself restricted again. He heard a muffled voice speaking through a megaphone in the distance. It sounded familiar…

"I repeat. This is Captain Rolland Malek with the Philadelphia Police Department. We have the place surrounded. Come out with your hands up or we will be forced to take action."

Mars groggily looked up from Big Sleep's ugly, dead visage. The movie theater had been replaced by a room not unlike the one that he previously saw onscreen. He was surrounded by the clown-cast of the film he was just watching, only now they looked the way he remembered from the Wiszniaks' house…

Spiro Ton was holding a pair of leashes with fake, life-sized Rottweilers posed in an upright, seated position tethered to the other end. Behind Spiro he saw Freddie Six-Toes' naked body lying, without a scratch, face-up and bespeckled with glitter. Judging by the look on his face, he had died of fright.

Mars was tied to a chair, yet again. Seated next to him was Big Sleep, who appeared to have died from the blast in Theater 3. The right side of his face was singed down to the bone. He was wearing a blond wig and hastily applied make-up.

Presto Ton was standing over Big Sleep and had been puppeting the dead man's corpse.

Whacko Ton ran into the room and overreacted, "They got the whole frickin' police department out there!"

"I told you we shoulda left," whined Presto Ton. "Didn't I tell him?"

"Shut up!" Vigo ordered. "I'm trying to think."

Mars was still feeling the effects of the hallucinogenic glitter that decorated his clothing. He thanked God that he was still dressed, though. He flinched and then hissed at the pain in his arm. He knew right away that it was broken.

He assessed his condition and determined that he had suffered burns from the explosion in Theater 3—maybe second or third degree to his face on the right side, and to his right arm. His right pant-leg was shredded up to the thigh; some kind of debris lodged in the meat of his calf. He couldn't get a good look to see how bad it was, but it felt pretty serious. He most likely had a concussion, too.

"I say we go *multiplier* on their asses!" said Bully Ton.

"Don't be ridiculous," Vigo scolded. "There's too many of them."

Ignoring his pain, Mars worked in secret to free his hands while the clowns argued amongst themselves. The Captain's voice came again.

"We know that you are holding one of our officers hostage in there!"

Mars sighed in response to the Captain's statement. His effort to free his hands, to survive this completely ridiculous ordeal, was invigorated by a sudden sense of belonging. It meant that, to some extent, the Captain and Shieldzie believed him. Finally, they believed him.

A phone rang shortly after. Following a brief discussion, it was decided that Spiro Ton would answer it.

Spiro played coy with the hostage negotiator, while his brothers listened via his responses, facial expressions, and body language. The negotiator asked if Officer Kersey was hurt. Spiro glanced over at Mars and replied, "He'll live."

"Does he require medical attention?" asked the negotiator.

"I said, 'he'll live.' What? You don't understand English?"

"If anything happens to Officer Kersey…"

"…you're gonna come in here wavin' your big blue dicks around like you own the place. Right?" Spiro mocked.

Vigo smacked Spiro in the back of the head and then pointed at Mars who was slumped in the chair. Mars had picked up on the discussion via Spiro's responses to the negotiator, and started playing up his injured state.

Spiro cupped his hand over the phone and mouthed to his older brother, "Was that really necessary?"

"Just listen," Vigo replied. "We tell 'em he's hurt real bad. They'll wanna do an exchange for the negotiator. Standard hostage-negotiating bullshit."

"So we switch one stinkin' cop for another? So what?"

"This pig here is on the shit-list with his people. He ain't worth much to us outside of keeping them off us for the time bein'. We get somebody in here that matters, like the negotiator, or the Captain, and get inside their head, and we can control the whole fucking lot of 'em. We'll throw them a curve-ball with this one here just to soften them up for the slaughter."

A curve-ball? Spiro said with his face.

"Bully knows what I'm talking about. Don'tcha Bully?"

Bully nodded and rolled his sleeves up to his elbows. His smile turned lascivious. He balled his fists and approached Mars.

Mars understood the big clown's malicious intent. He took a deep breath, tightened his body, and tried not to dwell on the size of Bully's approaching fists.

The first punch had Mars seeing stars. Through a blurry lens, he watched Bully's big fists rain down on him, and he could sense the jarring thrust of his body in reaction to each blow. But there was no pain. And then Bully slashed him in the face with a blade of some kind.

It felt like the blade had cut all the way to the bone. A terrible yelping sound leapt out of Mars' mouth. But the pain gave him a burst of adrenaline.

His left arm tore through the duct-tape and he slapped his hand over the fresh wound. He felt warm liquid draining through his fingers. His movement had been temporarily retarded by the assail of big fists, so when his mind said "Get up," his body replied with a short burst of strength followed by a prolonged bout of the lazies.

Mars fell to his knees. His right arm was still taped to the chair.

He floated in and out of consciousness while Spiro spoke to the hostage negotiator. He heard mention of the exchange... and of how Officer Kersey was in serious need of medical attention.

When the negotiator asked, "What happened?" Spiro hesitated for a moment, and then said with a naughty grin, "He tripped and fell."

***

Four evil clowns squeezed through the narrow, off-white corridor with purpose. The large one in the back carried a half-conscious Mars Kersey in his arms like some bare-chested romance novel hero cradling his damsel in distress. Mars' head was wrapped in gauze. A deep crimson stain darkened the left side of his face.

Mars appeared content in Bully Ton's arms. In fact, he was so out of it that he could barely hold his eyes open. The muscles in his neck employed minimal effort in holding his head up so he could see where he was going.

Vigo and Spiro walked side-by-side in front of him with Presto in the lead. Whacko Ton was moving through the connected stores spying on the cops and reporting back to Vigo. The police had no knowledge of the extent of the Tons' occupation of the Plaza, so he could move from window to window with impunity.

Mars' bouncing view was occasionally and briefly obstructed by Vigo's back and sometimes by Spiro's left arm as theirs and Bully's gates intersected.

Now that he understood Mars' specific usefulness, Spiro agreed on using the battered cop as a distraction, but to a different end than his older brother envisioned.

Spiro wanted to take it right to the humans while Vigo preferred a less impulsive strategy that would, in the long run, produce a greater reward.

"S'like he wants to be King frickin' clown or something," Spiro complained to Bully on the sly.

Bully, who was itching to "Go multiplier on their asses," nodded in agreement. Presto would've agreed, too, had they included him in the discussion. But not Whacko.

Whacko Ton was Vigo's bitch. No one dared even express a negative thought about Vigo in front of Whacko.

187

The lights went out.

"Aweeeee…" Spiro cooed. "They're trying to rattle our cages."

"They obviously don't know who they're fucking with," said Bully.

"You got that right, bro."

The security lights switched on seconds later.

A rather insignificant man was looking over Presto's shoulder. He had one arm around the rotund clown's neck. The other arm had a gun at the end of it, and he was holding it against Presto's temple. His top hat had fallen from his head and rested upside down on the floor.

Presto appeared incredulous and mildly worried, as did his brothers.

"Hooo-leee shit! Is that who I think it is," Spiro said.

"If I remember correctly, it's *US* who should be pissed at *YOU*, Sig," Vigo calmly stated.

"Don't gimme that shit!" Sig hissed. "I know it was you…fucking…*clowns* that took my family away from me!"

In fact it was only Spiro. He had paid a little visit to Sig's home a few months back and scared his poor wife to death. Sig's 14-year-old daughter Priscilla still languished in a coma because of what she had witnessed that night.

Vigo was clueless until he looked over at Spiro.

"You know something about this?" he accused.

Spiro's antsy reluctance answered for him.

"Goddamn it, Spiro!"

"Well, somebody had to pay for Harpo," he whined defensively. Harpo Ton was their baby brother whom Sig had accidentally dispatched back at the Toxic Brothers Traveling Carnival.

Vigo's eyes filled with anger. He motioned aggressively toward Spiro.

"IT DOESN'T MATTER!" Sig yelled. And when he got their attention…"It doesn't fucking matter who did it! I promised them that I would make you all pay. And you can betcher ass I'm gonna do just that."

Sig cricked his neck and settled into an oddly relaxed state.

There was flexion in his jawline from the grinding of teeth. He let his head fall back. Keeping watch through the bottoms of his eyes, he smiled in anticipation of an approaching storm.

"This time…I'm gonna enjoy every last second of it," he said in a much deeper voice than his own.

His disdain for the metamorphosis or "the change," as Sig called it, had been common knowledge among the carnies. It was the big payoff of his act back in the day.

A subcutaneous rumbling commenced in Sig's shoulders and traveled outward in every direction. Random pulsations erupted. A violent noise scored the event as bones shifted and popped from their sockets. Muscle fibers tore from their base and flailed like cephalopod tentacles. His limbs elongated. His torso expanded and stretched. His clothing started to rip.

Sig inhaled deep and then let forth an orgasmic groan. His voice lowered to an inhuman octave. He reached up and tore away the tatters of his shirt revealing a long torso with an inflated chest and a concave abdomen. His skin was an oddly waxen-texture and pock-marked with newly large pores that sprouted coarse strands of reddish-brown fur.

Despite the apparent trauma of the transformation, Sig maintained control as evidenced by the fact that he was still holding the gun to Presto Ton's head.

Presto and his brothers were cognizant of that fact and of the rather significant end result of Sig's metamorphosis.

"This is the last thing we need right now," Spiro whispered to Vigo from the side of his mouth.

"Thanks ta *you*," Vigo whispered back.

Convinced that he was seeing things, Mars Kersey let his head fall back and closed his eyes.

A hulking canine beast that used to be Sig stood a whole foot taller than its human alter-ego and was covered with fur. The cracking, and tearing, and pulsating flesh was localized to his head, his extremities, and a few random spots about his furry body.

His legs, from the knee-down, became long, thin, and strangely jointed, like a dog's hind legs. They held up dense, muscular thighs. His fingers grew long and thin. Fingernails became claws. He was still watching the clowns and still holding the gun to Presto's head.

A few feet behind the hulking, three-quarters-formed beast, Whacko Ton stuck his head out from the edge of a wall and put his finger to his lips, which were parted in a ghastly smile. His brothers looked away and hid their sudden optimism.

Whacko sneaked up behind the beast, tip-toeing like a cartoon and smiling like everything was a joke. He scooped up Presto's top hat from the floor, reached inside, and pulled out a baseball bat. He held the bat up for Vigo to see and made a face that said, "How bout this?"

Reacting on the down-low, Vigo shook his head, "No."

Whacko stuffed the bat back into the top hat and pulled out a golf club.

How bout this?

No.

He stuffed the golf club back inside and pulled out a chainsaw.

How bout this?

Possibly…

But then…

Whacko's eyes grew big at a sudden spark of inspiration. He stuffed the chainsaw back inside the hat and pulled out an even larger one that was made entirely of silver.

Vigo nodded in agreement.

Whacko flipped Presto's top hat onto his head and grabbed the chainsaw in both hands. He took a few, light steps closer to the beast and, in one motion, he snatched the rip cord and lifted the live chainsaw up over his right shoulder.

Sig, the werewolf, whipped around and caught sight of serrated, silver teeth just as they bit into his neck and traveled through to the other side. Whacko didn't expect the cut to be so smooth and he nearly toppled off-balance due to the thrust of his swing.

The werewolf let out a canine yelp before his head fell from his shoulders. The headless beast stumbled aimlessly and then collapsed to the ground and made a big noise.

"All right baby brother!" Spiro cheered.

Whacko stepped over the furry, convulsing husk and returned the top hat to the head of its rightful owner. And then he put his arm around Presto's shoulder and gave a supportive squeeze.

"Coulda done without the shenanigans," griped Vigo.

Whacko shot back a look of utter confusion.

"Sounds like something a human would say," he remarked somewhat sheepishly.

Vigo turned angry and Whacko surrendered his hands. "Sorry. You just kinda threw me with that one."

"He does have a point," Spiro added. "You *have* been kinda...subdued lately."

"What are you tryin' to say?" Vigo challenged.

"No offense, Veeg, but you're the one who's always makin' speeches about sellouts, and embrace your clowness, and all that. But you don't act like a clown at all. Not lately anyway. It's like..."

"Shut up! I don't wanna hear another word!"

Silence.

"Hello in there! Is something wrong!?" came a voice from the megaphone. "We're holding up our end of the agreement. The negotiator is waiting by the doors!"

A tight herd of police cars congregated in the parking lot 100-feet away from the Goldman Theater's shatter-resistant front doors. Police officers crouched behind the cars with their weapons drawn and their faces awash with uncertainty, and reluctance, and nervous excitement.

Captain Malek stood at the front of the herd holding a bullhorn and watching with baited breath as the Police Negotiator walked toward the doors with his hands in the air to show that he was unarmed. An eerie stillness amplified his footsteps.

A team of emergency medical personnel crouched in a real-world "Ready. Set," pose near the Captain, waiting to assist the injured officer that they expected to received as part of the exchange.

A single door cracked open and out stumbled a heap

of a man with a gauze-wrapped head that looked a lot like Detective Mars Kersey. The door closed behind him.

Mars cowered from the daylight like an old Hammer Films Vampire and listed on rubber legs with knees that buckled and then locked several times before he found the strength to maintain tension in his muscles. With his left hand, he applied considerable pressure to his bloodied cheek. A sizable blood-stain darkened the front of his shirt. Based on his appearance and on the amount of blood that colored his shirt, it seemed a wonder that Mars was still alive.

Mars turned and squinted at the gathering of his peers. The flashing lights atop their squad cars hurt his eyes and he performed an encore of his Hammer Vampire pose.

The negotiator scrunched his face at Mars' ugly condition while waving him forward. He was closer to the doors than Mars was to the herd of cops and flashing lights."

"Come on," said the negotiator. "Come toward me."

The emergency medical personnel made a move to assist and were ordered to stop by the Captain.

"Not yet!" he added. "It's too dangerous."

So they watched and waited like everyone else.

"You're gonna be alright, son," the negotiator, an older man whose face bore a similar construct to someone he knew, said to Mars as they passed each other. "Just keep going."

Mars looked up at the man as if the muscles in his face were frozen. The identity of that someone with the similar facial construct was buried under the shambles of Mars' punchy mind, but he knew that he had seen that person recently.

"You...don't know what you're getting yourself into," Mars slurred after a long, drunken pause.

The negotiator leaned toward Mars and said with a quiet voice and a knowing look in his eyes. "Oh...But I do." And then he kept on walking toward the wall of shatter-resistant doors.

Mars stopped to watch the negotiator enter the theater. He half-expected a giant hand or something to reach out and snatch the man inside. But nothing like that happened. Instead, the door simply pushed open one-body-wide and the negotiator walked in.

Five evil clowns boasting smiles that ranged from mischievous to outright sinister greeted the negotiator when he entered the Goldman Theater. They stood in a tight jumble at the mouth of the lobby. A 30-foot walkway separated the negotiator from the clowns.

"I'm unarmed," said the negotiator. He had his hands held high as he walked up the walkway toward them, and stopped a little more than halfway.

"How brave of you," quipped Spiro.

"How stupid is more like it," said Bully.

"Aren't you scared?" Whacko playfully asked in response to the negotiator's calm demeanor.

"My goal here is to resolve this situation in as peaceful a manner as possible, and to ensure the safety of all involved..." said the man. "Even a bunch of naïve, misguided, sorry excuses for clowns like you fellas."

Spiro's eyebrows jumped away from widened eyes. Whacko glanced at Vigo smiling and shaking his head at the negotiator's bravado.

"What did you just say?" asked Bully, who took immediate offense to the remark and was cracking his knuckles as if preparing to throw hands.

"Sounds like we've got ourselves an uninformed human," Presto remarked with naughty written all over his face.

Bully motioned forward, "It'd be my pleasure to... *educate* him," and ran into Vigo's outstretched arm.

"Don't be so hasty," Vigo warned. "Smells to me like he's got something up his sleeve."

Spiro smirked and looked at the floor. "I'm sorry, but you are like the biggest buzzkill lately, bro," he said to Vigo.

Vigo glared at Spiro. Whacko and Presto avoided Vigo's gaze when it came their way. Bully was too busy murdering the negotiator with his eyes.

"There's a reason for that, you know? Why your brother isn't acting like himself," said the negotiator.

"Shut him up!" Vigo nipped at the negotiator's last word, trying to talk over him.

Whacko and Spiro sprung toward the negotiator. Bully wanted to join them, but Vigo instructed him to stay back.

The negotiator moved to evade the charging clowns, but they were all over him in seconds. They grabbed him by the arms and manhandled him a bit. He struggled, and then...

An electric pop came out of nowhere followed instantly by a sustained buzzing/sizzling. The negotiator was crouched aggressively, his arms outstretched and connected to Whacko and Spiro Ton who were being electrocuted by his touch. Their bodies were rigid, yet alive with movement, convulsing and vibrating into and out of pointy starburst-pattern versions of themselves.

The negotiator let go of the two clowns and they went dancing to the rhythm of uncontrolled nerves and temporarily losing their consistency to residual electric tremors. Whacko was laughing the entire time. It was a fearful laugh, though.

Spiro hit the floor and lay there convulsing. Whacko followed soon after. He was still laughing.

The negotiator flung two Podeel Pocket Hand Buzzers to the floor, one from each hand. The objects were small and round and they fit into his palm.

Vigo yelled, "Get him!" with worry in his voice.

Bully lunged into a thundering sprint. Presto followed several steps behind him. He was running slowly, confident that Bully would handle the negotiator before he even reached them. And he was a little scared.

Bully barreled forward like a freight train. He was chuckling with devilish abandon.

The negotiator reached around his back, and pulled out a can of Podeel Pocket Whup-Ass, and sprayed it all over the big, angry clown. And then he sprayed it on Presto. They took a harsh ass-whuppin' and went down seeing stars.

The floor was littered with evil clowns. Vigo stared, in disbelief, at his fallen brothers, and then he took off running in the opposite direction.

The negotiator unwrapped a Podeel Pocket Bolas from around his waist, spun it over his head, and threw it at Vigo's legs. The bolas found purchase around Vigo's ankles, and he went down chest-first and slid a few feet.

"Never send a human to do a clown's job," the negotiator boasted.

"Drago?" Vigo gasped, in shock.

Reeling from electric leftovers and dizzied from aerosol fists, and elbows, and knees, and shins, and stomping feet, the other clowns reacted to the name with confused awe.

The negotiator dug his fingernails into the base of his neck and peeled his skin up and off of his head. There was a clown hiding underneath. His name was Drago Ton.

Drago smiled at the perplexed onlookers. He had black flourishes that pulsated with aggression and confidence around his eyes, a smile as big and creepy as it was wide, and purple hair styled like an average human white male.

"You've led these boys astray, Vigo," Drago said.

"I'm leading them to the truth!"

"Funny thing; the truth. Especially coming from you," Drago said.

"Don't listen to him! He's trying to turn you all against me!"

"All this cynicism and anger. It's not very clown-like. Now is it?"

The facial structure underneath Drago's white, clown base belonged to a familiar, fish-faced, chewed-headed individual, and at that moment, a connection that seemed obvious now was made in Spiro's mind.

"Shit, man. We had Podeel on our list," he thought out loud as he picked himself up off of the floor.

"So you had me figured out, huh?" Drago grinned.

"We knew Podeel was clownin', but we didn't know it was you."

"I knew!" groaned Vigo, seated on the floor with his knees bent and leaning, and his legs tied together.

"Did you, now?" Drago said. "We'll I know something about you, too. So I guess that makes us even."

"You're not one of us anymore," Vigo yelled. "You left. Remember?"

Drago's smile lost some wattage. A glimmer of regret lived in his eyes.

"I admit I could've handled my departure better, but I had to find my own way. Had I known it would lead to this…" As if waking from an unintended micro-nap, Drago jolted and stopped sudden. And then he said to Vigo with a smile reborn. "Why the hell am I explaining myself to you?"

"Lead to what?" Vigo challenged. "We were doin' just fine 'til you showed up."

Drago dismissed Vigo with a lingering, corner-eyed glare. A big, ghastly smile floated underneath it. And then he turned to address his other brothers, who were standing and kneeling, nursing bruises and perplexity.

"The problem is that you boys lack solid leadership. You think small. Picking pockets on the Carny circuit. Robbing customers' homes. Doin' jobs for the radicals."

"At least he didn't run out on his family," Spiro argued.

"So, we should just sell-out like you did?" said Vigo.

Drago had a minor epiphany…He pointed a scolding finger at Vigo.

"Thaaaat's what this is about, isn't it? You did a few jobs for the radicals, made some quick cash, and in the process, got caught up in their stupid, bass-ack-wards politics."

Drago's face took on a patriarchal guise.

"This isn't the way, boys," he said directly to Spiro, Whacko, Presto, and Bully.

"Don't listen to him!" Vigo yelled.

"We clowns…We've got a good thing the way it is," Drago continued. "With the humans we've got the world at our fingertips. And we're not bound by their limitations... Insecurity. Guilt. Shame. Remorse. What the hell is that? Think of all you could accomplish. Look-at-me. I'm makin' out like a fucking king. I got a Podeel Pocket what-cha-ma-fuck for everything you can imagine. I get to clown around all I want on my infomercials. Versus what; moping around like a human, so caught up in some…silly cause that you've forgotten what it is to be a clown?"

As he spoke, Drago Ton walked up to each of his younger brothers—save for Vigo—and looked them over with affection. It had been too long.

"We come out and reveal ourselves and we're gonna have us a biiig problem. One thing I've learned about the humans is that they don't like people who are...*different.*" Drago pointed to his face, and said, "And this is a bit more dramatic than brown skin or almond eyes. Wouldn't you agree?"

"Why should we have to hide who we are?" Vigo yelled.

"You really are delusional, friend," Drago smirked.

Friend?! Spiro frowned, confused.

"You working with the cops?" Whacko had been dying to ask Drago and mulling over whether or not he should.

"Yeah," Drago replied as if 'yeah,' translated to 'of course not, you dipshit.' "They made me Clown Commissioner."

The room erupted in laughter with the exception of Vigo, who used the distraction to try and unravel the bolas from around his ankles. It was going to take a while as the weapon was wrapped extremely tight.

Drago snatched away his laughter and replaced his cackling visage with a face-full of scrutiny, which he aimed squarely at Whacko. The other clowns stopped laughing, too. Whacko, who had suddenly become the center of attention, was smiling like he had missed the joke.

"Are you?" Presto sheepishly asked.

"Don't be stupid!" Spiro scolded Whacko and Presto simultaneously. "He's still a Ton!"

"Why *ARE* you here?" asked Bully.

"To reclaim what's mine. By that I mean, my family. You boys. Your big brother seems to think that you were doing just fine until I came along. To that, I say take a look outside. You're surrounded. Trapped. Sure, a handful of clowns should, in theory, make short work of a few dozen humans. But like I said, you boys lack solid leadership. As a result, you're overconfident. Careless. Sloppy. And to think, I was worried that you might be a threat. That's why I had the human team hit you first."

"You were behind that?"

Drago nodded, "Yes."

"In addition to testing you out, I wanted to prove a hunch that I had."

He looked knowingly at Vigo, and said, "Well, are you gonna tell 'em or should I?"

Vigo leapt to his feet and hurled the unraveled bolas to the floor. "You're a fucking liar!" he growled and charged at Drago.

Bully hurried forward and snatched Vigo up in a bear hug.

"Stop it, Veeg!" he yelled at his older brother, who was growling through clenched teeth and struggling in his embrace.

"Lemme go!"

"Ga head. Let him go," Drago teased. I wanna see how much he's learned about us?"

"I said, LET ME GO!"

Bully refused to oblige. Winded from his struggle, Vigo eventually calmed down and Bully released him from the embrace. Vigo snatched away from Bully and glared at him.

"What's he talking about, Veeg?" Spiro asked.

Based on the looks on their faces, Whacko, Presto and Bully, were wondering the same thing.

"Nothing! He's just trying to fuck with your heads! Don't listen to him!"

Drago shook his head at Vigo's defiance, and said, "You're really going to keep up this charade 'til the end, huh?" And then he turned to the other clowns. "Any-a-you boys remember a two-bit, hack illusionist with a hard on for clowns who called himself Sebastian Storm?"

"Shut up!" Vigo yelled, threatening to lunge at Drago.

Bully grabbed a clutch of his jacket and held him back.

"Yeah. I remember the jag-off," Spiro replied. "Veeg wasted 'em like a year ago."

Drago shook his head "No."

"That's what our brother set out to do, but that hack illusionist somehow managed to turn the tables on Vigo, and killed him."

"He's lying! It's not true!"

"And then he used his bag of tricks to assume Vigo's identity."

"No! I killed Storm! I killed him!"

"That's right," Drago said in response to his brothers' smiling wonderment. "Hoodwinked by a human. Stings a little doesn't it?"

Bully pulled Vigo close and pressed down on him with a frowning smile. He didn't see Vigo slide his hand into his pocket.

A sudden explosion of smoke detonated between Bully and Vigo. Bully turned his head away and shut his eyes. He let go of Vigo, who jumped backward and disappeared in the smoky cloud.

Determined not to let him escape, Bully reached into the cloud, felt around a bit, and then pulled Vigo out by the throat.

"It's not true what he said!" Vigo coughed and choked. He was trying, with both hands, to pry Bully's big mitt from around his throat. "I swear it! I swear!"

Bully wrenched Vigo's arm behind his back and held him still as Drago walked over and peeled off his clown mask under protest. A scared white man with short black hair matted by sweat was hiding underneath. He didn't look much like the cartoonishly arrogant showman smiling down from those old billboard advertisements for Sebastian Storm's 'World of Illusions' show at the Trump Taj Mahal in Atlantic City. But it was clearly him.

"Don't believe him! It's a trick!" yelled Storm.

"You asked why I'm here, Presto," Drago said. "I'm here for payback for my little brother. And I invite you all to join me."

As Sebastian Storm wriggled and thrashed against Bully's grip, four evil clowns closed in on him. They had vengeance in their eyes and smiles as big as they were ghastly.

Outside, Captain Malek had offered his version of an apology as Mars and the team of medics passed him on the way to the back of a waiting ambulance. Detective Shields did everything to avoid making eye contact. She was ashamed that she hadn't believed Mars, who was still too punchy to care about her feelings or the Captain's lame apology.

Twenty minutes passed with no communication from the negotiator, and no indication, good or bad, of what was happening inside the Goldman Theater. The police were getting antsy.

"You're going to have to keep still while I remove the gauze," the annoyed medic warned Mars Kersey a short time later. Mars was more interested in what was going on inside the Goldman Theater than having the gauze removed from his head.

Seated in the back of an ambulance, he peered over the heads of two dozen cops standing behind their squad cars watching the wall of shatter-resistant doors covered with faded posters at the front of the Goldman Theater. He adjusted his view accordingly as the medic snipped a section of the gauze and began to peel it away.

Mars could feel Shieldzie's eyes on him. He tried to let her know that it was okay, that despite her previous disbelief, there were no hard feelings on his part. Hell, he probably wouldn't have believed half of the shit he told her if he were in her shoes. But Shieldzie looked away when their eyes met.

His skin began to sting as the layers of gauze were peeled away. Mars tried to grab the medic's hand, but was stopped.

"Please," the medic said. "I'm almost there."

The second medic moved closer to the first and blocked Mars' view of the theater. He was holding a large swatch of fresh gauze soaked with some kind of antiseptic solution. It smelled like it was going to sting to high heaven when the man placed against the wound.

"Is it bad?" Mars asked.

"Nah," replied the first medic, but his eyes deceived him.

The second medic tightened his hang-jawed disgust when Mars glanced at him.

The first medic took extra caution as he removed the last layer. Mars hissed at the pain in his face and ground his teeth as the second medic came at him with the gauze. He groaned as the antiseptic solution soaked into the exposed subdermal tissue. He grimaced and leaned away from the second medic's hand as the man applied pressure to keep the flap of skin from falling open as the first medic tugged at the end of the gauze.

Static emenated from a radio inside one of the squad cars.

Mars craned his head to see over the medics' shoulders.

"Please hold still," the medic scolded.

Mars saw Captain Malek lean into his car and retrieve the hand-held transmitter from his dashboard radio. A spiraling cord connected the hand-held device to its base on the dash. "Hello!" said the Captain. "Come in! Is everything alright in there?"

"I'm okay." The negotiator responded after a long, suspenseful pause. "Sorry for the delay. I'm having problems with my radio."

"What's the situation in there? Are you hurt?"

"I'm fine. There's nobody here. I checked the whole place. They musta gotten away somehow."

Mars became animated. His sudden excitement dulled the pain. He shook his head, "No." The medics reacted so as not to let go of his face. And then they shared their annoyance with Mars, who didn't even notice.

"That's impossible. We've got the place surrounded."

"Hey. Beats the hell outta me how they did it. Come see for yourself."

Captain Malek ordered a team of six to enter the building.

Mars' gut told him that it was a trap and he tried to get up to warn them, but the medics held him still.

"Officer. Please!"

Mars feigned submission and then, when they relaxed their hold on him, exploded to his feet and ran. The flap of skin fell away from his cheek and bounced to a dangle. "No! Wait!" he cried. "It's a trap!"

The medics, who were running after Mars, were the first to react.

Mars spun in a circle thinking that someone was behind him, but there were only cops, and they were all looking at him like he was on fire or something.

Mars continued to whip his head in search of whatever it was that had everyone so spooked.

Then he heard Shieldzie cry out, "Oh my God, Mars!" He looked and saw her standing there, horrified, with her hand cupped over her mouth.

It finally occurred to Mars that half his face was hanging off. The pain came back and made him grimace. He attempted to lift the dangling flap of skin, but it hurt too much to even touch.

"He's…one-a-*THEM*!" yelled some random officer.

It took a moment for the statement to process. Mars froze with eyes full of fear. He was standing next to a squad car. Out of the corner of his eye he could see his reflection cast in the driver-side window of the vehicle.

Mars inched his eyes over and down and saw a man with two faces looking back at him. The right side was that of a battered and bruised Mars Kersey. The ugly, disfigured left side was hiding a clown face underneath his skin.

INDO AND THE KILLER ROCKSTAR

CLUB VENUS (Eye-in-the-sky surveillance footage)
August 23, 10:32pm

A creeping stratosphere of nicotine residue blankets the entire barroom. Club Venus consists of a large main room (bar, dancefloor, small stage up front, raised DJ booth) and a second floor loft that wraps around and looks down on the floor below. The mood on each floor is vastly different from the other, yet both contribute to the painfully typical nightclub ambiance.

In the main room, young and young-minded people press chest to back from the rear of the place to the foot of the stage up front, squeezed shoulder to shoulder from the wall beneath the DJ booth to the bar. They are waiting for something or someone. A banner hangs over the stage partially obstructing the view of the large video screen built into the rear wall. The banner reads,

WFBB Presents:
Jason Sydes – *Lovin' em to Pieces* Listening Party.

On the screen, a music video accompanies the passive-listening melody laid over a pulsating beat that sifts from speakers placed strategically throughout the building. It sates the crowd until the main event. Some of those gathered sway gently to the banal music while others simply stand facing the stage, their faces gleaming with anticipation.

The mood on the second floor is much more casual. There are people lounging on obnoxiously trendy furniture, leaning drunkenly against faux pillars, and mingling with sculptures welded and manipulated into pretentious designs. Their conversations are spiked with innuendo—quiet as they can manage without being drowned out by the noise downstairs.

A rainbow coalition of stage-lights peer down into the crowd and up at the ceiling, cutting through the residue blanket of smoke.

The crowd reacts to the portly, middle-aged man in a WFBB T-shirt who is working his way through to the stage.

His appearance (receding hairline, flashy tattoos, ponytail, circular shades) gives off the impression that he is trying hard to come off as younger than his years. They reach out and shout to him as if they know him.

He jogs up the three steps onto the stage and walks out to the center where a lone microphone stand awaits him, standing erect, its phallic head slanted downward. He wraps his hand around the microphone and jostles it out of the U-shaped bracket. He looks at his watch, then over at the DJ. Sliding his hand across his neck like a dull blade, he signifies silence.

The music is the first to go, then the moving images on the screen, and finally the voices.

"Any of you kids come to hear some Rock and Roll?!" he says.

The crowd roars with excitement. The portly middle-aged man looks momentarily annoyed at how long they take to settle down. He tries to talk over them. Fails. Tries again.

A chant creeps to the forefront of the noise. "We want Jason Sydes! We want Jason Sydes! We want Jason Sydes! We want Jason Sydes!"

The portly, middle-aged man rolls his eyes and signals to the DJ to start the record.

Silence…

The music starts. The portly middle-aged man walks off stage as the moving images resurrect themselves on the screen. Footage of Jason Sydes (aka The Insect), rocking out shirtless and sweaty.

Gentle finger-flicks tickle guitar strings. The gloomy wail sounds distant, echoed. A slow thump, like a muddled heartbeat, creeps forward. The guitar chords sink. A low organ bellow gives the melody some meat.

Jason begins the song in a whispering voice. His words are garbled by voices in the crowd (some of whom are singing along) and by the eye in the sky's poor sound quality.

The crowd is quickly entranced. They sway to the cadence of Jason's voice, especially the ladies.

The music snowballs to an angry peak, Jason's tone goes primal. The way he growls out the chorus sounds as if he's baring his teeth and gums.

I don't care what the *fucking police* says!
Instead of fighting -gonna love em' to pieces!
I don't care what the *Federal beast* says!
Instead of fighting – gonna love em' to pieces!
I don't care what that *hypocrite Priest* says!
Instead of fighting -gonna love em' to pieces!
I don't care what your *corporate release* says!
Instead of fighting – gonna love em' to pieces!

The chorus skips, and repeats. The DJ fumbles with his console to no avail.

Something comes over the crowd. It happens suddenly. It's the looks on their faces—the ones we can see—and the deep swell in their chests as they began to breathe heavily. They turn to each other, fake joy illuminating their faces and pouring from their strained eyes. It affects everyone within earshot.

"I love you," People chant to those standing closest to them before exchanging deep, open-mouth kisses, teeth gnashing and lacerating gums, lips slipping and sliding on saliva and blood as heads dance with violent passion. They wriggle and writhe, arms snaking human contours, constantly reestablishing their aggressive embraces.

"I love you, too," others reply.

Reacting with childlike glee to the feeling that has overcome them, they giggle, and laugh, and moan in euphoric delight. Speaking through emotional upheaval, they continue to turn to each other and chant. In a few of them we can see terror hiding beneath the happy masks.

"I love you."

"I love you, too."

The crowd begins to strip naked, bare flesh shining through the dim atmosphere, the storm of sex-vibes, and the nicotine residue. Standing upright, they continue to embrace, limbs twisting around limbs, blind digits probing the warm spots.

Instead of fighting – gonna love em' to piec-sez!
Instead of fighting – gonna love em' to piec-sez!

The crowd's actions are becoming more and more aggressive, bordering on savage. Joyous sighs and orgasmic moaning turns to screams laced with uncontrollable laughter.

Suddenly it is everywhere. Blood.

"I love you," they say as they lunge and bite down on their partner's nearest appendages. Lips and tongues, fingers and breasts and erect penises are thrashed away with passionate savagery. Flesh and muscle rubber-snaps back to newly opened wounds that cough and spit blood, and bile, and strangely colored fluids.

"I love you, too," others respond through bloody backwash and in-between dumbed-down cries of agony.

Bodies topple end over end from the second floor. Some are pushed or thrown. Some jump on their own, using their bodies as weapons. They rain down through the smoke and rainbow of the stage lights.

Bodies litter the floor. Some lie completely still. Some twitch, and scream, and laugh, all at the same time.

Bottles and chairs and uprooted fixtures are slung with brute strength. They crash down on unsuspecting skulls and shatter limbs. Knives and broken glass pierce flesh and cut through to the soul. Each and every one of them goes out with a smile, laughing through the pain, crying "I love you."

Instead of fighting – gonna love em' to piec-sez!
Instead of fighting – gonna love em' to piec-sez!

Those still standing kick and stomp on the fallen. A bloody sheen covers the floor and causes many to slip and slide, yet they persevere. When there is no more laughter, no more bodies twitching and writhing, they turn on each other.

"I love you!"

"I love you, too!"

***

One minute Jason Sydes, aka, The Insect, the former frontman of Insectisyde was in the middle of the best blowjob he'd had in years from some melancholy blond he met at Starbucks down the street, and the next he was being escorted, at gunpoint, to a back office at Club Venus by the Professor's personal bodyguard.

You've heard of the Professor. He's the manager, record producer, impresario of rock bands like Powerhaus, Sonic Tonic, and Insectisyde, and he was Jason's Svengali.

"You wanted to be more than 'famous?' Well, son, I'm gonna make you infamous," said the Professor, and then he forced Jason to watch via a bank of monitors as the crowd ripped each other to shreds to the first single from Jason's brand new solo album.

The critics were calling it a rebirth, a welcome maturation of his musical talents. An honest representation of Jason Sydes, the musician with a lot on his mind. It was all a sham, but it was of his making and not the Professor's.

Jason woke up sometime later in a storage room, coughing and barely able to breathe. Smoke. So much smoke. A door that led deeper into the place flexed and withdrew as if it was made of rubber. A draft of intense heat pushed through the space beneath the door and burned Jason's face and stung his eyes.

Something taped to his hand; a plastic gas canister, nearly empty.

Across the room, an "Exit" sign, floating on high, sliced through the rising wall of dense smoke.

Once outside Jason worked the tape from around his hand and tossed the gas canister to the ground. Then he ran away.

He prowled the backstreets and alleyways of Manhattan for hours, searching for an ally among his network of famous friends. Rain punched down like fists launched in anger. His shoulder-length, blond hair was tucked underneath a NYC baseball cap made for gullible tourists pulled down to his eyebrows, and a JC Penny's leather jacket made for men who'd given their balls away in marriage.

209

Disguises were nothing new to a celebrity of Jason's caliber. They were often necessary to mask his identity when he wanted to attend a sporting event (he was a die-hard football fan) or while he tried to enjoy a meal at some trendy restaurant.

The streets were nearly barren. When there were people, they hurried by shielding their heads as if from acid. No time for passing glances.

Jason had burned so many bridges over the years that none of his friends would take his calls. Not even his bodyguard Big Sumo.

When he showed up at his friends' residences they acted like no one was home. So he kept on moving.

Jason was walking down West 33rd when he heard a female voice sharing details about her sex-life without shame. He looked up, following some lizard-brain impulse, and accidentally locked eyes with a pretty-faced chubby girl with a cell phone pressed to her ear. She was sitting in the passenger seat of a late model Hyundai parked at the curb outside Cinnabon.

There was a spark of recognition and then the girl's eyes grew big. She stopped talking.

Jason looked away. It had been only seconds.

"It's him!" the chubby girl screamed. "It's Jason Sydes!"

Being a fucking rock God, Jason was well-educated regarding intense female vocalizations. This girl sounded like he had shoved his dick in her ass without warning. So Jason became like a ghost.

With his face pointed down, he ducked into Penn Station and tried to disappear into the crowd of busy-minded travelers.

He heard his name cut through the ugly collage of conversations, and hard-soled footfalls, and intercom gibberish.

"Is that…Jason Sydes?"

"Where?"

"Over there!"

Other people had heard it, too. Heads turned. Necks craned and elongated.

210

Jason made himself small so that his head was on the same plane as the shorter majority that surrounded him, and then, walking in a partial squat, he slipped down an intersecting hallway, sprung to his full height, and hurried down a flight of steps and onto a train platform. There was a train sitting idle. Destination: Philadelphia. Jason had an actor-friend who lived in Philly. Word around town was that this actor-friend was currently in Buenos Aires filming a Rom Com with some actress Jason had banged a few times. That meant the actor-friend's house would be empty.

Perfect.

***

Jason's actor-friend from Philly was actually more of an acquaintance with whom he had hit it off on a movie set a few years back. They had made plans to stay in touch, but as was often the case with onset relationships, things fizzled out once the cameras stopped rolling.

In the years since they had spoken, the actor-friend had gotten married, had two kids, and gone all Jesus freak. No way that kind of guy would be cool with a free-loading rock God with a history of drug abuse and sexual depravity. Jason's mind had conveniently omitted that part when he was standing on the platform in Penn Station desperate for somewhere to hide.

That was two days ago.

Now, Jason was standing half-naked in the master bedroom. He heard someone walk in the front door of the actor-friend's Society Hill Condo. The television was tuned to the News. His was the top story, followed by a recent wave of murders that had befallen the city's numerous gangs.

Jason had been meaning to alter his appearance by cutting his hair and shaving off his trademark goatee, but he just couldn't bring himself to do it. Even more than his talent, his "look" was the foremost component of Jason's damaged self-esteem.

As he had been living exclusively in the moment, Jason hadn't bothered to clean up the mess he made so there was no hiding the fact that someone was staying here.

Downstairs he heard a gasp and then an effeminate male voice.

"This bitch AGAIN?!" the effeminate man said to himself before calling out, "He ain't here, honey, and he won't be back for another month, so you might as well just bring your stalkin' ass down here before I call the cops!"

It didn't sound like the actor-friend's voice. A relative maybe? A friend? A gay lover? Jason didn't plan on sticking around long enough to find out.

He ran for the window, scooping up his new outfit along the way— baggy cargo pants, a T-shirt, a tracksuit top, and an Eagle's baseball cap fished from the actor-friend's wardrobe—and climbed out. Jason hated the Eagles. He was a Cowboys fan.

***

Jason was a shadow skulking along the murky urban corridors that most people avoided, drifting with the wind, which was slight and infrequent. The architecture was older in Philly and the blocks were shorter, but otherwise the backstreets and alleyways were strikingly similar to Manhattan's. Maybe they were similar everywhere.

He was constantly faced with banners for an African Art Exhibit currently showing at the Philadelphia Museum of Art. Dangling from lampposts, they flapped in the slight, infrequent breeze. Green text against a black and red background spelled out the particulars.

**REINHART GALLERY PRESENTS
THE ART AND MYSTERY OF AFRICA:
JULY 20TH – SEPTEMBER 3RD**

Strategically set in the forefront of a cluster of images from the exhibit, a wooden statue of a woman partially formed from the torso up and boasting a life-like expression, cast sad eyes down at Jason from every banner he passed under. Something about her eyes, and the distinctly African bone structure of her face kept calling to him to look up and appreciate her majestic beauty.

As he soldiered on, destinationless, Jason was haunted by ethereal News-Anchor busts communicating a mish-mash of inaccuracies about the events of two nights ago and about Jason in general.

Police are confirming today that the fire that burned Club Venus to the ground on August 23rd, was the work of an arsonist. The exterior doors had been locked from the outside trapping all 200 patrons inside. Bodies burned beyond recognition. Traces of an accelerant were found.

A security camera mounted above the back door of the club caught footage of the suspected arsonist, Jason Sydes, troubled former frontman of the hit rock group Insectisyde, as he fled the club in a disheveled state, discarding a canister that, according to authorities, contained the accelerant used to start the fire.

An All Points Bulletin has been issued for Sydes' arrest. Sydes' manager and mentor, record producer, Alton "The Professor" Raineagle is offering a reward of 1 million dollars for information leading to Sydes' capture. At a press conference earlier today, Raineagle, welling with emotion, offered his condolences to the families and friends of the victims, and went on to say of Sydes, "The drugs, they really changed him. They made him paranoid, unpredictable, to the point where he was almost like a different person. It became evident to those of us closest to him that he was using again. It's my opinion that the drugs played a large part in his falling out with me and the rest of the band. Had I known that he was capable of something so...so...awful...I would've taken steps to deal with it."

Later, Jason heard one of his songs coming from inside an Irish Pub as he walked past it. "Passion lick," was a raucous, kinetic tune, written during Jason's second stint in rehab back in 2003. One reviewer called the song "A nitric-kick of adrenaline," in that it inspired movement in everyone who heard it. The crowd inside the Irish Pub was strangely docile.

On closer inspection, Jason saw a roomful of people transfixed, heads tilted up, eyes scanning five flatscreens tuned to the same channel up on the wall. Jason squinted to read the text at the bottom of the screens.

BREAKING NEWS: JASON SYDES SPOTTED OUTSIDE 30TH STREET STATION.

The text was superimposed over a grainy, black and white photo of Jason exiting the northeast exit of the train station two days ago.

The screen cut to a street interview. The microphone floated at mouth level in front of a slightly built man with a pencil-thin beard and hair arranged in a faux-hawk. His mannerisms were big and unapologetically feminine. He was standing in front of a house that Jason instantly recognized as belonging to his actor-friend. At some point, the slightly built man held up a wallet that looked a lot like Jason's.

Jason gasped reaching for his back pocket. He felt around. No wallet. He looked up and thrust himself away from five smiling doppelgangers splashed across five wide, flat screens. It was his driver's license photo.

***

Jason wasn't sure how much time had passed. Maybe an hour. Maybe two or three. The neighborhoods had become more residential. They were smaller, darker. The alleys were barely wide enough to move through, clogged with weeds and refuse, and guarded by angry 'hood dogs who barked at anything that moved. So he stuck to the small streets. There was little human traffic save for the suspicious characters who congregated on corner stoops and wandered the dark spaces. Jason was one of them.

214

Feeling eyes on him, Jason assured himself that he was being careful and that it was all in his head, even as the hint of movement occasionally materialized in his peripheral vision. After a while, Jason looked for the glow of a television and tip-toed up to the window of a townhouse where the iridescent beam cut through the darkness. He peeked inside and spied a hairy, potbellied man masturbating to a Yoga Booty Ballet Infomercial.

A series of commercials played out on the next television he came to; this one in a neighborhood dive bar populated by old-timers. The front door was propped open. The smallish television set was mounted above the bar. Jason had a clear view of it from where he stood behind a parked van peeking through the passenger-side window.

The commercials ended and a solemn-faced anchorman appeared on the screen. Bold letters scrolled in from the left and out the right side of the frame just below the anchor's desk.

BREAKING NEWS: JASON SYDES SPOTTED IN UNIVERSITY CITY.

University City?! That's where he was right now.

The anchorman's voice was buried beneath the sounds of drunken merriment and 80s Dance, and R & B music that filtered out of the bar, so Jason couldn't hear what the man was saying. But he didn't need to.

Apparently people had snapped pictures of Jason with their cell phones as he skulked through University City. He wouldn't have believed it if he didn't see the photos right there on the screen.

***

Jason could hear people looking for him as he hid behind a corner store dumpster.

First it was the police, their cars crawling from block-to-block on silent lightstorm. At some point, wailing voices leapt out of the ether to accompany the flashing lights. Engines revved as squad cars accelerated and sprinted away

215

from where Jason hid, listening to their shrill voices fade into the night.

Next came random groups of males, on foot, looking for a big payday in the Professor's reward. They were talking shit about Jason's music and sharing fantasies about spending the reward money.

Somewhere in the background, deep-throated automobiles oozed down small streets, on creep, and trembling from heartbeats of slow bass-thumps pounding over grim melodies.

Jason waited behind the dumpster until he was convinced that the search parties had moved on to other locations. He got up and patted away the icky film that had settled on his clothing as he crouched there.

Someone standing behind him…Jason spun around.

"That's right, mothafucka!" said the gun pointed at Jason's head. A young man, not even 20-years-old, stood behind the gun, dressed like a thug. He had a horrible overbite and a gap between his front teeth that affected his speech. "Don't even think about running!"

"Please. I don't want any trouble," Jason threw his hands up.

"Coming from the nigga who burned down a whole club full-a-mothafuckas…"

"You don't understand. It didn't happen like they're saying," Jason said, attempting to back away.

"I know one thing. Yo crazy-ass better not take one more step or I swear-ta-mothafucking-God, I will—"

A car pulled up to the curb. Jason felt a momentary swell of relief. But then the gap-toothed thug waved the car down.

The Dirt Dawgs

Jason Sydes was squeezed between two thick, meaty brothas in the back seat of an 05' Lexus ES330. They were members of the Dirt Dawgs, a gang from the west side of town with a reputation for capping motherfuckahs at the drop of a hat. The gap-toothed thug was a member, too. There were five members present, but the Dawgs were 30-niggas deep according to the driver, a medium-skinned thug named T-Rah.

Gap tooth, who they called Smooth (pronounced Smoove) sat in the front, passenger seat spewing braggadocio about how he hunted Jason down, much to T-Rah's annoyance.

"So what-chu want, a muthafucking cookie, nigga?!" griped T-Rah, who had a scowl that could scare off the Devil. In this case, that scowl was aimed at Smooth, who took the hint and shut his mouth.

In addition to the meaty brothas who book-ended Jason, another thug called Trig was pushed up against the backdoor on the far left. Trig just happened to be a fan of Insectisyde. His favorite was "Hyperbadass Bitch Repellent," a song that Jason had written after his rather public breakup with that actress with the big ass. That one resulted in a trespassing charge and three days in the county lookup.

"That shit spoke to my ass, man," Trig said. "I was goin' through it with this half-Rican jawn at the time and—"

"Yo, man! Shut the fuck up!" T-Rah scolded as he turned that intimidating scowl of his on Trig via the rear view. And then he proceeded to chastise the guy for liking "all that corny-ass, headbangin' white music."

The meaty bookends sniggered despite their feelings of awe for being in such close proximity to a fucking rock God. Like the fact that their bodies touched made them somehow closer to all the A-List Pussy that Jason Sydes had pulled during his legendary career.

The bookend to Jason's immediate right wanted so badly to probe for details that he felt like he was going to explode. However his wanting paled in comparison to the reprimand that he would surely receive from T-Rah, who was secretly curious as well.

Jason tried appealing to Trig.

"What's this about?" he whispered, playing dumb.

Trig hesitated, and then, facing forward, he nervously parted his lips on the side to offer a response. His eyes darted and caught glimpse of T-Rah's scowl in the rearview, and that was the end of it.

Jason argued his case. He told them that he was innocent, that the Professor had set the fire to hide his little experiment.

They laughed at him and offered up their own humorous interpretations of "his little experiment."

Though reluctant to continue, Jason had nothing to lose, so he laid it all out hoping to appeal to the inner conspiracy theorist that kept angry, underprivileged black guys like these blaming the white man for all of their problems. He wondered if that made him racist. But only for a second. Hell, he had fucked his share of black chicks.

Jason told them about the Sklar Device and of its Nazi origins. But history was a foreign concept to these brutes. As such they reacted to his story with a moment of silence, followed by raucous laughter meant to demean. Only T-Rah remained straight-faced.

Feeling deflated and helpless, Jason escaped within himself as the conversation inside the car turned to someone or something that the Dirt Dawgs referred to as Indo. Jason was aware that Indo was sometimes used as street slang for marijuana, however they spoke of Indo as if it was a thinking, feeling entity to be feared; a ghost who had been haunting West Philly in recent weeks, and murdering gang members. He had worked his way through all the major gangs in the area. The Dirt Dawgs, The Westside Kingpins, and The Shadows were the only gangs left.

"Niggiz is droppin' like flies out here and you muthafuckahs is all slurpin' on this corny-ass nigga's dick like a bunch-a-lil' bitchiz," T-Rah scolded pointing a thumb at Jason. "What ch'all *NEED* to be worried about is collecting this reward. If there's a way to stop that spooky mothafuckah, I'm willin' to bet it's gonna cost money."

"Then his ass is ours," Smooth added.

"We gon be living laaaaaaarge!" sang one of the meaty bookends.

"No doubt," T-Rah replied quite emphatically. "But not if you niggaz don't get your headz together. Fuck this fake-ass rebel mothafucka *AND* his corny fuckin' music! He ain't no better than us. He ain't nothing but cash money. Y'nah mean?"

The Dirt Dawgs hummed and grunted in agreement and

then became all quiet and meditative.

Jason waited a few minutes and then leaned closer to Trig and whispered, "Who, the hell, is Indo?"

Trig scowled in the rearview, mouthed, "I ain't say nothing."

The scowl lingered and then went away.

To dissuade any further discussion, T-Rah turned up the volume on the radio. Some lyrically challenged, Autotune-enhanced rapper screamed at them for a while.

Jason looked down so as not to chance another meeting of his eyes with T-Rah's scowl, which occasionally floated into, and out of, the rearview and intimidated him. His head bobbled and bounced to an endless succession of potholes. Some were so deep that his ass left the seat. Everything about the song on the stereo insulted Jason so much that he felt the need to express his disgust on one of those "behind the artist" documentaries.

But that would have to wait.

"Whatever he's paying you, I'll double it!" Jason said out of the blue.

T-Rah drove on pretending not to hear him, but as the offer replayed in his underdeveloped, emotionally challenged mind, greed took hold. At the next red light, T-Rah placed the car in park, turned down the stereo, and turned around in his seat.

"So, how much we talkin'?" he asked Jason.

"Five million."

"Five million dollars?!"

"That's right."

The light turned green as T-Rah pondered all that he could do with that kind of money.

A Chevy Pickup rolled up behind them and honked its horn.

T-Rah turned his scowl on the Pickup's grill smiling at him through the rear window. For a moment it seemed like he was going to get out of the car and do something extreme to the impatient driver, but then after about 30 seconds, he just turned around in his seat, put the car in drive, and...

The car jerked forward and stopped. T-Rah had stomped the break to avoid mowing down a loose cluster of impatient pedestrians who had capitalized on his delayed response to the green light.

T-Rah thrust his palm at the horn and held his hand down.

"Get the fuck outta the way!" he yelled at the crowd and got back attitude in the form of frowns, and hand gestures, and mouthed expletives.

The Chevy Pickup honked again.

T-Rah squeezed the steering wheel in both hands. With his lips balled, he shook his head and muttered under his breath. He turned around to address the pickup when Smooth yelled, "Oh Shit," and shook the car with an explosion of movement.

T-Rah whipped around and locked eyes with a Lon Chaney Wolf Man mask. The mask wearer was a chubby, but solid man dressed in baggy pants and a thermal shirt. He was immersed in the glow of the headlights, standing dead center about a foot from the Lexus' front fender with a shotgun pointed at T-Rah's head. A similarly dressed man in a Karloff Mummy mask stood beside the Wolf Man flashing a gang-sign with his fingers. It was the letter "K."

"Kingpins!" T-Rah yelled and simultaneously turned his head away from a blinding flash that leapt out of the mouth of the shotgun.

There was a deafening boom. Glass shattered. Crystalline shards kissed T-Rah's cheek before his head was opened like a watermelon hurled against concrete.

As he scrambled over the seatback, Smooth yelped at the sound of the shotgun blast and shrunk away from the sticky, wet spray of viscera chunks from T-Rah's head.

"Go! Go! Go!" Trig yelled as he, Jason, and the meaty bookends wrestled and shoved for hiding space on the floor between the front and rear seats.

On his way down Trig glimpsed a tall, thin figure in a Bela Lugosi Dracula mask run up from behind the car and sink into a shooting pose outside the back door. Dracula was packing something that could spit serious rounds, too—an AR-15 or an AK. Trig couldn't tell which.

"They got T-Rah!" Smooth yelled to Trig as he landed on top of the pile of frantic limbs and torsos attempting to flatten. "We're fucke—"

A second blast snatched Smooth's voice away.

The remaining Dirt Dawgs were packed between the seats like wriggling sardines with red sauce from Smooth's lifeless body oozing downward. Jason was on the bottom of the shifting pile, facing up. Struggling to breathe, he feared he might suffocate from the weight pressing down on him.

He could hear people screaming outside the car. Hurried feet scuffed asphalt. Tires screeched. Engines revved as passing motorists stomped gas pedals to put some distance between themselves and the gunplay.

The rapid pop, pop, pop of automatic gunfire surrounded the car and the pitter-pat of bullets punching through the vehicle's outer shell made the remaining Dirt Dawgs groan and shout expletives in anticipation of bad things. Their fear amplified Jason's.

The unrelenting salvo of bullets roused a drastic swell in their voices. They flinched, and writhed, and made every attempt to escape the concussive punches and the terrible, terrible, stinging throb that followed each one. But there was no escaping.

Jason lost consciousness.

The Westside Kingpins

Jason's next memory was of a euphoric numbness. He was still inside the car, facing up. There was no sound. His eyes told him that he was moving backward or maybe upward in short, violent thrusts.

The air hit Jason and woke him up. Sound returned with a vengeance. Terrified eyes affixed, Jason moved his head quickly to take in all angles.

He was being dragged from the backseat of the Lexus by a man in a Karloff Frankenstein mask. A clog of traffic reached back from the Lexus. People had left their cars with the engines running and sought shelter in or behind the nearest structure. People were crouching behind cars and

221

hunkered down on the floor inside locked vehicles. Women were screaming. Police sirens wailed from a distance.

The Kingpins' masks were actually updated interpretations of the original movie monsters. Frankenstein was sans the flat top and with a face made of stitched together skins of slightly different shades. Dracula was more effeminate. The Wolf Man was sleeker and predominantly canine. The Mummy looked like a modern movie zombie peeking out through tattered bandages. Its mouth was full of long teeth and fixed in a snarl.

"Stay the fuck down!" Dracula yelled at the people hiding and fired his gun into the air to buy time while Frankenstein dragged Jason Sydes up to him. His and the other Kingpins' voices were muffled by their masks. "C'mon! Hurry up!" he instructed Frankenstein.

"He fucking heavy, man!" Frankenstein replied in a whiney tone that sounded like it belonged to a 14-year-old kid.

The Wolf Man fired more shots into the air and yelled. "He said *STAY*, the *FUCK*, *DOWN*! You wanna end up like them muthafuckahs?!"

He was referring to the Dirt Dawgs, who lay bloodied and in a heap of tangled and sprawled limbs. T-Rah was still sitting in the driver's seat. His lower jaw was all that remained of his head.

Jason made the mistake of looking and now his eyes were stuck on the bloody sight. Not more than five minutes ago they were alive. And now they looked so utterly lifeless. And there was so much blood.

"You can stand?" someone asked him.

A hand slapped Jason across the face when he didn't respond.

"I said, can you stand?!"

Jason looked up and saw Dracula staring down at him. He nodded, and said, "I think so."

Frankenstein helped Jason stand up.

No sooner did he get his balance than he was being pulled by the arm toward an alley where the Mummy and the Wolf

Man waited for them. Dracula was hot on their tail.

Dracula ordered the group back to the van. The Wolf Man had ants in his pants. He was bouncing like he had to pee and occasionally giggling at the rush of adrenaline. Rather than run toward the van like the others had started to do, the Wolf Man leapt out of the alley and into a wide-legged stance with the butt of his gun held against his groin.

"Tha fuck is you doin', man!" Dracula yelled, but his voice was drowned out by the Wolf Man's AR-15.

"Yeah muthafuckahs! You ain't seen nothing yet! The Kingpins rule this city now!" the Wolf Man bragged as he sprayed the air with bullets.

He back-stepped toward the alley shooting his gun and talking shit. Dracula nagged at him from the mouth of the alley.

"Are you fucking crazy?! I'm gonna beat your fucking ass if you don't get back here! We ain't got time for this shit!"

The Wolf Man was suddenly overcome with the need to cough. A series of dry heaves quickly graduated to a hacking fit. He stopped, and hunched, and gasped for air between violent, heaving outbursts. The coughing rattled his head and he began to stagger dizzily.

He threw down his gun and snatched off his mask. The man underneath was surprisingly normal looking. The expression on his face was that of someone who couldn't breathe and was fully aware of what that meant.

Dracula's threats trailed off into awed silence.

"What's the matter with him?" Frankenstein asked.

The Wolf Man was lurching violently. His face was red and swollen. His eyes were bulging and crackling with lightening veins. Spittle laced with vomit was propelled from his throat as he coughed, and hacked, and gagged.

And then…a puff of smoke. Wispy tendrils wafted upward from the corners of his mouth and from his nose and his ears.

"Indo," Dracula knowingly muttered.

Jason found himself suddenly unrestrained.

The Wolf Man's normal-looking alter ego stood up,

turned his AR-15 on the other Westside Kingpins and mowed them down.

Jason had just enough time to dive out of the way. Dracula fell on top of him. The dead weight was hard on Jason's lungs, but not nearly as hard as when he was on the bottom of the pile of Dirt Dawgs, so he managed.

The police opened fire when the Wolf Man whipped around to face the terrified spectators. Jason covered his ears to block out the horrible sound of bullets punching through flesh.

The Wolf Man's chest and abdomen were dotted with bullet holes. His back was a landscape of mangled exit cavities that exhaled puffs of smoke. The Wolf Man's arms dropped to his sides, his head slumped. He tipped on his heels and fell backward.

Smoke trailed from his mangled torso and settled into a living cloud aglow with aural light that hovered over the Wolf Man's expired corpse. Snaking tendrils swirled and twisted in and out of a pulsating center.

Jason stared in wonderment as the aural cloud worked itself into the suggestion of a man's head and left shoulder. The man was transparent, hovering wraith-like atop of a cloud of smoke. He turned a hollow-eyed stare on Jason, put a finger to hinted-at lips, and said, "Shhhhhhhhh."

Seconds later a breeze came along and reshaped the cloud-bust into a cluster of wisp strands and carried them away.

Jason made a strange sound that instantly reminded him of those old Casper Cartoons when people would realize that the little white boy with the big bulbous head was really a ghost. He was on his feet and moving quickly toward the other end of the alley. More than the figure in the smoke, Jason was running from the sound of hard-soled shoes approaching the alley. He speculated that the police hadn't seen him, and that, unless someone at the scene told them, they had no reason to think that Jason Sydes, the killer rockstar was running with a gang from West Philly.

The alley spit Jason out onto a nearly empty parking lot. He ran right past a blue van sitting idle. A neo-retro "Creature

From the Black Lagoon" sat behind the wheel with his head sticking out the driver-side window.

"Hey!" he yelled at Jason, who heard the voice and knew that it was directed at him, however he assumed that it was a cop, so he kept on running.

The van reversed and then rocketed forward. Traveling at a wide arc, it blew past Jason, spun around up ahead, and came barreling at him. He was stunned, having looked right into the headlights before turning away. As he stumbled, momentarily blinded, Jason expected to feel the van's grill punch him in the side and shatter his weary body. But that didn't happen.

The van skidded to within inches of Jason. The creature behind the wheel leaned out of the half-opened door and pointed a gun at him.

"Tha fuck you think you're goin'?! Where the fuck is everybody?! I heard gunshots!"

Jason was afraid that the truth would anger the creature, so he just stood there avoiding the creature's fixed glower and shaking his head.

"Hey! I'm talkin' to you, Muthafucka! Did something hap—"

"Freeze!" came a voice from the mouth of the alley.

The creature stepped on the gas and Jason found himself diving out of the way, once again. Within seconds he was back on his feet and running.

The police let loose on the van and its masked driver. The van accelerated and swerved out of control. The tires stuck and the van rolled over several times and then slid on its roof and into another parked car.

The cops swarmed the van when it came to rest, upside down. Jason heard them yelling at the driver.

***

Jason was in no way built for running. That was for sure. His legs were made of stone. A cramp stabbed him in the side and his lungs were about to burst from his chest. The last time he had run as much was when he was trying to impress an actress he was dating.

Jason wanted to stop running a long time ago, but the ever-present echo of sirens kept him on the move. Block after block of old architecture gone 'hood-neglect. Cozy little pockets that shined through the urban grit were bullied by an overwhelming sense of disparity.

The banners for THE ART AND MYSTERY OF AFRICA Exhibit were heavy in this area, at least two-per-block, flapping in the breeze from lampposts and telephone poles. The partially-formed majestic beauty on the banner cast judging eyes down on him, or so it seemed.

At one point, Jason was spotted by a carload of drunk girls on their way home from a Nicki Minaj Concert. They chased him for a few blocks, leaning out the windows and screaming, "I love you! Come party with us!"

They might have caught him, too, if it weren't for the sleeping homeless man lying outstretched across the pavement. Jason was so intent on getting away that he didn't see the man until he had already tripped over him and fell behind a row of parked cars. It happened so fast that the drunk girls didn't see where he went. Jason remained as still as possible until the girls gave up looking and drove away in a huff.

The homeless man hadn't as much as flinched. Jason worried that he might have injured him…or worse.

"Hey. You alright?" he whispered to the homeless man.

Then he reached out to the man when he didn't respond.

"Take off yer damn shoes in my house," the homeless man said in a drunken, half-awake voice.

Jason kept moving. He eventually came to a trash-strewn city park with more homeless folks asleep on benches under blankets made of newspaper. Fatigue began to trump the need to get away, and the idea of a rest stop seemed quite appealing.

Jason found an unoccupied bench in the back. He fished yesterday's newspaper from one of the trash receptacles, sat down, and peeled it open. The plan was to rest long enough to catch his breath, and then continue moving. Where he would go was as good a guess as any.

He began reading from the first section his heavy eyes landed on—Sports. He didn't see his picture plastered across the front page beneath a headline that read, THE HUNT FOR THE KILLER ROCKSTAR. Consciousness escaped Jason without his knowledge. He felt his head bounce, his eyes flutter. He blinked and there was someone sitting on the bench across from him, a girl, who looked too healthy to be homeless. He must have dozed off because he didn't remember her walking up and sitting down.

The girl was looking at him as if trying to place a familiar face. The paper had fallen from his face leaving it exposed. He didn't realize this right away.

"You're Jason Sydes, aren't you?" she asked.

A million things ran through Jason's mind. None of them were a response to the girl's question.

"It *is* you! I know it is!"

Jason panicked.

"I didn't do what they're saying! It was my manager! He's trying to set me up! I swear!"

"I knew it," the girl said as if she had been arguing that very point just moments ago. "I knew you could never do something like that."

The girl looked all of 16-years-old. After the accident in Tulsa, Jason was careful to avoid being seen in the presence of under-aged girls.

And then, out of the blue, the girl asked, "You need a place to stay?"

Jason stared at the girl and she stared at him. He was trying to decipher her motives.

"What about your parents?"

"I live with my mom. She never comes out of her room. She kinda big."

The girl had a somber maturity that played out sad and a little creepy. Her eyes bore the weight of responsibilities beyond her years. Jason envisioned the mother as some morbidly obese shut-in who depended on her daughter for every little thing.

But what if it's a trick? What if she's just trying to lure you to her house so she can call the cops on you and collect the reward?

"I don't get out the house much, so I don't have any friends...In case you're worried that I'm gonna tell somebody..."

"Why are you helping me?"

"Sometimes...I just wish she was like a normal mother," the girl said as if she was ashamed.

In a way Jason could relate. Even with all the money, and the fame, and the pussy in the world, he often wished for a normal life filled with normal people with everyday problems.

"Sometimes I stand in the window watching the days go by. It's like that line from 'Sister Charlotte; the one where you talk about being a ghost among the living."

"Sister Charlotte" was the first single from Insectisyde's second album, "DDT." It spent 10 weeks at number one on the Billboard Charts back in '08.

"Nobody who writes lyrics like that could do what they're saying."

In fact Jason didn't write that one.

"Be nice if everybody felt that way."

"They will."

The girl's confidence was inspiring. Jason dared hope. And then he heard in the distance, sirens.

"What's your name?"

"Shauna."

Shauna told Jason that her house was only two and a half blocks from here and that she liked to sneak out to the park to "smoke weed and escape," after her mother fell asleep.

"How old are you?"

"Old enough."

It was a common answer and one that Jason's inner cynic translated to mean exactly the opposite. But what choice did he have?

***

This would be the part where God laughed, if Jason believed in God. He was sitting on a king-sized bed with a creaky wooden frame in the basement of a most-likely underaged girl's house in the 'hood. He couldn't have dreamt up a more unlikely scenario.

A gaudy-chic, Formica endtable clashed with the old-school wood of the bedframe. On top, a dollar-store clock radio facing away. Flashing red digits giving him the side-eye. In the drawer he found baby-wipes and a 24-pack of LifeStyles Extra Strength Condoms.

Strange. The girl he had just met didn't strike him as the sexually active type. Certainly not to the extent that she would need a 24-pack of condoms. Jason catalogued it as "to be reviewed," and filed it away in the back of his mind.

The dank, gloomy basement was longer than it was wide. Giant craters in the walls bled concrete dust. The old stone floor was cracked and soiled by dirty soles. The ceiling was a patchwork of exposed pipes criss-crossing each other. A single light bulb dangled from a broken fixture in the middle of the room providing the only lightsource. Directly underneath it, a rickety card table held up empty beer bottles and an ashtray full of cigarette butts and cigar entrails. More cigarette butts on the floor. Folding chairs pushed away from the table suggested that the last occupants had left in a hurry. A narrow, wooden staircase just beyond the table. And another bed/endtable set-up way on the other side of the basement, where the light barely reached.

Shauna had told Jason that she slept down here and that her mom hadn't left her room in months.

Then who sleeps in the other bed?

Shauna came downstairs with a cup of water, a sleeve of Pringles chips, and a glass votive candle with a modest flame dancing on its wick. She placed them on the endtable, pulled a folding chair up to the foot of the bed, and then said, "Gotta go check on momma. Be back shortly."

As he watched Shauna's feet disappear up the staircase,

Jason remembered to ask about the other bed, but it was too late.

He drank the cup of water in one gulp, grabbed a handful of chips and ate them as he lay back on the bed. The pipes vibrated to Shauna's footsteps on the floor above. Jason followed the muted thump and the squealing of floorboards until they stopped.

As he lay there snacking on Pringles, Jason came to accept his monumental naïveté in thinking it would be so easy to walk away. Fame had given him a false sense of security. He saw himself as untouchable. Invincible.

Even now there was a part of him that figured he would land on his feet in the end. A very small part. On the surface, he hadn't even figured out his next move. He was too tired to think strategically. He dozed off a few times.

"It's just me," Shauna said when she came back downstairs a while later eating a bowl of instant noodles. She sat down in the folding chair and glanced over at the cup and the sleeve of Pringles. Both were empty. "Can I get you something else?"

"I'm good," Jason groggily smiled and then lay back down.

Sleep was all he wanted. But Shauna was ready to talk. He could feel her eyes on him, probing as if to validate that a Rock God was really lying there in her bed. She had a look that was common among fans, running thoughts in search of the best question to ask. It was usually something stupid.

"Is it true that you communicated with Jimmy Hendrix during a séance?" Shauna asked.

The Professor had started that rumor to help market the single, "Realeyes." It was one of several songs that the Professor had written for the band.

"Don't believe any of that shit you read in the magazines."

"I heard it on Entertainment Tonight."

"Even worse. It's all a big scam, Shauna. The whole fucking thing! They brainwash you into believing that these people are larger than life until you crave them like a drug. People like me! They make up lies to mold us into a character and then they force-feed us to the public. I wouldn't go along with their *game-plan*, so they turned on me."

Jason was mindful of Shauna's expression as he feared that he might lose her support at any moment. Currently she was wondering who "They" were, so Jason told her.

"The Professor...He said that he was washing his hands of me because of my constant lack of gratitude. That he was gonna make an example of me because of my arrogance and disrespect. He said it like it was nothing. Like I was just some asshole off the street."

"The Professor always seems kinda sneaky when I see him on TV or in magazines'n stuff," said Shauna. "The way he be smilin' and everything. Kinda like a white Don King."

Jason nodded marinating on Shauna's comparison. He had never heard a more appropriate one of his manager/mentor.

"It wasn't the fire that killed all those people," Jason said. "It wasn't?"

Jason shook his head "No," while mustering the courage to review the image and the fortitude to withstand its impact, and then he said rather sheepishly, "I watched them tear each other apart."

And then he glanced over at Shauna, curious as to how she would react to the morbid revelation. She was nursing a quizzical expression.

"Was there a fight or something?"

"Something like that," Jason replied wanting to say more.

Considering the scope of the conspiracy that he was about to drop on this poor girl, Jason felt it necessary to compile the awful memories in the most plausible manner before presenting them.

Jason was about a year into his run as an A-List Celebrity when he started to hear about Sklar.

"Have you seen the light?" or "You down with Sklar?" People would whisper in his ear at random A-List events.

The Sklar Wave Manipulator was used by all levels of the entertainment industry—music, television, film, theatre. Knowledge of the technology was a privilege of Hollywood's A-list.

Jason told Shauna as much as he knew about the technology. It was as much as anyone knew. Discarded mind control technology invented in 1959 by Dr. Richard Sklar. A relic of Cold War Clandestine Research. Uses wavelengths to create a physiological dependence via images and sound.

Fame had come with blinders that allowed Jason to ignore the obvious warning signs of a downside, and drugs did their part to further sedate that function. He managed to avoid aligning himself with the Sklar Machine or with its devotees and their weird, plastic enthusiasm until his first solo album went gold in two days of its release, and suddenly Jason Sydes, the former frontman of Insectisyde, gone solo, was a bonifide Rock God.

He came home one night to a trio of studio executives waiting for him in his living room. The Professor was with them.

"We're troubled by your resistance, young man," said one executive. "Whether you know it or not, you owe a great deal of your success to the Sklar Technology."

"Nobody gets to where you are without a little…push," said another. "Or did you really believe you were that talented?"

Jason glanced at the Professor, looking for an ally, and found him standing with his arms crossed, communicating "I told you so," with his body.

"We're happy for your success, Jason. But as a show of gratitude, we urge you to reconsider your decision not to rejoin the band," said the third executive.

Jason had quit the group citing the Professor's controlling nature as the reason, and vowed never to return. He viewed the success of his solo album as the final nail in the coffin that was Insectisyde.

"At least one more album," said the Professor. "Then we handle your departure the right way. No hard feelings."

"You mean the Sklar way, right?" Jason replied.

"You're part of an exclusive club now, Jason," said the first executive. "One that requires the utmost loyalty from its members."

They presented a contract for Jason to sign.

"Did you sign it?" Shauna asked.

"No way, man! They gave me a day to think it over. I called my agent. I called my old bandmates. Nobody wanted to help. I didn't know that the Professor had my phone bugged the whole time. He heard me running my mouth about how I would never go back to the band, how I don't do cults...I was all, 'How dare you question my talent. Don't you know that I'm a fucking Rock God? Rolling Stone Magazine even said so.' I didn't say all that, but that's the vibe I was on. I told him I was gonna to go to the press, the police even, to get the execs off my back, if I had to. And I meant it, too. So stupid. So fucking stupid."

"So what are you gonna do?"

"That's a good question," Jason replied, staring up at the ceiling as if the answer was written on it. "That's a good fucking question."

A few silent moments passed and then Shauna said, "I'm gonna go check on momma."

"Okay," Jason replied. It was a delayed response as he was lost in thought.

The next time Jason opened his eyes the room was much darker. With the intensified darkness came another level of quiet. Shauna had come and gone as evidenced by the wool blanket that she had draped over him as he slept. *How nice of her.*

Muffled noise from upstairs as if from a television...

Jason's mind had put him through the ringer while he slept. His heart-rate was elevated and his clothing was sweat-soaked. Thankfully, he didn't remember much of the dream. His mouth was dry, his head cloudy, and his body felt weighted down. His mind and body begged for more sleep. But he had been up long enough for his waking thoughts to reset and reacquaint him with all the drama in his life. Sleep seemed less likely and Jason became strangely afraid of that fact.

At some point he tried to move and was caught by surprise. Someone had tied his wrists and ankles to the bedpost with nylon rope. Jason loitered in disbelief and then burst into a fierce struggle. The bedframe lifted and dropped and scraped the cement floor, but the restraints held fast.

Jason let out a desperate call.

"Shauna?! What did you do?! Shauna!"

He waited for a response, and then called out again when none was given.

"Shauna?! Please?! You can't do this?! Shauna?!"

Out of the moments echo came a wincing of old floorboards from above. Footsteps grew out of the creaking chatter and approached the basement door.

A rectangle of light cut into the darkness. It was slanted in Jason's view due to his limited range of motion.

A shadow darkened the doorway and cast a shapely silhouette on the wall next to the basement steps.

"Shauna?! What the FUCK?!" Jason yelled at the shadow. "I thought we were friends!"

The shadow descended the stairs morphing along the way into a girl that Jason didn't recognize.

"Shauna?"

This was the girl that Shauna became in her dreams. As such, the idea that he might still be dreaming crossed Jason's mind. A quick tug at his restraints belayed that thought.

The new, improved Shauna walked up and stood at the foot of the bed. She looked older—maybe 18 or 19. She wore just enough make-up to feminize the masculine way in which she held her face and clothing that accentuated her curvaceous figure. Her skin possessed a confident sheen that hadn't been there before.

"Please don't be mad at me, Jason. I really am a fan."

Shauna's voice was different, too, sans the pitiful tempo from earlier and imbued with self-assuredness. Her apology sounded sincere, which only served to amplify Jason's confusion.

"What the fuck is going on?! Why'd you tie me up?!"

"I was just doing my job. It was nothing personal. I want you to know that."

"Your job?! What the fuck are you talking about?! You

nuts or something? Just tell me you didn't call the cops?!"

"I didn't call the cops."

"Then what THE FUCK is going on here?! Zis some kinda fantasy fulfillment thing?! Huh?! Is that what this is?! Cause you coulda just asked!"

Shauna side-eyed the surrounding darkness and said as if speaking directly to it, "Guys?"

The Shadows

The darkness came alive with the shapes of four men with nightmarish, bugged-out faces. They oozed into the light, heavily armed and wearing black, their faces hidden behind gas masks.

"You're property of the Shadows now, homie," said the one in front, his voice muffled by the mask.

"Another gang?" Jason cried out in complete bewilderment.

"*THEE* gang, son!" said another one whose voice was similarly affected.

"What the fuck, man?! Did I do something to piss you people off?"

Jason winced realizing his poor choice of words.

"You people?" one of the shadows accused.

"I didn't mean it like that. I was talking about gangsters er...bangers er... gangbangers! Whatever I did or said, I swear I didn't mean any harm!"

"It's nothing like that," said Shauna.

"Then somebody please tell me what I did?!"

"You just wiped out a whole night club and you got the nerve to ask that?" said another shadow.

"But I didn't. It wasn't me. I swear."

"It was the Professor and his mind control device, right?" quipped the lead shadow.

"That's right," Jason said nodding enthusiastically, and then it dawned on him that he was being mocked.

That fact was made evidently clear when the lead shadow replied with a chuckle in his voice, "I'll make sure to ask him about that when he gets here."

Jason's chest tightened and his heart stuttered into high gear. He felt a sharp pain from the sudden acceleration. His skin became so sensitive that the surrounding air, still as it was, gave him a tickle, and then a chill.

Jason addressed Shauna in desperation. "The Professor?! He's coming here?! OhmyGod! You HAVE to untie me! PLEASE?! You don't understand! HE'S GONNA KILL ME!"

"That ain't her problem, homie," the lead shadow said quite coldly.

"Whatever he's paying you—"

"You'll double it, right?"

"That's right! I will! Triple it! You just name the price! Anything!"

"He said that your bank accounts have been frozen; in case you tried that one."

"He's lying! He's a liar! Whatever he told you! You don't know him like—"

"I don't trust any-a-y'all mothafuckahs," the lead shadow cut in. "But, for the record, his story was *waaay* more believable than yours."

Jason was, for the moment, without options and feeling thoroughly defeated. His eyes darted. They grazed Shauna who immediately looked away.

The nylon restraints became impossible to ignore. A claustrophobic swell provided his mind with a rough chronological breakdown of the time he was likely to spend stuck in this position before the Professor arrived and ended him in some horrific fashion.

There was no way that the Professor would risk Jason revealing Hollywood's dirty little secret. Jason was, for all intents and purposes, a dead man.

Anxiety whittled down Jason's nerves and chased every last bit of patience from his rigid body. He squeezed his eyes shut and held his breath in one final attempt to thwart the flood of intense emotions. In that moment there was no time. He was numb, both mentally and physically, so there was no physical pain. But his respite was short-lived.

Jason's eyes shot open. He screamed and thrashed until his body could no longer sustain his mind's demands and then he lay there in tears, spent, and reeling from dizziness. His wrists and ankles were rubbed raw. His view of the dark room was slightly altered due to the bed's new position five feet to the left.

And he was alone...again.

Jason took deep breaths to settle his churning stomach. Voices speaking through gas mask filters trickled down from upstairs. Shauna was up there with them, laughing and having a good old time. Why wasn't she wearing a mask?

Jason drifted in and out of panic over the next few hours. A speculative period followed each tantrum.

Shauna occasionally came down with a glass of water and five-minute blocks of concern for his well-being.

"How old are you anyway?" he asked her on one occasion.

"Twenty-three."

On another, Jason appealed to Shauna to let him go and she gave him some bullshit about loyalty to the gang—"But I meant what I said about your music. If I could, I would let you go in a heartbeat."

Jason wanted to strangle her ass.

"Did you feel that way when you lured me here with that lonely girl act?! And don't give me that shit about you would if you could! 'Would if you could' doesn't do dick to get me outta here! 'Would if you could' ain't gonna stop the Professor from offing my ass the first chance he gets! If you really thought I was cool then you'd cut these ropes. You can make it look like I got away. They'll never know."

Shauna was tentative in her response, which gave Jason hope that she was considering his plan or at the very least that her decision against it caused her great pain. In a very small way that, in itself, was a hopeful sign.

"I'm sorry, Jason. I can't," she said with troubled eyes.

Lingering in a weird calm, Jason began to tremble, erupting from the inside out. His skin became flushed. His eyes bugged out and, baring teeth, he yelled, "Fuck you! Fuck you all! Go back to your FUCKING gang so they can pass your dumb ass around like the FUCKING WHORE that you are!"

Shauna reacted as if from a slap to the face. She cast a hang-jawed frown down at Jason. When he showed no sign of remorse, she put on an unaffected expression, walked over to the stairs, and climbed them while Jason yelled at her back, then her legs, then her feet. When she was gone he yelled at her footsteps on the ceiling.

"And if you think the Professor's really gonna pay your friends, then you're as stupid as they are! He'll just as soon kill them all! He'll kill you, too!"

***

The Professor's voice was like a stimulant in that it had a way of inspiring heightened anxiety from dead calm in Jason. When he heard that voice coming from upstairs, Jason began to sweat profusely. By his best estimate he had been tied to the bed for two days, anticipating this very moment.

The pipes shook from the footsteps of several men. They spoke in muted voices to an older man whose voice was colorful and unrestricted. The basement door opened and cast an oblong rectangle of light clogged with a jumble of shadows.

The Professor was doing his usual passive-aggressive jabbing as they descended the staircase and walked up to Jason's bed.

"Love the costumes," he commented.

"It's not a costume," replied one of the shadows.

"If you say so. You boys do business outta this place, huh? More power to you."

"Sorry it ain't the Four-fucking-Seasons, old man," replied another shadow.

"The girls bring their tricks here," said the leader.

Jason thought of the condoms and the baby wipes in the drawer, and of the bedding he was lying on, and began to itch all over. But he could have been on fire and it wouldn't have fazed him anymore. He was physically spent from multiple freak-outs. His wrists and ankles were chaffed, and raw, and stinging. His brain was jelly from too much time left alone to face his imminent death.

"You can't do this to me, Rain," Jason pleaded. "I know I've said and done some fucked up things, but I don't deserve this."

"I'm afraid you've done this to yourself, son," replied the Professor. "I'm just sorry I didn't see the warning signs sooner."

"I'll sign the contract. I'll do whatever you want."

"Contract? Do you even realize what you've done? Two hundred people, Jason. All dead because of your drug habit."

"No! You're lying. He's lying. I've been clean for over a year and you know it!"

"You need help, Jason. I prayed that I find you before the police did."

"You never prayed a day in your life..."

"Sorry to interrupt your little family moment here," the lead shadow interrupted, "but we need to discuss our payment."

"Ah yes. The reward," said the Professor and then he turned to another man standing behind him and said, "Mr. Jacklyn..."

Mr. Jacklyn was a tall, thin man dressed like a Fed on casual Friday. He had a briefcase in his hand.

"Jacklyn's here?" Jason said in a worried voice, straining to lift his head and see.

Jacklyn stepped forward and offered the briefcase to the lead shadow, who stepped forward to grab it.

Three bursts of light came in the blink of an eye. Violent noise followed.

Jason squeezed his eyes shut, turned away, and grunted in anticipation of being shot.

The room became silent. Footsteps on the ceiling rapidly approached the basement door.

Jason stopped grunting and opened his eyes.

Two of the shadows were dead. The lead shadow was just standing there with his arms by his sides, breathing heavily

239

through the gas mask.

Jacklyn held the briefcase by his side. A handgun had jumped out of his sleeve and right into his other hand. He was still holding the gun on his last target, the lead shadow. "I pegged him," said a confused Jacklyn. "I know I did!" "Well shoot him again, Goddammit!" yelled the Professor, ducking behind his tall, thin protector.

"Awe Shit! Y'all ain't have to shoot him," Shauna cried, thinking that Jason had been shot.

She came running down the steps, her eyes adjusting along the way. She stopped halfway and screamed when she saw the bodies.

"Run Shauna! Run!" Jason yelled.

Shauna turned and took two steps in retreat before Jacklyn shot her in the legs and she went down screaming.

"No! Don't hurt her!" Jason yelled.

In that same motion Jacklyn turned the gun on the lead shadow, and fired several times. The bug-eyed shadow stumbled backward and then stood there motionless, breathing heavily.

"What the fuck?!" said Jacklyn.

"Shoot 'em in the head!" yelled the Professor.

"I did! Twice!"

Jacklyn squeezed the trigger again, but the gun was empty.

The lead shadow exploded forward without warning, aural mist trailing from his wounds.

Moving quickly, but not hurriedly so, Jacklyn tossed the gun away, snatched another, larger handgun from inside his blazer, and swung his arm into a point.

The lead shadow grabbed Jacklyn's arm before his aim was set. Jacklyn resisted. The lead shadow pushed forward and they stumbled, intertwined into the wall. The Professor was knocked sideways. He ran over to the stairs hiding behind his arms, and looked back fearful that Jacklyn had finally, after 22 years of dedicated service, met his match.

He glanced movement and looked up the stairs. Shauna had managed to crawl to the top of the staircase and was halfway through the door. A bloody trail marked her path.

Jacklyn squeezed the trigger by accident and the bullets followed the trajectory of his and the lead shadow's violent dance. They danced into walls and through cheap furniture, toppling beer bottles that bounced and shattered against the cement floor. They fell onto the bed with Jason, who turned his head away from them, closed his eyes, and groaned from deep within as they rolled on top of him, punching, clawing and grabbing, and off the other side of the bed.

The next time Jason looked, the lead shadow was slamming Jacklyn into the wall. Jacklyn became dizzy from the concussive blows. His shoulders slumped and much of the fight had left him.

The lead shadow held Jacklyn against the wall and snatched off his gas mask. The young man underneath was light-skinned with dead eyes and a head chewed by bullets. Blood drained from the large wound in his head and down the left side of his face.

With his mouth held open, the light-skinned man lurched, and then vomited an aural mist all over Jacklyn's face. A second later his lifeless body crumbled to the floor as if he had no bones.

Jacklyn came alive, coughing and whipping his head away from the finger-wisps of aural smoke that probed his orifices and forced their way inside him. He wheezed, lemon-faced, and stumbled forward, choking and shaking his head as if from a constipated sneeze.

Jacklyn wrapped his hands around his throat and let out a terrified wail. There was a deafening pop, like a water balloon bursting, and in an instant Jacklyn was gone.

Jason was smacked about the body and face by a warm, salty fluid that was dark in color. A few feet from his bed, the left and right walls were painted with a litmus configuration of the same dark liquid, tiny flecks reaching out beyond the main body. It was blood. Jacklyn's blood.

Floating in Jacklyn's place was the aural suggestion of a man with a bald head, hollow eyes, and an Africanized facial structure. Hovering on a tail of kinetic mist, the aural man aimed his hollow-eyes at the bound, blood-soaked Rock God.

Blue eyes trembling in shock stared out from a bloody mask as Jason lay there, a hostage to the moment, unable to run, or even turn away. The aural man looked on Jason as a curious human would an ant struggling to carry something much larger than itself.

An anguished whimper cut through the silence. It had come from upstairs.

Shauna! Jason thought.

The aural man looked up.

A thump on the ceiling. A dragging sound. A feminine whimper.

Wafting upward, the aural man dissipated into a shapeless mass of kinetic mist and disappeared into the busy cross-section of pipes.

A minute later Shauna let out a horrible scream. There was a loud crash and then it became very quiet.

Jason burst into another escape attempt, pulling, and twisting, and yanking at the ropes. Jacklyn's blood was like a lubricant that enabled Jason to squeeze his hands through the knotted loop around his wrists.

He sat up, exuberant, and untied his feet. His wrists and ankles burned. His fingers were numb and sore.

His eyes grazing the darkness, caught view of a body slumped at the foot of the stairs. It was the Professor. The light from the basement doorway shined down on him and exposed a peculiar expression frozen on his face. A stray bullet from Jacklyn's gun had found purchase in his forehead. A steady stream leaked from the tiny hole.

Jason derived no joy from the sight. With the Professor dead, who would believe his story? They'll spin it to look like *HE* did it.

What am I going to do? WHAT, THE FUCK, AM I GOING TO DO?!

There were other bodies, dressed in black and wearing gas masks. There was blood everywhere. Pieces of Jacklyn scattered about. The smell was horrible. If he'd had more time, Jason might have considered vomiting.

Jason's clumsy, half-dead fingers fumbled with the rope around his ankles. It took some time, but he was eventually able to loosen the knots and pull his feet through the loops.

He rolled sloppily from the bed and, after a number of slippery, noodle-legged false starts, Jason ran over to the Professor's body, took him by the lapels of his Wool-blend Bomber Jacket and violently shook him.

"Wake up, you bastard! You have to tell them the truth! You have to tell them what you did!"

Sirens in the distance. Jason stopped shaking and listened. The sirens were getting louder. It became clear to him that the Professor wasn't going to wake up, so Jason let go of his lapels and ran up the basement stairs.

On his way out the back door, he glimpsed Shauna's body lying in a broken heap in the dining room. Her head, which he could not see from where he stood, was painfully tucked underneath her body, blood had pooled around her shoulders.

Jason mourned a little bit for Shauna, who was probably as smart, and as thoughtful as she portrayed herself in the park, but stuck in an environment that had no use for those traits.

He wasn't even sure what day it was, just that it was late, about the same time of night as when he met Shauna, so to some degree, it seemed like the past few days could have all been a waking dream. If that were true then he wouldn't be covered in blood and his wrists, and ankles wouldn't burn like they did.

Some time passed.

Jason sat, thinking, at the top of a short staircase recessed into a side entrance of an abandoned warehouse. It smelled like five years worth of funk marinated in piss, but it offered temporary shelter from prying eyes.

A sleek, Azurite Blue car pulled up to the curb 15-feet away. Jason didn't lift his head to see who it was because he didn't think the driver could see him.

He heard a window roll down.

"You there," a man with a familiar voice called out. "Are you in need of medical attention?"

243

Jason looked up and saw the Professor sitting behind the wheel of a Jaguar XJ. The bullet that should have killed him was clearly marked by the hole in his forehead that leaked blood...and finger wisps of smoke.

"I am not the man you know as the Professor," Indo said in the Professor's voice.

"Whatever beef you've got with these guys...I swear. I've got nothing to do with them! They kidnapped me! I wasn't even—"

"I have no quarrel with you."

"Oh," Jason said pleasantly surprised, but not yet relieved. "I didn't do it. What they're saying on the news. It's not true."

"I know."

***

"Your Professor had not yet expired when I entered his body," Indo/Professor said.

The Azurite Blue Jaguar with tinted windows was parked in a well-lit area with ample pedestrian traffic. The Philly after-hours scene was in full swing. Jason was slouched way down in the back seat of the Jag stressing over that fact and wearing another man's blood like a soggy blanket slowly hardening as it air-dries. Luxury cars weren't uncommon around here, but you didn't usually see them parked on the street.

Jason's eyes were tuned to all the potential threats that passed by his window. His ears were tuned to Indo/Professor's voice.

"But he was dead when I left him" Jason said, lingering long enough on Indo to express his wonderment before returning to his fixation with the people on the other side of the tinted window.

City folks typically wore blinders with only their destinations in sight, but Jason was waiting for that one errant glance to wander his way. That's all it would take.

Indo/Professor, in the driver-seat, faced forward as he spoke. He didn't seem at all concerned that they were too visible.

"He appeared dead. But there was life left in him," Indo/ Professor said.

"Did he say anything to you?! Did he tell you that I'm innocent?!"

"Indirectly. Yes."

"So you know that he set me up?!"

"Yes."

"You have to help me, then!"

"We can help each other."

"Dude! You just wiped out three badass street-gangs with no problem and you're asking for *MY* help?"

"I am."

"Look, man...I'm not a fighter. I've never fired a gun. I might act all big-n-bad, but I'm just a pampered fucking celebrity." Jason gave Indo/Professor a moment to ponder his admission and then he said, "Still want my help?"

"Yes."

Jason nodded and then he quietly pondered.

"So, ah...what are you, anyway? A ghost?" he said to Indo/Professor a minute later.

"I am one who is summoned to right wrongs. I have spent lifetimes bound by doctrine that I can no longer serve. Because of this doctrine I have committed despicable acts in the name of my summoners. I have been complicit in the murder of entire families. Entire villages. Men. Women. Children. I have turned a blind eye to their dying pleas for mercy, to their cries for help. But for the love of a woman I would still be a slave to this destiny that was thrust upon me."

Jason nodded his head, trying not to look completely thunderstruck.

"The woman that I speak of...She is there," Indo said looking up, through the windshield, at a banner for THE ART AND MYSTERY OF AFRICA Exhibit hanging from a lamppost that stood over the Jag. "We were together before I was summoned. With her is where I long to be."

"No offense, but what's stopping you?"

"The benefactor of the exhibit is an art collector named Miles Davenport. During one of his expeditions to Mali, where my people are from, he acquired L'amulette de Ciel et de Terre. He used this amulet to summon me and to imprison my Atieno in that statue when I refused to do his bidding."

"What did he want you to do?"

"Kill his ex-wife, and her new family."

Indo/Professor's compassion rang peculiar to Jason given the brutal manner in which he had dispatched of the Dirt Dawg's, the Westside Kingpins, and the Shadows just hours ago…or was it days…

"He meant to use the amulet on me as well, but I escaped. The exhibition is an attempt to lure me out of hiding. He knows that I'm out there, following them from city-to-city, watching from afar. As long as he posses L'amulette de Ciel et de Terre, I can do nothing to help Atieno."

"The gangs…How do they play into all this?"

"Until I am reunited with my love, I must atone for the sins of my past."

"So you're kinda like a vigilante?"

"Call it what you will."

"What do you want *me* to do?"

Indo/Professor turned and looked at Jason.

"There is another way to reach Atieno."

***

Two days later, Indo/Professor walked into the Beverly Hills Police Department and asked the desk Sergeant, "Do you know who I am?"

The sergeant looked up and was underwhelmed by the man with the bloated, ill-fitting face, whom he instantly recognized.

"Yeah. So?"

"I'd like to turn myself in."

"For what?"

"I didn't realize makin' bad music was a crime," an officer eavesdropping in the background joked.

The desk Sergeant turned a glare on his colleague.

"Murder," said Indo/Professor.

Two detectives escorted Indo/Professor to an interrogation room, where he spent the next few hours educating them about the Sklar Device. His presentation included, black and white, archival footage of Dr. Sklar working with the Nazis, and later with the United States Government. There was a lavishly produced tutorial video meant for new initiates, footage from the Club Venus incident, and a list of famous names and their donations to a "charity" called, The Film Preservationists' League (FPL). The FPL was a front for Sklar Industries.

"You're saying Sydes was set-up?" asked one of the detectives.

"But what about the surveillance footage from the back door of the club?"

"We...that is myself, and Mr. Jacklyn...rendered him unconscious and placed him in the back room before the fire was set. The gas canister was taped to his wrist."

The detectives looked at each other.

"That explains the duct tape," one said.

It was as if the air had been sucked out of the room. The officers stood, speechless, exchanging thoughts via facial expressions and looking all kinds of baffled.

"We're gonna have to bring the Feds in on this," one leaned over and whispered.

"I'll make the call," the other detective replied and then he left the room.

"There's something else," Indo/Professor said to the detective who remained.

The man gave the Indo/Professor a funny look and replied quite sardonically, "What's that?"

"I sent an identical package to all the local News outlets."

***

As they were complicit in the scandal, the News Media attempted to cover up the Professor's story, but the Internet bloggers had already caught wind.

The Feds came down hard on the alleged perpetrators in

response to the public outcry for justice. They rounded up two dozen A-list actors on live TV. Escorted them down the red carpet in hand-cuffs as they left some gala event, and into waiting police vans while "Thanks for the Memories," poured from overhead speakers. By shaming them like that, the Feds meant to send a message.

"...and that message is that no one is above the law," barked the Deputy Director of the FBI. "Not even Holly*weird* Royalty."

The indictments kept coming. Studio heads. Record company executives. Respected journalists. Politicians. All your favorite singers and actors.

Town hall meetings were held. Medical experts addressed the publics' concerns regarding prolonged exposure to the Sklar Device.

"Based on what we know so far...Migraines. Memory loss. Blindness. Seizures. Dementia," said a prominent neurologist. "We suspect that it may play a role in the rise in obesity as well, but that's yet to be verified. There's also been some evidence to support cancer as a side effect. But again... that has yet to be verified. There's just so much to learn. You have to understand that from a strictly science perspective, the possibilities for advancement that this technology represents are—"

"—Maybe you people should spend more time looking at it from the *victims'* perspective," came a voice from the peanut gallery.

The crowd cheered.

"There isn't one of us on this panel who doesn't own a TV, a radio, or a computer," the neurologist spoke over the raucous.

Entire industries struggled to survive and regain the public's trust. No one went to the movies or watched TV anymore. Computers became glorified word processors as Internet usage saw a massive decline.

Celebrity became a poisonous word. Several celebrities were attacked in the streets for their affiliation with the guilty parties. Angry crowds pelted their vehicles and homes with eggs and rocks, and whatever else they could throw.

Sometime during all that...

"Knock it off!" Big Sumo complained under his breath as he walked around the Philadelphia Museum of Art trying not to look out of place.

He wore a pair of clunky spyglasses and an earpiece microphone through which he communicated with Jason Sydes.

"My bad," Jason replied.

"I'm shittin' bricks over here, man. The last thing I need is you whistling in my ear."

"Alright! Relax. Just try to act normal."

It was easy for Jason to say from the comfort of his new Condo in downtown Philly, whistling the melody from the new song he had been working on while he watched through Sumo's eyes via a laptop on the coffee table.

With Indo's undying love for Atieno as inspiration, the structure and lyrics of the new song flowed with impunity from his brain. Jason couldn't remember the last time they came so easily.

"I stick out like a sore thumb in this place."

"What? Big, beefy, powerlifter-looking dudes can't admire art?"

As his story was prominent in the Sklar scandal, the public viewed Jason as a victim. When a prison guard found the Professor's lifeless body hanging in his cell, everyone assumed that Jason had something to do with it. The autopsy turned up the bullet lodged in the Professor's forehead. Someone had attempted to conceal it with make-up.

It looked like a hired hit. The theory was that the Professor was murdered by another inmate, and then hung up in his cell to look like a suicide. And Jason had motive coming out the ass. But the police couldn't prove anything.

To the public Jason was the guy who stuck it to "the man." Thus he was given a pass.

Still he wasn't taking any chances by going out in public.

"I feel like people are staring at me," Sumo whined.

"Well, yeah...Look at you. You're as big as a house. But

so what! It ain't like we're in LA, where people know who you are."

Sumo kept complaining, and Jason kept consoling him as he moved from exhibit, to exhibit, feigning interest in things that he found mostly uninteresting.

Jason cringed at Sumo's awkward social skills when he was forced to interact with people.

"It's like the artist is daring you to join him on a whimsical journey of color and technique," one woman said of a painting. "What do you see?"

Sumo tilted his head from side to side studying the painting, and then replied, "Looks like somebody puked and then smeared the puke all over the place, to me."

"Dude! You're supposed to be a fan of this stuff," Jason scolded through the earpiece.

There were more exhibits on the second floor. Sumo spent less time with each one. He passed through a large doorway into a dark room filled with African Art. A velvet rope cordoned off a familiar-looking statue in the back.

"There she is," Jason said, his voice full of reverence.

Several admirers crowded the exhibit. Too many. Most of them were lingering around the statue.

"I don't know, man."

"Just hang tight until it clears up a little. Look around or something. You're an art snob, remember?"

Sumo walked around the exhibit feigning interest. The African Masks were an exception. They were cool.

"What if I fuck up the pronunciation?" he mumbled like a ventriloquist. "You kept goin' on about it yesterday. S'got me schitzin'."

The incantation to free Atieno was to be spoken in an African dialect. Jason had scribbled the short verse on a piece of paper and given to Sumo.

"You're not gonna fuck it up. Just do it like we practiced."

"What if somebody interrupts me before I can—"

"Sumo!"

A silent moment.

"Yeah..." Sumo replied, suddenly calm.

"Listen to me. You can do this. Now just take a deep breath. I'll be right here with you the whole time. Okay?"

"Okay."

Sumo made his move once the crowd subsided. Jason watched on pins and needles.

"She's beautiful isn't she," Jason commented to Sumo, who was standing just beyond the velvet rope preparing himself to recite the incantation. "I can see why Indo—"

"Shhh!" Sumo scolded. "I'm trying to concentrate."

"Sorry."

Sumo dug the paper from his pocket, unfolded it, took a deep breath, and then recited the incantation just as he and Jason had practiced.

He exhaled when it was over. He folded the paper, slid it back into his pocket, and then turned and smiled at a woman who had been staring at him.

The woman reluctantly smiled back.

Fearing that something big was about to happen, Sumo started to back away from the velvet rope.

"Wait!" Jason yelled in his ear.

Sumo winced at the sound of Jason's voice. "For what?"

"Just give it a few seconds. I wanna make sure—"

A sound jumped out at them, like an old tree working out the kinks from such a sedentary existence. It had come from the statue.

Seconds later, a crack appeared in the statue's face. Sumo jumped back and watched as a tendril of smoke began to rise from the fissure.

"It's happening," Jason smiled.

251

DRUG RUNNIN'
BLUES

One pound = 454 grams
Standard price for 1 pound of weed $1800 -$3000
Price per lb. for high grade weed (aka Sticky Bunz) = $2800
100 pounds of Sticky Bunz stashed in hidden compartments throughout Subaru Outback.
100 lbs. of Sticky Bunz = $280,000
Penalty for intent to sell in Ohio:
-anything over 20,000 grams = 8+ years (2nd degree felony) $15,000 fine
-near school or minor = 10+ years (1st degree felony) $20,000 fine
100 lbs. = 45,400 grams

Gabriel Benjamin swooned behind the wheel and the Factory Gray Subaru Outback swerved into the next lane and cut off an SUV made for giants. He tightened up at the squeal of brakes that followed, expecting a nasty collision. A big engine roared, and seconds later, an ambush of honking came from behind.

Gabe stared straight ahead and played dumb, hoping that the angry driver, whom he assumed was as big as the vehicle he drove, would give up and blow past him. But the driver kept honking.

The SUV was much closer now, nipping at Gabe's bumper. The vehicle's enormous shadow darkened the back window of the Subaru. But that threat was sedated by the echo in his head.

100 lbs. = 45,400 grams
-anything over 20,000 grams = 8+ years
45,400 grams = 16+ years

Sixteen years was a long time to spend locked in a 6' x 9' box, away from his family and friends, away from Tara, his girl of three years. He pictured Tara's reaction and heard the pain in her voice when she said goodbye to him for the last time. He watched her dainty features contort, her eyes well-up…

The SUV was still riding Gabe's ass and honking at him like he had killed someone. Gabe was trying to ignore it.

The SUV and its horn was only one thing on a long list of problems. In the grand scheme, it wasn't even near the top.

The backs of automobiles came at him startlingly fast on the Pennsylvania Turnpike. Gabe struggled, under pressure from the SUV, and its constant honking, to focus on the road, the yellow divider lines, the mile-markers, the turnpike signs, the flat landscape melting by on either side of the car, and the quaint little Pennsyl-tucky towns that time forgot.

Quaint little Pennsyl-tucky towns probably had minors living there. The larger ones probably had schools, too.

Anything over 20,000 grams near school or minor = 10+ years.

45,400 grams = 20+ years

Without warning, Gabe swerved into the next lane and hit the brakes. He made sure to check that there was nothing coming up the lane first. The SUV blew past him.

Gabe pulled over to the shoulder of the road, put the car in park, and spent a moment trying to return to some degree of composure.

Up ahead, 200 feet, he saw that the SUV had pulled over to the shoulder, too, and was sitting idle. He could see the outline of the driver's head and shoulders. The man appeared smaller than Gabe had pictured. He turned his head enough for Gabe to see the brim of a red baseball cap jutting out from his brow, but the driver mostly just sat there facing forward, probably watching Gabe through the rearview.

Tha fuck's with this guy? Gabe thought as he sat there waiting to react.

The angry driver appeared to do the same.

Five minutes later, the engine revved, and the big SUV drove away kicking up gravel and dirt.

***

Gabe pulled into the next rest stop and drove around to the general parking lot. There he saw the big SUV parked at a slant. There was no sign of the angry driver. He was probably inside, relieving himself.

People walked around on stiff legs, having been seated for extended periods. They wore trance-like expressions, like zombies hungry for greasy food, bad coffee, and going to the bathroom. Most of them were horribly overweight.

Gabe parked far away from the SUV, and behind a minivan, to ensure that the angry driver didn't see his car. He sat there trying to convince himself that it was okay to leave the car for a few minutes. High on his list of plausible negative outcomes of the job were 'the stolen car', and 'the stolen weed' scenarios.

Who the hell's gonna steal a Subaru Outback when ya got a fucking Mercedes over there, and a Mustang there, and a Range Rover, he scoffed, scanning the other cars in the lot.

Gabe got out of the Subaru and took a big whiff. The air was laced with truck exhaust and petrol fumes. He walked toward the rest stop with eagle-eyes, fearing a confrontation with the angry SUV driver. Then he realized that the man never got a look at his face, and transferred his anxiety back to the job.

He checked the time on his phone. It was 8:30am.

The job was $15,000 for an 11-hour run from Philly to Fort Wayne, Indiana. Gabe was scheduled to drop the car off at Hugh's Auto Parts in Fort Wayne at 9pm sharp. He was seven hours in, two and a half hours from Toledo, Ohio, where his friend Sam was waiting to take over should Gabe receive that sign from God he was waiting for. He had left early to give himself a window of time to drive into Toledo if need be. Currently that window was at an hour and a half.

Sam had done this before. In fact, it was Sam who turned Gabe on to the opportunity.

"It's a high like you can't imagine," he told Gabe. "Knowing what'll happen if you get caught. Dealing with hardcore criminals. I mean, these dudes scare the scary guys. Real calm and cold-like. The Pick-up Men are suspicious of everything. You meet them at the drop-off point. They'll check and double check your ass while another dude holds a gun on you, and another one stands there staring you right in the eyes like he's trying to read your thought's-n-shit. It certainly ain't for everybody. Most people can't handle that kinda pressure. But the money is *sooo* good."

$15,000 for Nine hours of work...
16+ years for 45.440 grams
20+ years if near school or minor

Gabe walked past the entrance of the rest stop and toward the sound of an angry voice he recognized coming from behind the main building, where the big rigs and the RVs parked. It wasn't a voice that he had actually heard before, but one that he imagined to fit the angry SUV driver; a deep, baritone pitch with a nicotine-stained drawl. It sounded like he was angry, which made sense.

Gabe looked around to see if anyone else cared, but there were only overweight zombies.

He had to walk around to the back of the main building to see it; two men standing in front of an old, Gulfstream RV that looked like it had driven through a warzone. The man doing the yelling was medium-sized with a scruffy beard and wearing a Philadelphia Phillies Baseball Cap. It was the angry SUV driver. He was giving it to some chubby-face older fellow who looked completely caught off guard.

"Well then you'd better *GET* used to driving that thing," the angry driver scolded the chubby faced man.

"I'm sorry. Please? I don't want any trouble," Chubby face replied. He seemed strangely preoccupied with something inside the RV.

"Sum-bitch tries to run me off the road and he's askin' for trouble."

"I told you. It was an accident."

"Accident, my ass."

"But it was. I swear—"

"You looked right at me when I honked my horn."

"Please. I was distracted. You don't understand."

The angry driver shoved the older fellow up against the RV and got right in his chubby face.

"You calling me a liar?"

"No. Please," Chubby face replied. "I would never do that. Please. Just let me go. I don't want any—"

"Pussy," said the angry driver as he let go of the man and walked away huffing and puffing.

He walked right past Gabe, who looked down and pretended to scratch his head. The angry driver glanced at him, and then looked away.

On his way to the bathroom, Gabe watched the angry SUV driver chew out some poor cashier at Roy Rogers for no apparent reason.

If ever anybody deserved to have their food spat in, it's that guy, he thought and gave the deflated cashier a nod of support when the boy looked his way.

Gabe took a long, satisfying piss and then inhaled one of those mini pizzas from the Pizza Hut Express. On the way back to his car, he noticed that the angry driver had not yet returned to his SUV. He had seen the man leave the rest stop a few minutes before he did.

Upon mental review, Gabe remembered seeing the angry driver turn right instead of left, where his SUV was parked, after walking out the front doors. That way led around back to the Truck/RV Lot.

Standing within arm's reach of the Subaru Outback, Gabe was comforted by the fact that the car was still where he had left it, and still in one piece.

I should just get in this car and be on my way, he mused.

It was only 8:45am. His window was now at an hour and fifteen minutes, which was still doable. At the moment Gabe was feeling optimistic, though. Like he was going to see the job through to the end. If that was the case, he had an hour and fifteen minutes to spare.

Gabe skulked between tractor trailers seeking a better vantage point to spy on the angry SUV driver, who he saw snooping around the outside of the Gulfstream RV. The chubby faced driver was apparently still inside the rest stop. Gabe had seen him in there earlier.

Gabe came to a gap between a truck cab and trailer and peeked through it.

The angry man had managed to pry the RV door open and was peering into the dark interior of the shabby vehicle.

Maybe I should do something? Gabe thought, but he was too concerned with calling attention to himself.

Something reached out of the darkness…a hand…It was big, with cracked skin around its joints and fingers that completely engulfed the angry driver's head as they wrapped around it, squeezed, and then yanked the flailing man inside the RV.

Gabe backed away and slammed into another parked truck. It startled him and he whipped around.

The RV door slammed shut. Gabe spun back toward the RV and wound up slightly dizzy.

Could someone be that big? he thought envisioning the hand as he stared at the side of the shabby RV. *They would have to be what…like 10, 15 feet tall? There's no way.*

A voice came at him sideways.

"Looking fer something', son?" asked a squinty-eyed man with deep wrinkles who walked up to the tractor trailer Gabe was standing beside.

"Ah…no. Sorry," Gabe replied, backing away nervously. "I was just—" and then he remembered the job…and then the time…It was 9:08.

Shit! His Toledo window was down to under an hour. And Gabe was on another down surge in confidence. In fact, the stress had him seeing things. That's not good. Not good at all.

* * *

The signs for Toledo were plentiful now that Gabe was only 40 minutes from the first exit. That was the one he would take to get to Sam's place. He still hadn't decided yet, but as of this moment, he was leaning toward finishing the job. The past hour and twenty minutes had been uneventful, which was good in one sense, yet bad in that it left Gabe alone with his thoughts for far too long.

$15,000 for Nine hours of work…vs. 16+ years for 45.440 grams

20+ years if near school or minor

He attempted to fill his head with music, but the radio

260

conspired against him with songs about prison-life. The theme was 'lost loves' when he tried the same thing earlier. So, he turned the damn radio off.

Thirty minutes until the point of no return. Gabe was burning up. He turned on the air conditioning and cranked the knob to full blast. He fumbled with the buttons, taking his eyes off the road in short spans, until the air finally came out of the vents directly in front of him.

Gabe settled back into his seat and reset his focus on the turnpike. There were a few cars evenly dispersed among the four lanes. Tractor trailers to his left; two of them, riding nose to tail.

The tractor trailers eventually pulled ahead of him and there was the beat up Gulfstream RV cruising along in the next lane over. The tractor trailers had concealed it from Gabe's view until now.

Gabe eased into the next lane and coasted 20 feet back from the shabby vehicle and to the right of it. There, he watched the thing rattle and shake as if it might fall apart. At some point it occurred to him that maybe the chubby-face old man was doing a "job," too. Gabe remembered the old man's preoccupation with something inside the RV as the angry driver bullied him. Maybe that's why he didn't retaliate.

Up ahead…

A rectangular window slid open near the back of the RV. Something red fell or was thrown from the window. It hit Gabe's windshield before passing right over the roof of his car. In the rearview, Gabe saw the object—A Philadelphia Phillies Baseball Cap; red.—hit the street and roll with the wind.

There was a smear of red liquid where the baseball cap made contact with his windshield. Tiny droplets trembled in the wind that pushed them upward and over the roof. It looked like blood.

Twenty minutes to the point of no return. Gabe was riding alongside the RV, glancing up at that rectangular window when he could.

Something was staring back at him the next time he looked, an instantly recognizable face. It was huge, revealed

261

in rectangular swatches, as the window wasn't tall enough to frame the entire face at once. But as it moved, leaning and tilting its head to get a better look at Gabe, Gabe got a pretty good look at the thing.

He wasn't ready to accept that Jesus Christ, himself was staring at him from the window of a beat up RV, and that Jesus was somehow a giant. He dismissed the thing as a figment of his stress and looked away.

The face was still there when Gabe looked again, staring at him as if trying to ascertain whether he was friend or foe. It looked like a statue, but it didn't move like one. Its head was long and skinny with eyes a washed out shade of blue and with no depth. Tears of rust streamed from its eyes and over red cheekbones and narrow lips. Its skin was a smooth, yet rough, and lumpy texture with tiny cracks around the corners of its orifices. A crown of thorns rested on top of its head. Inert trails of red-orange blood over a painfully furrowed brow.

With Gabe locked in its focus, the statue thrust its face toward the window and frowned and squinted. And then it lifted its head so that its narrow, hinted-at mouth was framed by the window. It raised a giant finger to its lips and said, "Shhhhhhh."

Gabe swerved to avoid ramming into the back of the car that suddenly appeared in front of him. He briefly lost control, and was able to steer the skidding vehicle over to the shoulder of the road, where it came to rest in the gravel.

His eyes immediately darted to the turnpike. The RV was up ahead some ways. He watched it until the shabby vehicle disappeared over the horizon and then he sat there for a moment.

Gabe took a deep breath. He turned on the windshield wipers and became hypnotized by their dance as they wiped the red liquid away. He was almost sure it was blood.

Gabe dug his phone out of his hip pocket and dialed Sam's number.

Sam picked up on the first ring and said in a satisfied tone, "So what made you change your mind?"

"Remember that sign from God I was talking about?"

ANDRE DUZA is an actor, stuntman, and a leading member of the Bizarro movement in contemporary literary fiction. His writing has been described as horrific, bizarre, smart, funny, and fast-paced, with lush, finely-detailed prose. He is fond of collaborating with artists to create macabre illustrations for his books.

Andre's novels include DEAD BITCH ARMY, JESUS FREAKS, NECRO SEX MACHINE, and his graphic novel, HOLLOW-EYED MARY. He is the co-author of SON OF A BITCH co-written with Wrath James White, and the comic book OUTER LIGHT, co-written with television writer/producer Morgan Gendel.

Andre has also contributed to such collections and anthologies as BOOK OF LISTS: HORROR, THE BIZARRO STARTER KIT, UNDEAD, UNDEAD: FLESH FEAST, and THE MAGAZINE OF BIZARRO FICTION.

Andre is also a Certified Fitness Trainer and a Kung Fu Instructor. He lives in Philadelphia with his wife and four children.

deadite press

"Header" Edward Lee - In the dark backwoods, where law enforcement doesn't dare tread, there exists a special type of revenge. Something so awful that it is only whispered about. Something so terrible that few believe it is real. Stewart Cummings is a government agent whose life is going to Hell. His wife is ill and to pay for her medication he turns to bootlegging. But things will get much worse when bodies begin showing up in his sleepy small town. Victims of an act known only as "a Header."

"Red Sky" Nate Southard - When a bank job goes horrifically wrong, career criminal Danny Black leads his crew from El Paso into the deserts of New Mexico in a desperate bid for escape. Danny soon finds himself with no choice but to hole up in an abandoned factory, the former home of Red Sky Manufacturing. Danny and his crew aren't the only living things in Red Sky, though. Something waits in the abandoned factory's shadows, something horrible and violent. Something hungry. And when the sun drops, it will feast.

"Zombies and Shit" Carlton Mellick III - Twenty people wake to find themselves in a boarded-up building in the middle of the zombie wasteland. They soon discover they have been chosen as contestants on a popular reality show called Zombie Survival. Each contestant is given a backpack of supplies and a unique weapon. Their goal: be the first to make it through the zombie-plagued city to the pick-up zone alive. But because there's only one seat available on the helicopter, the contestants not only have to fight against the hordes of the living dead, they must also fight each other.

"Muerte Con Carne" Shane McKenzie - Human flesh tacos, hardcore wrestling, and angry cannibal Mexicans, Welcome to the Border! Felix and Marta came to Mexico to film a documentary on illegal immigration. When Marta suddenly goes missing, Felix must find his lost love in the small border town. A dangerous place housing corrupt cops, borderline maniacs, and something much more worse than drug gangs, something to do with a strange Mexican food cart...

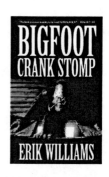

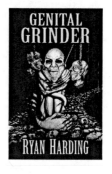

CPSIA information can be obtained at www.ICGtesting.com
Printed in the USA
BVOW02s1314180314

348017BV00004B/12/P